THE WAGER (A MENAGE ROMANCE)

A MENAGE IN MANHATTAN NOVEL

TARA CRESCENT

My editor Jim takes the comma-filled words that emerge from my keyboard and shapes it into a story worth reading. As always, my undying gratitude.

Additional thanks for Miranda's laser-sharp eyes.

Cover Design by Eris Adderly, http://erisadderly.com/

FREE STORY OFFER

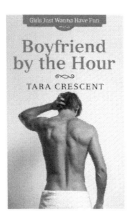

Sadie:

I can't believe I have the hots for an escort.

Cole Mitchell is ripped, bearded, sexy and dominant. When he moves next door to me, I find it impossible to resist sampling the wares.

But Cole's not a one-woman kind of guy, and I won't share.

Cole:

She thinks I'm an escort. I'm not.

I thought I'd do anything to sleep with Sadie. Then I realized I want more. I want Sadie. Forever.

I'm not the escort she thinks I am.

Now, I just have to make sure she never finds out.

THE WAGER

A steamy ménage. A secret baby.

My life is falling apart.

I've been fired from my job. My new stepbrother has promised to ruin me. The only people on my side are Hudson and Asher.

I shouldn't have given in to temptation. I shouldn't have slept with them.

One night, they said. No promises. Just pleasure.

But the condom failed.

What am I supposed to do now?

> **Note:** The Wager is a full-length MFM ménage romance that is all about the woman. This story is about two

damaged men who fall in love with the same woman. No cliffhangers.

The Wager was previously titled Wagering on Wendy.

1

For time and the world do not stand still. Change is the law of life. And those who look only to the past or the present are certain to miss the future.

— JOHN F. KENNEDY

Wendy:

I've been a divorce lawyer for six years, and in that time, I've learned one thing. All men are lying, cheating bastards.

Okay, *okay*. Maybe not all men. Maybe I'm wrong, and maybe my profession has skewed my perception of the gender. Divorce lawyers don't exactly see couples at their best, after all.

Take Howard and Sandi Lippman. They've been married twenty-five years, and in that time, Sandi raised three kids and was the perfect wife and mother. Then Howard Lippman decided to cheat on her with his twenty-two-year-old assistant. To add insult to injury, he hid the bulk of his assets so he wouldn't have to pay his ex-wife her fair share in the divorce.

My goal today? Find the hidden money with the help of my uber-awesome hacker friend Miki. Demonstrate to the judge that Howard Lippman is a cheating son of a bitch, and my client Sandi deserves half of his assets. Win, and win big

THE STREETS of New York are almost quiet as I make my way to work. It's a little after seven in the morning, and when I push open the frosted-glass door to the reception area of Johnson Nash Adams, I'm expecting to find the place to myself. To my surprise, Beverly, the assistant I share with two other lawyers, is already at work, as is Lara Greaves, who sits next door to me.

I raise my hand in greeting, and head to my office. Five minutes later, there's a knock on my door and Lara sticks her head in. "Hey Wendy," she says. "A few of us are going to *Nerve* tonight to celebrate Pam's birthday. Do you want to join us? All of New York's rich and famous will be there."

"That's not exactly a selling feature," I reply dryly, thinking of Howard Lippman.

She rolls her eyes. "The drinks are excellent. Dante is the best mixologist in the city."

I'm tempted. I've been working crazy hours in the last couple of months, and I'm overdue for a night out. *Nerve* is Manhattan's newest lounge. It's very exclusive, and I'm dying to find out what the buzz is about.

Unfortunately, there's a large mound of paperwork in front of me that needs to be dealt with. "I can't," I tell Lara regretfully. "Jonathan Stern's lawyer just dumped several boxes of evidence on me before Amber's first hearing next week."

She shakes her head but doesn't try to argue. Lara's trying to make partner too. We both know that work comes first; it always does, and it always will. "I'll put you on the list," she says. "Just in case you change your mind."

Before I can reply, my cell phone rings. It's Miki. "I have to take this," I tell Lara, who nods in understanding and shuts the door. Once I'm alone, I pick up the call. "Tell me you have good news for me, Miki."

We're down to the wire here. Miki is a financial hacker, and she's excellent at what she does, but Lippman's systems have stymied her so far. She's been working around the clock to find me proof of Lippman's missing four hundred million dollars.

"I hit paydirt, Wendy," she announces, her voice layered with triumph. "Shell corporations, offshore bank accounts, you name it, I found it. I'm emailing you the details right now."

"Yes." I punch the air in delight. The idea of Lippman getting away with his ruse has been gnawing at me. Now, he won't. "You," I tell my friend, "are a fucking goddess. A rock star. This is fantastic."

She laughs. "Sorry it took so long," she says. "The company Lippman hired to hide his assets are pretty good at covering their tracks. In fact, I'm fairly sure that my snooping has been detected."

That could be a problem. "How long do I have before Lippman moves the money?"

"A day or two," she replies. "The trial's this afternoon, isn't it? You should be fine." She hesitates for a brief moment, then continues. "This is the third guy in the last two months I've investigated for you. You're making enemies, Wendy. Please be careful."

Miki is rarely paranoid, and this behavior is unlike her.

"Miki, this is my job. If I do it right, the ex-husbands want to punch me. It goes with the territory. I'm used to the hatred."

This *is* my job, and I *am* used to the hatred, but this time, it's a little more personal. Sandi reminds me of my mom. They're the same age. Same honey brown hair, fading to gray, same caramel brown eyes. Same lousy taste in men.

Thirty years ago, my father swept my mother off her feet in a whirlwind affair, conveniently forgetting to mention to her that he was married. Then Janet Williams found out she was pregnant. When she told Paul Hancock, he'd given her ten thousand dollars and told her never to contact him again. Too poor to hire a lawyer and fight for child support, my mother raised me on her own, sacrificing everything to give me a stable, loving home.

I have no power to change the past. I can't help my mother, but I can help Sandi. "Don't worry," I repeat. "I've got this."

Judge Hadid takes one look at the evidence Miki has secured for me, says several stern things to Howard Lippman and his lawyer Katrina Schroeder about lying to the court, and rules in Sandi's favor.

Outside the courtroom, Sandi hugs me tight. "Thank you, Wendy," she says, her voice thick with gratitude. "I didn't think you'd be able to pull this off, but I should have had more faith."

I shrug, uncomfortable with her praise. "I'm just doing my job," I tell her with a smile. I watch her leave, then turn on my phone to check my messages. There is no voicemail for me to deal with, but there's a news alert that stops me dead in my tracks.

Paul Hancock has died.

I scan the article for details. My biological father has succumbed to cancer caused by the tumor growing in his brain. His wife Lillian died six years ago, but he's survived by a son, Thorne Hancock.

My good mood evaporates. Paul Hancock never once acknowledged the daughter he conceived. I never met him, and now, I never will.

I don't know how to process the complicated cocktail of emotions I'm feeling, but if I go home, I'll just end up brooding all night. I dial Lara's number. "You guys still going to *Nerve*?" I ask her when she answers. "I'm joining you."

Dante had better mix up a mean drink. I'm going to need alcohol tonight.

2

Open your eyes, look within. Are you satisfied with the life you're living?

— BOB MARLEY

Asher:

I'm staring at my schedule, wondering why on earth I'm supposed to be at Miguel's new lounge on a Monday night, when my assistant Vivian knocks at my door. "You have a visitor," she says, sounding harassed. "A Mr. Engels. I tried telling him you don't see people without an appointment, but he wouldn't leave."

I go very still. The last I heard, Levi Engels was in jail, locked up for a year for his role in a scheme involving bad checks and forgery. He's lucky it wasn't longer. My childhood friend has become something of a career criminal, and we haven't spoken to each other in almost fifteen years. Why is he here now?

I force a smile on my face. "Is he waiting in Reception?"

She nods. "Do you want to see him?"

Not really. Levi Engels is trouble with a capital T. I don't have a good feeling about this at all. "Yes, please. Could you send him up?"

"Ash Doyle," Levi's voice booms out as he walks in. He looks around my office, taking in the expansive space, the large windows that overlook Manhattan and the modern art on my walls. "You're a big shot now, aren't you, buddy?"

There's a trace of hostility in his voice. I ignore it. "Long time, Levi. How've you been?"

"I'd have been better had my lawyer been any good," he says. "All lawyers are fucking thieves, am I right?"

Bullshit. His defense lawyer was a genius. It was Levi's third arrest, and he should have been locked away for five years. I disregard Levi's dig at my profession; he's trying to get a rise out of me, and I refuse to let it work. "What can I do for you, Levi?"

His expression turns serious. "I need a place to stay for a month or two, Ash. Just until I'm back on my feet." He swallows, sounding vulnerable. "I want to clean up my act, but it's hard when I'm surrounded by temptation."

For years, I've been waiting for him to ask for help. "Of course," I reply instantly. "I can arrange..."

"No." His voice is vehement. "I don't want your charity. Can I crash at your place? You have a spare bedroom, don't you?"

Several. Bedrooms are not the problem. As much as I want to believe Levi's change of heart, there's always a chance that he's going to get seduced by crime, by the promise of easy rewards. And I can't be involved with that. I won't risk everything I've worked for.

But Levi's expression is hopeful, and I can't turn him away. "Sure," I reply. "My place isn't far away. If you have some time now, I'll get you a key, introduce you to the doorman and show you around."

"Thanks, buddy," he says fervently. "You want to grab a beer later?"

I look up at that, surprised. "Can you go to a bar when you're on parole?"

He shrugs indifferently. "My parole officer's an idiot. He'll never find out."

Trouble already. Thankfully, I have an excuse to avoid Levi tonight. "I can't," I reply. "A client just opened a lounge in SoHo. I promised him I'd drop by."

Levi doesn't look too put out by my refusal. "No worries," he says. "Some other night, yeah?"

"Sure."

I'm pretty sure I'm going to regret this decision.

~

Hudson:

"Want to bet that we're getting fired today?"

Nadja Breton, my second-in-command, and the only woman I truly trust, frowns at me. "That's defeatist," she chides. "We could be reading this situation wrong."

The two of us are in the small conference room in our SoHo office. The floor-to-ceiling windows give us a great view of the city while shielding us from the noise and the chaos. We moved into these offices four years ago, and when I signed the lease, I knew I'd made it. I'd grown Fleming Architecture from a one-man operation to a prestigious design firm that had twenty-five employees and was projected to make fifty million dollars by the end of the year.

On the glass table in the center of the room, there's a scale model of the skyscraper I've designed for Jack Price and Ian Schultz. It's gorgeous, among the best work I've done. I eye it dispassionately. "Jack Price received box seats to the Knicks yesterday, courtesy of Kent and Associates. I'm not an idiot, Nadja. I can read the writing on the wall."

"Doesn't it bother you?"

"I'm not going to bribe Price for this job," I say flatly. Fleming Architecture is extremely successful, with an abundance of happy clients. While I'd prefer not to lose this account, my intuition tells me the Clark Towers project is bad news.

There's a lot more I could add. I could remind Nadja that after Megan, my gold-digging ex-wife, I'm leery of people that are only interested in me for my money.

Nadja, who's been staring out of the window, takes a seat at the table. "Some of the newer architects are restless."

I raise my eyebrow. "Why?"

"They think you should be bidding more aggressively for work. Branch out in new directions."

This argument again. I'm willing to bet money that Colin Cartwright is behind the discontent. Colin believes I should have picked him over Nadja to be my second in command, and he's doing everything in his power to undermine me. I'm getting tired of it. "We're a boutique firm, Nadja. We only bid on projects that are a good fit for us."

She sips at her coffee. "I'm not the one you need to convince," she replies.

I make a mental note to have a conversation with Colin. If he doesn't stop his bullshit, his days at Fleming Architecture are numbered.

Jack Price and Ian Schultz frown when they see the model of the skyscraper in the middle of the room. Nadja, noticing their discontented expressions, exchanges a look with me. *Fired,* she mouths.

She's right. Ian Schultz looks up. "I have to be honest, Fleming," he says bluntly. "This isn't working."

Translation: I didn't bribe them. "You seemed perfectly happy with our design during the last meeting."

Jack Price has the grace to flush. "Things change," he mutters. "I'm sorry, Hudson. We're going to have to let you go."

The two of them watch me warily. If they're waiting for me to react, I'm not going to give them the pleasure. "That's your call to make, gentlemen." My voice is pleasant, but underneath, I'm simmering with fury. "Have you decided on a replacement firm?"

They look away, unable to meet my gaze. "Kent and Associates come highly recommended," Price says finally.

I doubt it. Kent and Associates doesn't have much of a track record when it comes to delivering projects on time and on budget. In a few months, when Clark Towers starts to fail, Jack Price is going to regret his decision. "Give my regards to George. I assume you'll see him at the Knicks game tonight?"

Price's head snaps up in shock. I rise to my feet. "I'm not a fool, Jack," I say evenly. "Don't ever take me for one. You know the way out."

Once they've left, Nadja sighs heavily. "What a day," she says with a grimace. "I think I'm going to leave early, Hudson. This mess will be waiting for us tomorrow morning."

She looks dispirited. We've both put in months of work into this project, and it sucks to see it go to waste. Still, there will be other clients. "The new 3D printer finally came in," I tell her, in an attempt to cheer her up. "If you're looking for a new toy to play with, it's all yours."

My attempt works. Her eyes sparkle with excitement. "Oh good. I've been dying to load up our designs on it and test it out. Remember the all-nighters we used to pull in college when we had to assemble models?"

"Oh God. Don't remind me. Glue, craft sticks and cold pizza. I'm glad those days are behind us."

She chuckles. "Me too. See you in the morning, boss."

I get back to work, losing myself in a preliminary sketch for a museum. I don't notice the setting sun or the darkening sky. Nothing disturbs my concentration until a knock sounds at the door. "I was afraid I'd be interrupting you," my friend Asher says, stepping into my office and giving the crumpled up sheets of paper on the floor a pointed look. "But you look ready for a break. Want to get a drink?"

"Sounds good." I stand up and stretch, my muscles creaking with protest. "What's the plan?"

"One of my clients just opened a new lounge." He grimaces. "I'm duty-bound to make an appearance. It'll be loud and pretentious."

"You're doing a great job selling this." I stuff my laptop into its bag and sling it over my shoulder. "Fortunately for you, a beer sounds pretty good at the moment."

"Don't hold your breath," Asher advises. "Miguel told me he hired the best mixologist in the city. I doubt they serve anything as uncomplicated as a beer."

"Damn it, Doyle," I grumble. "You owe me for this. You're buying tonight."

Asher laughs in agreement. "It seems the least I can do."

3

We must let go of the life we have planned, so as to accept the one that is waiting for us.

— JOSEPH CAMPBELL

Wendy:

The door to *Nerve* is guarded by a burly bouncer in a black suit. He gives me the once-over, taking in my shimmery gray silk dress and my silver hoop earrings before he nods and allows me entry.

I make my way inside, trying to find Lara. The club is beautiful. I'd been expecting black and chrome, but instead, the walls are a soft burnished gold. Hundreds of glass globes hang from the ceiling, filling the space with a warm light. A jazz band plays on a corner stage, but the acoustics are perfect, and the music isn't too loud. It's half past nine, too early for the dance floor to be crowded, though the bar area is packed with people, all waiting for Dante the *mixologist* to make them some fancy concoction.

My bra digs into my sides, and my toes, squeezed into a pair of painful Louboutins, feel like they are on fire. I scan the crowds for my coworkers and don't see them. I'm debating going home to Netflix and ice-cream when I hear Lara call out my name from a table at the far corner. "Wendy," she greets me with a broad smile. "I'm so glad you changed your mind about coming."

There's one empty chair, and I sink into it with a sigh of relief. Damn shoes.

"What happened with the Lippman case?" Matt Vella, who's sitting next to Lara, asks me. He's also a lawyer at our firm, though I don't know him very well.

"We won," I reply absently, trying to catch the eye of the bored looking waitress who's taking drink orders a couple of tables away.

"Excellent." Pam Prickett turns to Matt, holding out her hand. "Come on, Matt. Pay up."

Matt grumbles as he takes a hundred dollar bill out of his wallet and passes it to her. I give Pam an astonished look. "You bet on the case?"

She tucks the bill in her purse. "Of course I did," she chuckles. "A fool and his money are easily parted. Matt, next time, don't bet against the Barracuda."

Matt grins lazily. "I should have known better," he agrees. "Wendy, you want to dance?"

I shake my head. "Not in these shoes," I say ruefully. "And not before I get a drink."

Matt wanders off to try his luck on the dance floor. Pam, Lara, and I gossip rather aimlessly about work as we wait for the waitress to acknowledge our existence when Lara suddenly grabs my arm. "Oh my God," she breathes. "Look who just walked in. That's Asher Doyle."

I turn around. Asher Doyle is something of a legend in

our profession. He started out his career as a district attorney, and then he changed direction and became a corporate lawyer. His hourly rate is two thousand dollars, and his firm supposedly has more work than they can handle.

"He's wasting his time as a lawyer," Pam mutters. "He should be a model."

"An underwear model," Lara adds. "Can you imagine?" The two of them dissolve into a flood of giggles.

I might not trust men, but I'm still human. I like eye candy as much as the next woman *and damn.* Asher Doyle doesn't look like a lawyer. His shoulders are broad; his dark hair is tousled, and his cheeks are covered with stubble.

"Sex on a stick," Pam says dreamily.

I'm staring at the man with my mouth open. I snap it shut hastily, lest I start drooling. "He's probably very boring," I say dismissively. "The hot ones usually are."

Lara shakes her head. "Haven't you heard the stories?" she asks me, lowering her voice. "He's not boring at all. The word is that he likes to share women with his best friend, Hudson Fleming."

"Who just walked in as well." Pam looks like she's about to faint. "Wendy, check him out."

Damn again.

Asher Doyle looks like a bad boy. Hudson Fleming, on the other hand, is smooth and sophisticated. He's wearing dark jeans and a gray button-down shirt with the sleeves rolled up to his elbows. My eyes fly immediately to his strong forearms. Yeah, forearms. I have a thing for rolled-up sleeves, okay? *Sue me.*

The two men go up to the bar, and space clears for them instantly. The bartender, a blonde wearing a very low cut blouse, smiles seductively as she pours them their drinks.

I can't stop staring. I notice the way Hudson rolls his

eyes at Dante's contortions. I notice the way Asher Doyle's strong fingers curl around the crystal base of the glass he's holding, the way his thumb almost seems to caress the cool surface. When he laughs at something Hudson says, my stomach clenches with desire. It's their body language. These men are confident and powerful, and unexpectedly, it's turning me on.

Lara says something to Pam and me; I barely listen. The two of them join Matt on the dance floor. The waitress finally notices that I need a drink, and bustles up to take my order.

An hour later, I'm ready to go home. I've lost sight of the eye-candy, and Lara, Pam, and Matt show no sign of slowing down. The glass in front of me is empty, and I'm fighting the urge to check my phone for further updates on Paul Hancock.

You can't leave already, I scold myself. *You came out to have fun, so have fun, damn it.*

What I need is another drink.

I get up and make my way to the bar. Dante's making blush-pink cocktails for a giggling group of women. I find an empty spot and wait for someone to notice me. Next to me, a woman in a red cocktail dress is thumbing through her phone. She catches sight of Dante and rolls her eyes. I bite back a grin at her reaction, so similar to my own.

"Hi there, honey." A man with gel-slicked hair sidles next to her and gives her what he thinks is a winning smile. "Can I buy you a drink?"

"No thank you," she says politely, drawing away from him as he inches closer. "I'm waiting for someone."

Hair-Gel Guy is oblivious to her body language. "No harm having a drink while you wait, is there?"

She gives him a tight smile. She obviously wants to be

left alone, but the guy's not picking up on her signal. "No thanks," she says again.

"Are you waiting for a boyfriend?" He lays his hand on the woman's ass, and she flinches. Her eyes dart around the room, looking for someone to help her out of this situation.

That's my signal to intervene. There's a special place in hell reserved for guys who refuse to take a hint. "She said no," I tell him, not bothering to conceal the disgust in my voice. "Which part of that wasn't clear?"

He turns red. He moves right next to me, hovering threateningly, inches from my face, and I can smell the booze on his breath. "No one was talking to you, bitch," he snarls.

I position myself in front of the trembling woman. "Leave her alone."

He grabs me by the wrist to yank me out of the way. When I first moved to New York, I'd taken self-defense classes. Our instructor had taught us how to handle this. As his fingers clench around my wrist, I twist my hand, hard. His shoulder wrenches, and he grunts and lets go, stumbling back a few paces, pain etched on his face. "That was a big mistake," he says. "You're going to pay for that."

Shit. I'm in trouble now.

Suddenly, two men appear out of nowhere. Asher Doyle and Hudson Fleming fill the space between my assailant and me. Asher grabs the guy by the collar and pushes him back. "I believe the lady told you to leave her alone," he says icily. He seems to make a gentle movement with his fists, and the man goes flying across the room, landing in a heap next to a black leather couch.

The band stops mid-note; a hush falls over the room. People scramble out of the way of the fight. A couple of people take out their phones to take photographs. Of course.

Hair-Gel Guy rises to his feet slowly, shaking his head. I'm hoping he's had enough and is ready to walk away, but instead, he bellows with rage and charges for Asher. I inhale sharply, but my concern turns out to be entirely unnecessary; Asher repeats his movement and the man goes down again.

"Once more?" Asher's eyes gleam with anticipation. He almost appears to be enjoying himself.

Before the man attacks for the second time, a bouncer appears and grabs him by the collar and drags him to the door.

Hudson Fleming, who's been watching the fight intently, turns to me once the threat of danger has passed. "Do you want to press charges?" he asks. "We saw him grab your wrist. We're happy to be witnesses."

I shake my head. It seems more trouble than it's worth.

The band starts playing again, and the dance floor fills with people. Asher approaches the two of us. "Thanks for the help," he grumbles to Hudson.

Hudson laughs. "You seemed to have the situation under control," he responds. "Besides, two on one doesn't seem sporting."

Asher flips him off with a grin. He signals to the bartender, then turns to me with a probing look. "Are you okay?"

My heartbeat, slowly returning to normal after the fight, speeds up again. I thought they were good looking. Up close, they are so much more. They're gorgeous. "I'm fine," I stammer.

Pull yourself together, Wendy. Tongue-tied is not a good look.

The bartender appears in front of Asher. "Mr. Doyle,

what's your pleasure?" she simpers, thrusting her boobs into his face. Subtle.

Asher doesn't appear to notice. "Can I buy you a drink?" he asks me.

"No," I protest. "This round's on me. Thank you for your help."

Asher shakes his head. "It was nothing," he replies. "Honestly."

The bartender's waiting for us to order, so I ask for a glass of their house red. Asher orders a beer, as does Hudson. Once she's moved away to get our drinks, Hudson gives me an amused look. "If you're going to pick a fight with a drunk guy," he chides, "Pick one your own size. That guy weighed two hundred pounds."

I'm grateful for their help. Really, I am. I'm not going to lie—it felt good having two guys charge to my rescue. But I can't get used to it. Men cannot be trusted to stick around. *Just ask my mom.* "I could have handled the situation," I insist.

"Is that so?" Hudson looks amused.

"I've been taking boxing lessons," I tell them solemnly.

Asher's eyes twinkle. "Really?" he drawls. "And how many lessons have you attended so far?"

Busted. "None," I admit sheepishly. "I signed up for the classes but I haven't had time to buy a pair of gloves."

Asher chuckles; Hudson laughs openly. "We haven't introduced ourselves," he says. "I'm Asher Doyle. And this is Hudson Fleming."

I feel the urge to laugh hysterically. Everything about these two men is gossip-worthy. Where they went. Who they were seen with. Who they're sleeping with at the moment, and *oh, did I know they like to share women?*

With heroic effort, I keep my tone neutral. "Wendy

Williams," I reply, shaking their hands, first Asher's, then Hudson's. A tingle runs through my body at their touch, and my insides do a little flip. *Whoa there.*

"Wendy," Hudson says, not letting go of my hand. His thumb strokes my palm; his gaze remains on my face. "Do you come here often?"

Our drinks appear, and I take a big gulp of my wine to try and calm myself. "No, it's my first time here," I admit. "I only got in today because my colleague put me on the list."

"Your colleague?" Asher asks. "What do you do?"

"I'm a divorce lawyer."

"You are?" His eyebrow arches and he surveys me openly from head to toe. "You don't look like one."

He's checking me out blatantly; they both are. I should be offended. I should walk away before I do anything I might regret. These men have a reputation that precedes them.

But the arousal that washes over me is so very unexpected. I can't remember the last time I was this turned on. Hudson's touch on my skin sets my body throbbing. My cheeks are flushed, my nipples hard underneath my dress.

I shift my weight from one foot to another to keep my raging hormones at bay. *Say something, Wendy. You're just gaping at them.* "What do divorce lawyers look like?"

Hudson coughs. "Asher, I beg you, don't answer that question." He grins at me. "You'll have to excuse my friend. He's not the most tactful person in the world."

My lips twitch. "He gets a pass," I tell Hudson. "After all, you guys did save me. My heroes."

The wine is going to my head. I'm flirting with them. If my anthropologist friend Bailey were here, she'd tell me that my body language is giving me away. I'm leaning toward them, smiling into their eyes. I haven't pulled my hand free of Hudson's grip.

I should go back to my table. I don't.

Asher stares at me. "Have dinner with us."

"What?"

"Dinner." His eyes gleam with amusement. "You've heard of the concept? There's a meal involved, usually some wine, good conversation?"

"I know what dinner is," I respond. An evening with Hudson and Asher. Is this what Cinderella felt like when the prince picked her to dance with at the ball? My heart is racing; my mouth is dry. "With *both* of you?"

"Ah." Asher takes a half-step closer. "From the emphasis you placed on the word *both*, I take it you've heard stories."

He's direct; I'll give him that. "You like sharing women." It feels so naughty to say those words aloud.

They nod. "You're not running away screaming," Hudson notes. "Are you intrigued?" His finger traces soft circles on my skin.

I swallow. A devil-may-care urge grips me. My father died today. I've been trying not to think about it, but the news plays about at the edge of my consciousness, trying to sneak into my thoughts when I'm not paying attention.

I could use a distraction. *Two distractions.* "Dinner sounds lovely."

"How about tomorrow night?" Asher pulls a business card out of his wallet and hands it to me. "Call me, and we'll work out the details."

"Tomorrow?" My voice comes out in a squeak. "That soon?"

"Why wait?" Hudson asks.

I can barely breathe. I argue cases for a living, but words have deserted me. I'm afraid I'm staring at them with my mouth open, like a drooling idiot. Before I embarrass myself further, I nod hastily and make my escape.

In the cab home, I finger the crisp edges of the business card Asher gave me, and close my eyes. I can't believe I've agreed to a dinner date with them. Is this what I want? Though Bailey, Piper, and Gabby are in ménage relationships, I've never seriously contemplated a threesome.

Until now.

4

You will not be punished for your anger, you will be punished by your anger.

— BUDDHA

Asher:

When Wendy shakes my hand, a spark of awareness surges through me. When she thanks me for helping her, I want to stay at her side and fight her battles for her, but bitter experience has taught me I can't do that. Once upon a time, I was in love with a woman and I wanted to protect her from the world, but it ended in disaster. Lauren killed herself, and the man responsible for her suicide got away scot-free. *Never again.*

Her blonde hair is the color of the sun on a winter's morning, and her eyes are the most unusual shade of pale blue. She's not conventionally beautiful; her face is too narrow and her forehead is too wide, but somehow, I can't tear my eyes away from her. Though most women can't wait to get into my bed, they like to act disingenuous about my sexual tastes. *Not Wendy*. Her candor is refreshing and rare.

Hudson and I watch her leave. Once she's out of sight, Hudson gives me a speculative look. "That was *interesting*," he says contemplatively.

I raise an eyebrow. After Hudson's disaster of a marriage a year ago, he's been more reclusive and less trusting. I thought he was interested in Wendy, but maybe he's not ready to put the Megan Klinsmann shitshow behind him. "Are you having second thoughts about dinner?"

He shakes his head immediately. "It's been a while; that's all." We drink our beers in silence. Finally, Hudson breaks it. "Is something bothering you?" he asks. "You look troubled."

Hudson and I have been friends since college. I'm not surprised he would pick up on my mood. "You remember my buddy Levi? He's out of jail again. He asked if he could stay at my place until he got back on his feet."

Hudson stiffens. "Tell me," he says slowly, "that you said no."

"I said yes."

Hudson curses loudly. "Damn it," he snaps. "Levi Engels beat his ex-girlfriend's new boyfriend half to death and tried to pin the rap on you. He's bad news. You know that. You need to cut him loose."

It's not quite that black and white. I hit Jason too. I wasn't entirely innocent.

"I can't do that," I reply. My foster father liked to use his kids as a punching bag when he was drunk. Levi would intentionally provoked him so he'd be the target, not me. Now, it's my turn to help my friend.

"Asher, you're a lawyer. Unless it involves a client of yours, you're obligated to report a crime. If you hang out with Engels and he does something dodgy, can you turn him in? Give the guy money, for fuck's sake. Just don't let him back in your life."

His argument is logical. I should listen to him. I gulp my beer down in two long sips. "Let's change the topic."

Hudson frowns, his unhappiness clear. "Fine," he concedes. "Did you see the news? Paul Hancock died this afternoon."

"He did?" I ask sharply. I've been in meetings all day, and I haven't had a minute to check the news. "No, I didn't know."

Both Hudson and I have history with the Hancocks. Many years ago, through some slick and unethical corporate maneuvering, Paul Hancock stole a large piece of land in Staten Island from Hudson's father, Nathaniel.

My beef is with Paul's son Thorne, who is, if possible, even more vile than the father. My fingers grip the long neck of my beer bottle. "I suppose Thorne Hancock will inherit his father's money?" God, that makes me furious. After what Thorne did to Lauren, he should be in jail for the rest of his life. Instead, he's walking around, free as a bird. And Lauren's dead.

"I suppose he will," Hudson answers, giving me a sympathetic look. He was there with me at Lauren's funeral. He'd seen Lauren's mother sob with grief, and rage at my inability to convict Thorne. Though ten years have passed, I can still feel the sting of the icy-cold wind on that February afternoon. I can still see Lauren's family somberly shoveling dirt over the coffin of the twenty-one-year-old.

I failed Lauren. I still feel guilty. I still feel responsible.

"The old man has kept Thorne on a pretty tight leash all these years," Hudson is saying.

"That's bullshit," I snarl. "Paul Hancock used his money

to buy his son out of a rape conviction. Paul Hancock lied and cheated, and cut your father out of the biggest deal of his life, almost bankrupting him in the process. Don't make him out to be an angel. He's not."

"I didn't say he was." Hudson's tone is mild.

The damage is done. I'm angry and frustrated. Life's not fair, but the idea of Thorne Hancock inheriting his father's millions just infuriates me.

"I'm leaving," I say shortly, tossing a hundred-dollar bill on the counter. "I'm going to bed."

"We still on for dinner tomorrow?" Hudson calls after my retreating back.

Of course we are. I need a distraction. Wendy Williams is exactly who I'm looking for.

5

Wherever you go, go with all your heart.

— Confucius

Wendy:

I find it difficult to concentrate the next day. I've arranged to meet Asher and Hudson at a private club in the Village called *Residence*. My mind keeps straying from my work, and I pass the hours in a state of nervous anticipation. Finally, at five, I give up and leave, promising myself I'll stay late at work the rest of the week to catch up on my caseload.

"There's are a couple of packages for you, Ms. Williams," my building's doorman says as I walk in. He lifts a large bouquet of candy pink roses from his desk and hands it to me, grinning from ear to ear. "There's this too," he adds, pulling a cardboard box wrapped in silver from a drawer at his desk. "You need a hand with this?"

"No thanks, Andy. I can manage." I arrange the flowers

on top of the parcel while slinging my laptop bag over my shoulder.

Andy gives the precarious arrangement a dubious look. "Are you sure?" he asks. "It'll be a shame to break that vase."

He's right. The cut-glass vase holding the roses is beautiful. The crystal catches the light in the lobby, slicing it into a thousand glittering shards. It looks expensive, and I'd hate to break it. "I'm okay," I tell him, and inch my way toward the elevators. Thankfully, there's a couple waiting at the doors, who press the button to my floor for me when they realize I have my hands full. It's a little trickier at my front door, but I manage by setting the parcel and the flowers on the floor while I fumble for my keys.

Inside, I rip open the wrapping paper and lift out a pair of red and black boxing gloves. There's a note from Hudson and Asher. "For the next time you get into a fight."

My lips twitch. The roses are lovely, and the vase is spectacular, but the boxing gloves show that they have a sense of humor. I like their sense of style.

After a quick shower, I dress for my date in a midnight blue dress with a softly draped neck and a fluttery, asymmetrical hem. I'd seen it in the window of a high-end boutique last year. Unable to resist, I'd bought it, but since then, it's been sitting in the back of my closet. My life isn't usually exciting enough for pretty cocktail dresses.

I pin my hair up in a loose knot. Tendrils escape from the bun and curl around my face, and when I glance in the mirror, I don't look like a barracuda in the slightest.

My heart pounds in my chest. I can't remember the last time I was excited by the prospect of a date. The men I've gone out with in the last few years have been uniformly disappointing. Most of them are intimidated by me, and the few that aren't intimidated are jerks.

This isn't a date, Wendy, I scold myself. *This is the prelude to a hookup. Your panties match your bra, and you've shaved everywhere. Be honest, you're getting ready for sex.*

Am I? Despite my bravado, I'm as jumpy as a skittish kitten. I have no idea what tonight is going to hold.

I'm getting ready to leave when there's a knock on the door. Wondering who it is, I peek through the peephole, but I don't recognize the young man standing outside my door, wearing a rumpled suit. "Who is this?" I ask warily. How did this guy get past Andy at the front desk?

"Is this Wendy Williams?" he asks, his voice just as cautious as mine.

"Yes."

"Ms. Williams, my name is Derek Greene. I work at the law firm of Anderson Massey Dodd. Our firm has been retained to be the executor of Mr. Paul Hancock's will."

I open the door, and the lawyer thrusts an envelope in my direction. A sense of disquiet fills me. In the years I've been a divorce lawyer, I've learned to trust my instincts, and right now, they're telling me that whatever this package contains, it isn't good. "The reading of the will is on Friday afternoon," he says. "You'll find all the details in the envelope."

My father didn't acknowledge my existence once when he was alive. He had thirty years to reach out to me; he never did. And now he never will. There's no more time left. No second chances. I will never be able to look into his eyes and ask him how he could abandon his child without a second thought.

I'm being summoned to the will reading? I couldn't give a damn about the will reading. Fighting my anger, I shake my head and hand the papers back to him. "I'm not interested," I tell Derek Greene dismissively.

A nervous look fills his face. "Ms. Williams, please. Your presence was specifically requested by Mr. Hancock. It's vital that you attend." He swallows hard. "My job is on the line here, and my wife just had a baby. Please..."

Damn it. Though I'm angry at Paul Hancock's presumption, I don't want to get this kid fired. "Fine," I snap, ready for this conversation to end. I have a date tonight, damn it. "I'll be there."

"Thank you." He lowers his voice and leans toward me. "Just between you and me, may I offer a word of advice? Bring a lawyer to the reading."

"I'm a lawyer."

"You're a divorce lawyer," he responds. "Bring someone who knows estate law. Or better still, corporate law."

Corporate law? Why would a corporate lawyer be required for a simple reading of a will? My feeling of unease deepens, but before I can demand an explanation, Derek Greene hurries away.

6

It is one of the blessings of old friends that you can afford
to be stupid with them.

— RALPH WALDO EMERSON

Hudson:

Tuesday is hell.

Our weekly staff meeting takes place on
Tuesday mornings. I used to hold them on
Mondays until I realized that my team was coming in on the
weekends to prepare for it. We work hard at Fleming Architecture—our client load has increased faster than my ability
to handle it, and I've been working until midnight two days
a week—but I also want us to play hard. An architect gets
inspiration from the real world. If we spent all our time
huddled in our cubicles, our work would quickly get stale.

The six architects file into the room. Nadja's first to
arrive. It's a little after nine, but she already looks exhausted.
"Dobson's driving me insane," she complains. "Please tell

me you're going to hire more people. I can't handle everything on my plate."

"I'll have two architects here before the end of the year," I promise her.

"December can't come soon enough." She sinks into her chair. "I've been in here since six."

Colin Cartwright, Heather Maskov, and Mark Summers arrive together. Colin nods curtly at the two of us. Heather gives me a tentative smile, but Mark doesn't meet my eyes, doodling instead on his yellow legal pad. I raise my eyebrow at Nadja, who shrugs in response. *Who can tell what's going on with these three,* she seems to say.

Once the other two have arrived, I get going. "A quick update on the Clark Towers project," I tell them. "The clients have decided to go elsewhere."

Raul, my most recent hire, looks up in surprise. "Where?"

"To Kent."

"We lost another one to Kent?" Colin erupts. "Damn it, Hudson. This is getting ridiculous. At this rate, we're going to be the laughing stock of the city."

Mark and Heather both nod in agreement of Colin's sentiment, but Alyssa, who's been with us for three years, shakes her head. "Everyone knows Kent is garbage," she says. "Word on the street is that *all* of their current projects are running late. In Morocco, the guy who chose Kent just got fired because of the delays."

Ignoring Alyssa, Colin gives me an accusing look. "You passed up on Stanton Towers, and Kent got the contract instead. You refused to bid on Pine Gardens, and Kent picked it up. Not to mention the airport redesign in Bamako. And that's just in the last six months."

Cartwright is an idiot. "Jackson Stanton doesn't pay his

bills," I counter. "The firm that designed his last building is still trying to get paid, five years later. I don't want to spend the next decade in court. Mali is a war zone, and the government is on the verge of getting overthrown. That airport is never going to get built. And Pine Gardens is one of Mikhail Vasiliev's projects, and I'm not going to work for the Russian Mafia." I give Colin a cold stare. "Any others?"

"You're too ethical," he snaps back. "Would it have killed you to give Price a fucking box seat to the Mets game?"

"Price is a basketball fan, not baseball," Nadja cuts in, her voice hard. "It's the Knicks he likes. But tell me, Colin, how do you know what Kent offered Jack Price?"

He doesn't meet her gaze. A chill creeps up my spine. I dislike office politics. I don't spend a lot of time dwelling on Colin's imaginary grievances, but it appears that my indifference has come at a cost because Nadja's right. *How does Colin know?*

The silence grows. "Colin?" I prompt. "Anything you want to tell me?"

He finally looks up. "I met with George Kent last week. He made me an offer." He regains some of his lost bluster. "Not just me. He made Heather and Mark an offer as well."

I go very still.

"It came with a sign-on bonus," he adds. "Fifty thousand dollars if we start right away." He gives me a challenging glare.

"Are you looking for me to counter Kent's offer?" I ask. My gaze swivels from Colin to Mark and then to Heather, who both look like they want to be anywhere else right now. "I'm not going to do that."

"It isn't just about the money, Hudson," Mark pipes up. "We'd all like to lead larger projects."

Mark's last design was a shitshow. If Nadja hadn't bailed

him out, he'd have been seriously over budget. He needs more experience before he's ready to lead. At least, he does at Fleming Architecture. George Kent clearly has lower standards.

"Stop explaining yourself, Mark. Hudson's not going to change." Colin rises to his feet. "I quit. I'll be out of here at the end of the week."

I don't think so. I don't respond well to threats. "Not the end of the week." I get up as well. "The three of you have made your choice. Security will stand by as you clean out your desks. Now."

Two hours later, I call Nadja into my office. "That was fun this morning," she says. "I've been thinking about how we're going to manage. Alyssa can take on Mark's projects and some of Heather's as well. Raul's going to have to come up to speed fast, but he can take the remainder of Heather's work. Which leaves the two of us to deal with Colin's clients."

"That's not why I wanted to meet," I tell her. "I wanted to ask you about Kent. He didn't make you an offer?"

She meets my eyes frankly. "One of his recruiters called me a couple of months ago, and I shot him down. I'm happy where I am, Hudson. You pay me well, and I get to work on interesting projects. I'm not going to give up what I have for the chance to work for a slimeball like George Kent. I do have principles."

Nadja is an amazing architect, but more than that, she's a good person. I don't know what I'd do without her on my team. "Thank you. I don't tell you this enough, but I appreciate your loyalty."

There's a sheen of tears in her eyes. "Don't you get all sentimental on me," she quips. "I won't recognize who you are."

I chuckle. "Our workload's going to be hell."

"I know." She sighs. "Still, we'll be fine as long as we don't take on any more projects."

"Sounds good to me. Okay, let's sort out who's going to work on what."

She shakes her head. "I have to meet Dobson in ten minutes," she says. "How about later this evening? I told Seth I needed to work late, so he's taking the kids to Coney Island."

Tonight, I have dinner plans with the intriguing Wendy Williams. "I can't," I reply. "I have a date."

She looks curious. "Anyone I know?"

Nadja hated Megan from the first day she met her. I wonder what she'll think of Wendy. Not that I have any intention of introducing them; I'm not interested in getting involved with Wendy Williams. I'm just looking for something casual. "No."

"How about tomorrow morning?"

I wonder if Nadja is resentful that she's giving up an evening with her family while I'm out on a date. I doubt it; she's far too nice. Still, I feel a stab of guilt. This is the worst possible time to pursue a woman. If I were smart, I would cancel my dinner plans with Wendy and spend the next forty-eight hours at my desk.

I'm not going to. I hope I don't end up regretting my decision.

7

If you are not willing to risk the unusual, you will have to settle for the ordinary.

— Jim Rohn

Wendy:

On the way over to *Residence*, I get angrier and angrier with my father's presumption, and my earlier lust evaporates. By the time the cab pulls up in front of a building with darkly tinted windows and no signage, I'm half-tempted to tell the driver to turn around.

A valet hurries forward and holds the door open for me. Thanking him, I walk up a short flight of stairs, where a woman waits for me. She's dressed entirely in black and her dark hair is scraped back in a tight ponytail. "Ms. Williams?" she asks with an arch of her perfectly plucked brow. "Mr. Doyle and Mr. Fleming are waiting for you upstairs. Please follow me."

I'm a little intimidated as I trail after her to an elevator.

We ride in silence to the top floor. She leads me down a long hallway and knocks on the door at the end.

Hudson opens it immediately. "Thank you, Naomi," he says politely to the hostess. He smiles at me warmly. "Wendy, come on in."

He's gorgeous, and my heart does a little pitter-patter at that smile of his. Resolutely, I steel myself against his charm. *Even if we do hook up tonight, it's just sex,* I warn myself. There's no need to respond to his smile.

Stepping in, I let my eyes wander around the room, which is empty apart from Hudson and Asher. A black leather sectional fills the space, and the floor-to-ceiling window opposite me has a view of the waterfront. The floor is covered with a plush gray carpet, and candles are scattered on the surface of the coffee table, filling the room with a soft glow.

Asher's seated on the couch, reading something on his phone. When he catches sight of me, he puts it aside and rises to his feet. "You look nervous," he comments, with a wicked gleam in his eyes. "We don't bite."

Of course you do. "This isn't quite what I expected when you invited me to dinner," I reply.

Asher gives me a searching look. "What did you expect?"

Any other day, I'd have bitten my tongue, but Derek Greene's visit has made me cranky. "Well, this club looks like the kind of place where the mafia shoots the lawyer for knowing too much, while the dark-haired woman disposes of the body."

Asher chuckles, low and smooth, while Hudson laughs out loud. "That's very imaginative of you," Hudson says, his eyes twinkling. "Sadly, nothing that exciting has ever happened at *Residence.* Asher and I are protective about our privacy; that's all."

I think back to Lara and Helen's gossip, at the way the bartender at *Nerve* had flaunted her boobs in their faces. I can see how they might get tired of that. "Thank you for the flowers and the boxing gloves," I remember to say.

Asher's lips lift in a grin. He moves over to a side table containing an assortment of bottles. "Do you like champagne?" he asks, gesturing to a silver bucket.

My eyes widen when I catch sight of the label. The Krug Clos du Mesnil is a thousand-dollar bottle. *Toto, we aren't in Kansas anymore.* "That's too nice a bottle to gulp down like two-buck-chuck," I mutter ruefully. Of course, I'm still going to down it like there's a global shortage on champagne.

"Why do you want to gulp it down?" Asher asks. His eyes search my face, and he frowns, his voice softening with concern. "Wendy, are you okay?"

No, I'm not. My emotions are in turmoil. I'm trying to forget about the will reading. *Damn my father.*

I give them a little nod and take the glass Asher hands me, tipping the champagne down my throat. God, that's good. The liquid tastes like a million drops of sun-warmed grapes dancing in my mouth.

Hudson sits next to me, close enough that I can feel the heat emanate from his body. "Wendy," he says soothingly, placing his hand over mine. "There's no pressure, I promise. Nothing needs to happen. You don't need to drink yourself into a stupor to have sex with us."

I give him a startled look. *That's why they think I'm drinking?* "That's not why I'm upset," I mutter. "I received some unsettling news this evening."

Asher settles himself down on the couch as well, across from us. "Want to talk about it?"

Do I? If Bailey, Piper or Miki asked me that question, I'd spill my guts, but I don't know these two men well enough to confide in them. "Just a messed up family situation," I say with a shrug. "It's no big deal, really. I'm silly to let it bother me."

A skeptical look crosses Asher's face. "If you say so," he replies. He leans forward with the bottle and refills my glass. "You hungry?"

My stomach growls at that moment, answering Asher's question. Hudson rises easily to his feet, crossing the room in long steps. On a side table next to the booze, appetizers have been set out, cheese, olives, and cured meats, veggies and dip, and much more. Hudson fills a plate with food and sets it on the coffee table. "Dinner should be served in thirty minutes," he says.

I reach for a piece of cheddar. "This place serves food?"

"Very good food," Hudson replies. "It's not quite at the level of your friend Piper's restaurant, but Rinaldo Oliviera does a very good Brazilian-inspired tasting menu."

I haven't mentioned Piper to them. I lift an eyebrow. "You googled me?"

"Of course," Hudson says readily. Asher's sipping away at his champagne, watching me with unnerving attention. "Does that come as a surprise?"

"Not really." My cheeks flush under Asher's scrutiny. "I googled you as well."

"What did you learn?" Hudson shrugs off his jacket and loosens his tie. He uncuffs his shirt and rolls up his sleeves, and I swallow as his strong forearms flex. Warmth floods my body, and I can't tear my gaze away from his big, callused hands, caressing the fragile stem of his wineglass.

I drag my focus back to his question. "You were married," I tell Hudson. "You got divorced last year."

He stiffens imperceptibly. "What else?" he asks, his tone deliberately casual.

The topic of the divorce is off-limits, evidently. "You're an architect. You've been nominated for the Pritzker Prize twice. You've been hired to build your third skyscraper in New York, the design of which is going to be unveiled next month."

"Clark Towers?" He shakes his head, his lips twisting into a wry smile. "Unfortunately, we just lost that deal. It's not public knowledge yet, so I'd be grateful if you kept it to yourself."

I have to admit; I appreciate the gesture of trust.

"What about me?" Asher speaks up. "What did Google uncover?"

My smile widens. "Well, I did find out that both of you were featured four years ago on the Village's annual list of New York's most eligible bachelors. Number 10 and 12, if I remember correctly."

That elicits a groan from both of them. "We're never going to live that stupid article down," Asher quips. "What else?"

I snag a cracker and spread some Brie on it. "Your billing rate is two thousand dollars an hour," I say. "Which is pretty damn impressive. But that's not what has me intrigued."

"What does?" Asher stretches his legs out and leans back. He looks like a predator sizing up his prey, biding his time, waiting for the perfect moment to pounce. That thought sends a shiver through me, and once again, I have to force my mind back to our conversation.

"What I really want to know is why you gave up on being a public defender ten years ago and became a corporate lawyer."

His eyes darken. "There's more money in corporate law," he replies smoothly.

Another deflection. I don't think Asher is telling me the

truth. This is a very nice club, and Asher wears very expensive clothes, but I still think there's something more.

"My turn," he says. "You went to Yale Law on a scholarship, and you graduated in the top ten percent of your class. You had over a dozen offers with some extremely prestigious law firms, but to everyone's surprise, you picked Johnson Nash Adams. So tell me," he asks, his eyes resting on me. "Why does someone who could have worked at any law firm in the city end up becoming a divorce lawyer?"

"You found all of that on the Internet?"

He shakes his head. "Peter Reyes was in your class at Yale."

Of course. Pete works at Doyle and Miller. I'd forgotten that. "Nice guy, Pete," I say blandly. "Very driven."

There's a knock on the door, followed by a white-clad waiter, who wheels a cart into the room. He sets three exquisitely plated portions on the coffee table in front of us. "Charcoal-grilled octopus served with a cauliflower puree and vinegared peppers," he announces. "Bon appetit."

It looks delicious, and I'm starving. "You eat seafood, I hope?" Hudson asks. "Sorry, we should have checked if you have any food restrictions."

"I eat everything," I say frankly, flushing red as soon as the words leave my mouth.

Asher's lips curl up in an amused smile. "Good," he says. "Let's dig in."

The conversation flows easily over dinner. Hudson and I chat about architecture; Asher and I talk about mutual acquaintances. While we don't move in the same legal circles, there's a handful of lawyers that we both know. I discuss my latest case, telling them how Miki helped me find Lippman's missing money. We talk about books and movies, and the latest shows on Broadway.

To my surprise, we also talk about our families and where we grew up. Hudson's from Manhattan. It's clear from his description of his childhood that he's always been wealthy. Asher, on the other hand, is from Scranton, New Jersey. "I bounced around from one foster home to another," he says when I ask him about his family. "My parents lost custody of me when I was five. They're dead now."

I must look astonished because he raises an eyebrow. "Not what you expected, Wendy?"

I can't lie. "No," I tell him. "You wear the wealth well. You look like you were born to it."

He laughs. "Not if you talk to Hudson's friends on the Upper East Side," he quips. "They're all discreetly fascinated by me. I'm the bad boy they want to bed."

"You don't sound bitter by it." I grin at him. "Sounds like you use your reputation to your advantage."

Hudson laughs openly at Asher's expression. "It's very refreshing to see someone mock Asher," he comments. "What about you, Wendy? Where are you from?"

"Fredonia," I reply with a shudder, thinking of the small town where I grew up. "And I wanted to escape it as soon as I could."

"Do you still have family there?" Asher asks.

"My mother." Before they can ask, I blurt out, "My father wasn't around growing up."

I don't want to think of Paul Hancock right now. Thankfully, they don't probe.

My anger has faded over the course of the excellent dinner. I've just finished eating a fantastic mango crème brulee, and I want to retain the warm glow I feel. The meal and the champagne have relaxed me and loosened my tongue.

"So, Wendy." Hudson gives me a look that I can't quite

decipher. His voice lowers, and I lean toward him almost instinctively. "I know what you do for work. Tell me, what do you do for pleasure?"

I can feel my cheeks flood with color. "Pleasure?" I ask, unable to meet either of their gazes. There's a distinct tremble in my voice, and the heat that vanished because of Derek Greene's visit comes roaring back in a blaze. "Not a lot. I'm not as exciting as the two of you."

"Really?" Asher looks unconvinced. "Three of your close friends are in ménages. What about you?"

I shake my head mutely.

"You've never been tempted?" Hudson murmurs.

"In my fantasies, maybe," I whisper.

"But not in reality." Asher gets up to refill our drinks, and when he sits back down, he settles next to me. I'm now sandwiched between the two of them. "Why not?" He brushes a strand of my hair back from my neck, and his fingers linger over a vein beating in my throat.

I bite my lower lip nervously, but don't pull away. "I don't understand it," I confess. "I don't understand *why* you share women."

Asher and Hudson exchange glances. Hudson's finger-tips brush my forearm, and I shiver again, goosebumps rising on my skin. "I don't think of it as sharing," he says, his voice pitched low. "I think of it as giving pleasure. One orgasm after another, until your legs tremble and you think you might never be able to stand again. Until you can't remember your name, until every bit of need is replaced by fulfilled desire. Until you are replete, satiated."

My breathing catches at the heat in Hudson's eyes. Asher's hand lifts to my hair, and he starts pulling pins loose. "Do you ever give in to your fantasies, Wendy?" he says, his breath hot against my ear. "Do you ever let your hair down?"

The pins fall to the floor, the sound muffled by the weave of the carpet. I inhale sharply, my fingers clutching at the stem of my glass for strength as Asher's fingers run through the strands of my hair. "What are you doing?"

Desire is in the air. Desire, with a hint of danger. These men are not in my league. I should be sensible; I should gather my belongings and run before I'm tempted to do something stupid.

"Kissing you," Hudson replies simply. Then his lips crash down on mine.

The need I've held at bay all night blazes free. The kiss is gentle at first, giving me time to pull away, but I don't want to. I groan, parting my lips, leaning into him, giving into my desire. His tongue slides into my mouth. Through a daze, I feel Asher tug the champagne flute from my grip, and then his mouth trails hot kisses at the back of my neck.

The hardness of their bodies blanketing mine causes my head, already spinning from the champagne I've consumed all night, to whirl and gyrate in dizzying circles. I close my eyes and give in to the moment. Hudson's hand—*or is it Asher?* - is on the back of my neck, tugging me closer. I feel another touch on my shoulder, and fingertips glide, maddeningly slow, down my neck, to rest at the valley between my breasts. "This dress," Asher mutters, his tone thick with lust. "All night, every time you've leaned forward, I've been able to see your bra." His fingers ghost over the silk. "It's a very sexy view."

"Please..." I breathe, almost overwhelmed by the dazzling sensations that explode over my body at his touch. My vibrator, handy though it is, can't do this. "More..." I shift my legs, and my heels brush against the coffee table.

An empty bottle of champagne falls to the floor with a dull thud, the thick carpet cushioning the drop and preventing the glass from shattering.

But the sound cools their lust. The two men exchange glances and pull back reluctantly. I blink, confused at the sudden change in mood. They're aroused; I can tell. Their cocks are hard and thick, the outline clear through the fabric of their pants. *Why have they stopped?*

"Wendy." Asher's voice breaks the silence, regret etched on his face. "I want this. God knows I want this, but…" His voice trails off, and he picks up the bottle from the floor, setting it down once again on the table in front of us. He gestures to the four empty bottles of champagne. "You're upset. You're more than a little drunk. We shouldn't take advantage of you."

I'm not *that* drunk. It feels like I've been drenched by a bucket of ice-cold water. Yikes. I'm such a fool.

"Listen to me." Hudson puts his finger on my chin, tipping my face up. "We're trying to do the right thing. Have dinner with us on Friday, please."

Friday is the day of the will reading. That thought is sobering. "Yes." I accept before I change my mind and do something sensible. I won't let Paul Hancock interfere with my life from the grave.

Asher smiles warmly. "Before dinner," he suggests, "would you like to go to our boxing gym?" His eyes twinkle. "What do you say, Wendy? Want to break in those gloves of yours?"

God knows that after the will reading, I'm going to need to punch something. "I'd love to," I reply. "But I've got to warn you. I don't know what I'm doing."

Asher chuckles. "You're a divorce lawyer. You already know how to fight. You'll catch on quickly."

They call a cab and accompany me home. They walk me to my apartment and wait for me to fish my keys out and open the front door. *Asher's a corporate lawyer,* I think, as they prepare to leave. *Ask him for help on Friday. Derek Greene's warned you that you're going to need a lawyer.*

I stay silent. Asher and Hudson appear trustworthy. But I've never yet trusted a man enough to be vulnerable, to ask for help, and the habits of a lifetime aren't changed easily. I'll manage on my own.

8

Do not dwell in the past, do not dream of the future, concentrate the mind on the present moment.

— Buddha

Asher:

Thursday afternoon, Vivian buzzes me. "You have another unscheduled visitor," she says. "This one's a cop. He says it's about Mr. Engels."

"Of course it is." Three days with Levi at my place and cops are already visiting me. I wonder what I have to look forward to in a month. "I'll see him now," I tell her. "Can you delay my three o'clock meeting?"

A large man with graying hair and black rimmed glasses enters the room. "Sorry to bother you without an appointment, Mr. Doyle," he says, reaching forward to shake my hand. "I was in the neighborhood, and I thought I'd drop by. My name is Patrick Sullivan."

"No problem," I reply, waving him to a seat. "What's this about?"

"You're probably wondering who I am," he says. "I'm Levi Engels' parole officer."

"Is Levi in trouble?"

The cop shakes his head. "Not yet," he says heavily. "Look, can I be honest with you? Deep down, Levi's a good guy. His heart is in the right place. But every time he gets out of jail, he starts hanging out with Beecham's gang, and sooner or later, he gets into trouble."

I fish a couple of bottles of water out of the refrigerator and hand him one. "Why are you telling me this?"

"Because I'm counting on you to keep an eye on him," he says. He gives me a serious look. "Word on the street is that Lloyd Beecham is planning a big heist."

"Levi's a grown man, Mr. Sullivan," I tell the cop. "I can provide him a place to stay, but that's about the limit of what I can do. I can't keep him from his friends."

"This isn't just about keeping Engels out of jail, Mr. Doyle." Patrick Sullivan leans forward and fixes me with a piercing gaze. "This is about keeping him alive. You see, Beecham doesn't know it, but the warehouse he's thinking of robbing belongs to Mikhail Vasiliev."

Ice trickles down my spine. Mikhail Vasiliev is the head of the Russian Bratva. He's the most dangerous man in the New York Metro area.

"I see from your reaction that you know who Vasiliev is, Mr. Doyle. Then you know how serious the matter is. There are consequences to stealing from the *mafiya*."

"What do you want me to do?"

"Watch Levi," he says. "If you find any sign that he's slipping back in with Beecham," he slides a business card across my table, "contact me right away."

I take the card and tuck it in my wallet. Sullivan rises to his feet. "Have a good day, Mr. Doyle."

∾

Hudson:

I spend most of Thursday catching up on work, but my thoughts keep drifting to Wendy. The way she'd stepped in to defend that woman at the club without a thought about her own safety. The abandon with which she'd kissed me. The passion with which she'd talked about her work.

She intrigues me. I can't wait to see her again.

Is this wise? My conscience prods me. Wendy is a good person. All I'm willing to offer her is a temporary fling, and she deserves so much better than that. She deserves the full, undivided attention of someone who wants to make her happy, and I can't be that man. Not after Megan.

I get back to my apartment just as the sun begins to set. Roger, the doorman in my building, waves when he catches sight of me, and I detour toward his desk. "A gentleman dropped this off for you, Mr. Fleming," he says, handing me a large envelope. "He said it was urgent."

"Thanks, Roger." The damn thing looks like it's from a law firm. My thoughts instantly go to Megan, and I bitterly wonder if she's run out of money. It won't be the first time. I've had to fend off more than one attempt to renegotiate our divorce settlement.

Exhaling with frustration, I rip the cover open. It's not from Megan's lawyer. It's from a law firm I don't recognize, Anderson Massey Dodd. The letter tells me that their firm has been appointed the executor of Paul Hancock's will, and request my attendance at the reading of the will, which will take place on Friday afternoon. I'm welcome to bring my lawyer, but the event is otherwise private.

I don't understand what's going on. My father had done business with Paul Hancock, but he cut ties with the man after the Staten Island deal, and never spoke to him again. I can't think of any reason for me to be invited to tomorrow's gathering. *This can't be good.*

I call Asher. "Something's happened," I tell him grimly when he picks up the phone. "I've been named a beneficiary in Paul Hancock's will."

"What?" He sounds shocked. "Do you think it's connected to Staten Island?"

"It has to be, but why now, after all these years?"

My heart aches when I think of that land in Staten Island, about the many conversations my father and I had had about his plans for the property. He'd wanted to build a mixed-use complex in the borough, with senior housing, low-income housing and enough retail to make the project profitable for a developer. "When you become an architect, Hudson," he'd tell me, "you can design it for me. Deal?"

"Deal," I would reply, though the project had never been as real to me as it had to him.

In the three painful months following his death, I'd worked on those drawings, night and day, until I was done. It had been my way of mourning him. No one has ever seen those sketches, not Nadja, not even Asher, but it is my best work, a way to honor the man who had raised me to be a decent human being.

Asher doesn't reply to my question. "How did you find out about being a beneficiary?" he asks.

"The law firm managing his estate sent me a letter. The will reading is tomorrow at two."

"Did they say something about being able to bring a lawyer? That's routine in cases like this."

"Yes." I re-read the letter in my hand. "Can you make it?"

"You bet." He sounds grim. "If there's even the slightest chance that Thorne's not going to inherit his father's money, I'm going to be there."

I hear someone say something in the background, and Asher mutters a curse. "Got to go, Hudson. There's a crisis here. I'll swing by your work tomorrow, and we can ride up together, okay?"

I'm about to hang up when something strikes me. "Will Thorne Hancock recognize you?" I ask my friend. I'm always hesitant to mention Lauren to Asher. Some wounds cut deep, and none had cut deeper than her death. "From the trial?"

"I doubt it," he replies. "It was ten years ago, and we only met once in court. He's unlikely to remember my name."

Something tells me things won't be quite as simple as that. Something tells me that tomorrow is going to be very, *very* complicated.

9

Life is 10% what happens to you and 90% how you react to it.

— CHARLES R. SWINDOLL

Wendy:

I'm a divorce attorney. I know how to dress for battle. Friday morning, I choose my most severe gray suit and pair it with a pale blue silk blouse. Four-inch heels complete the picture. I apply my makeup with a careful hand. Today, I need to look formidable.

Beverly whistles when she sees me. She beckons me over. "Are you interviewing at another law firm?" she asks me in a hushed voice.

"What?" I give her an astonished look. "What would give you that idea?"

"It's Friday, and you're all dressed up," she points out. "Also, you've been leaving work earlier than normal all week."

Oh, good grief. I've probably become the topic of gossip for the entire firm. None of the lawyers leave before eight in the evening. Working long hours is par for the course. Even if I make partner, I'll still be expected to put in a minimum of sixty hours a week.

Is this what you want to do for the rest of your life?

I dismiss that uncomfortable thought. *I love my job,* I tell myself firmly. I love helping people in trouble. I've worked hard for it. But a nagging feeling of discontent remains.

A little after one, I head to the nearby offices of Anderson Massey Dodd and ride the elevator to the thirty-third floor. The young woman at the reception looks up with a smile as I march up to her. "Can I help you?" she asks pleasantly.

I discreetly wipe my palms on my skirt. I'm nervous about today. Being asked to show up for this reading is so unexpected, and I have no idea what to expect. "I'm here for the will reading of Paul Hancock," I reply. Even though law offices are familiar surroundings for me, I feel out of place here. I'm waiting for someone to call me an impostor. What connection do I have with Paul Hancock, after all? One sperm managed to penetrate one egg thirty-one years ago. Does that make him a parent? Of course not.

"And your name is?"

"Wendy Williams."

I must be on a list because she nods immediately and rises from her chair. "Let me show you to the conference room."

I follow her down a short hallway to a large meeting room. There's a round table that can seat about twenty in the center of the room. About a dozen people are already there, standing around the table in groups of twos and threes, engaged in quiet conversation. When I enter, muted whispers break out, and a couple of people stare openly at me.

If the receptionist senses the tension in the room, she doesn't let on. She leads me toward the food-covered tables lining one wall of the room. There's coffee and juice, a tray of sliced fruit, and an assortment of pastries. "Please help yourself," she says. "I'll fetch Mr. Greene."

I'm not sure if anyone knows who I am, and I'm not ready for conversation. Butterflies are doing the Lord of the Dance in my stomach. Though I skipped lunch, I'm too nervous to eat, so I pour some hot water into a mug and find a bag of green tea. While it steeps, I nibble on a piece of pineapple, staying in my corner.

A minute later, Derek Greene hurries into the room and makes a beeline in my direction. "I thought I told you to bring a lawyer," he hisses into my ear. "They're going to eat you alive."

"I can take care of myself," I lie. My heart is hammering in my chest. The looks people are giving me aren't friendly, and I have a bad feeling about what's going to come next. I wish belatedly that I had asked Asher for help. Me and my stupid pride.

"You're being a fool," Derek says bluntly. The door opens again, and he stops talking abruptly. A tall man with slicked-back blond hair and an unpleasant glare on his face walks in. I've never met him, but I have seen photos of him online. This is my half-brother, Thorne Hancock.

Thorne walks around the room, greeting the people there. When he catches sight of me, a frown appears on his face. "Who the heck are you?" he snaps. "And what are you doing here?"

I wonder what would happen if I tell Thorne the truth. I feel no obligation to keep Paul Hancock's secret. Lillian

Hancock, Paul's wife, is the only person I might want to protect, but she's been dead for fifteen years.

An innate sense of caution keeps me quiet. Information is power, and until I know why I've been invited today, I'm going to hold my tongue.

A gray-haired man standing nearby intervenes before I can think of an answer. "Your father wanted Ms. Williams here." He holds out his hand in greeting. "My name is Bill Anderson," he says. "I'm the executor of Mr. Paul Hancock's estate. I'm so glad you could make it here today." He turns to my half-brother, who's still glowering at me. "Thorne, why don't you take a seat? We're just waiting for one more person and then we can get started."

Everyone moves to a seat. No one sits next to me; the chairs on either side are left vacant. *We might as well be in high school again.*

A couple of minutes after two, the receptionist pushes open the conference room door. Two men walk into the room, possibly the last two men I expected to meet at my father's will reading. Hudson and Asher.

You've got to be kidding me.

I'm shocked to see them, but not as shocked as they are to see me. Hudson stops dead in his tracks. Asher, a half-pace behind, almost collides into him before drawing up short. I'm looking right at them as they enter and I can see the flare of astonishment on both their faces.

Bill Anderson springs to his feet and shakes Asher's hand. "Mr. Doyle," he gushes. "What a pleasure it is to meet you. I don't know if you remember me, but we were on a panel together last year at the Law Society."

Asher smiles politely. "Of course," he replies. "Tort reform, wasn't it? Good to see you again, Bill. Sorry we're late."

"It's my fault," Hudson says, moving to the vacant seat on my left. "Work was a little crazy this morning."

If my presence caused a stir in the room, it's nothing compared to the consternation that Hudson's arrival causes. Multiple conversations break out in the room. The man sitting next to Thorne taps on his shoulder and says something urgently, his gaze never leaving Hudson's face.

Hudson ignores the chaos and ducks his head in my direction. "What are you doing here?" he asks in a low voice.

Asher settles himself at my right and leans toward us, trying to overhear my answer. I take a deep breath. I've never told anyone who my father is. I've kept Paul Hancock's secret my entire life. Until now.

"You remember when I said my father wasn't around growing up?" I ask them. "It was Paul Hancock."

They are visibly shocked. "Does Thorne know?" Asher asks, a note of urgency in his voice. "Does he know there's another claimant to the estate?"

I shake my head. "I don't want to be here," I confess in a whisper. "I'm not going to claim anything."

Hudson's hand closes over mine. "Be careful," he warns quietly.

Bill Anderson rises to his feet, and the room falls silent, cutting off our conversation. "Everyone's here," he says. He gestures to the massive monitor hanging on one wall. "Let's get started. Please direct your attention to the screen."

Asher and Hudson lean back, their expressions carefully neutral. Bill Anderson fiddles with a remote, and my father's face fills the screen.

My breath catches. I've never seen the man. He should mean nothing to me, but seeing his face, lined with pain as he struggles to sit up in the hospital bed, I feel strangely emotional. His skin looks deathly pale, and his breathing is labored. He's clearly dying in this video. What was he thinking in his last few days? Did he regret never connecting with me? It's too late to find out.

"Hello everyone," he says before he's seized by a coughing fit. A nurse comes into view and fusses over him, but he waves her away and turns to the camera once again. "If you're watching this video, I'm dead." His lips twist into a wry grimace. "Please don't feel sorry for me. I've had a better life than I deserve. I've done so many things I'm ashamed of."

His voice trails off and he stares into the screen sadly for almost a minute before continuing. "But as my clock ticks down and the end approaches, I want to make amends."

A cold dread prickles at the back of my neck. I have a sudden premonition that I'm standing on the threshold of something big—something that is going to transform my life.

Sure enough, he says the words I've waited an entire lifetime to hear. "When I was younger, I had an affair with a woman who worked for me," he says. "That affair produced a child I've never acknowledged. My daughter, Wendy Williams."

There's an audible gasp in the room. Thorne jumps to his feet, his chair toppling over with a loud crash. "Are you fucking kidding me?" he snarls. "Bill, what the fuck is this?"

"Sit down." Anderson's voice is curt. "Let your father speak."

Paul Hancock keeps talking on the screen. "I haven't been much of a human being," he says. "I spent my life building my company. I devoted everything to Hancock Construction. And now that I'm dying, I find myself at a crossroads." There's another long pause, and he takes a sip of water before continuing. "Who should run Hancock

Construction after my death? Is it my son Thorne, who has been my second-in-command for the last four years? Or my daughter Wendy?"

My body goes cold. *Please*, I pray silently. *Please don't do this.*

He's doing this. "Hancock Construction employs ten thousand people." My father's eyes, the same unusually light blue color of my own, shine with emotion. "People whose livelihoods depend on me making the right decision. I've thought about what to do for many months, and I've finally reached a conclusion."

Everything is going very badly wrong. *No, no, no. Please, no.*

Under the table, Hudson's hand rests on my thigh. Asher moves closer to me, solid and reassuring. "We're here," he murmurs. "You're not alone."

"I've set aside two projects," my father says on the screen. "A complex in Staten Island and a highway in South Carolina. I want Wendy to run the Staten Island project, and I want Thorne to run the one in Beaufort. You both have a year to complete the projects. The person that does the best job at the end will inherit my company."

At the mention of Staten Island, a look of understanding dawns on Hudson's face. I'm about to ask him when Thorne flings his cup of coffee in a shocking gesture of violence at the monitor. Shards of glass fly everywhere and a web of cracks appear on the screen, radiating from the point of impact. People jump to their feet.

"I've heard enough," my half-brother rages. He addresses me directly, his expression intensely hostile. "You're not the first gold-digger I've come across in my life," he says. "And you won't be the last. I don't know what you did or said to my father to convince him to set up this insane contest, but if you think I'm going to stand by and allow this to happen, you're wrong. I will take you to court, and I will ruin you."

Shocked whispers erupt at Thorne's tirade. I'm too shell-shocked to react. "Thorne Hancock," Bill Anderson says sternly. "The will is valid. I was there when your father made it. These are his wishes."

"Fuck his wishes," Thorne barks. "Hancock Construction is my birthright." He leans over the table, an almost crazed look on his face, and he looks into my eyes. "If you want to survive," he warns me, "Walk away from this mess. Leave now, and we'll pretend this never happened."

Well, that got ugly pretty quickly. At my side, both Asher and Hudson tense, and Hudson pushes himself to his feet, his face inches from Thorne's. "You threaten Wendy again, and I'll make sure you regret it." His voice isn't loud, but there's so much menace layered in his tone that the hair on the back of my neck stands up.

Bill Anderson clears his throat. "Do you want to hear the rest of the terms or not?" he snaps at Thorne, who settles back in his seat, giving Hudson a look of loathing. Anderson continues, ignoring the coffee slowly dripping down the screen. "Here's how the contest is going to work," he says. "Ms. Williams, Mr. Hancock recognized that his son, who has worked at Hancock Construction since college, has many built-in advantages. However, he recruited a team of people to help you." He clears his throat and looks at Hudson. "Given the history of the Staten Island plot, he hoped that Mr. Fleming would agree to be the architect."

What history? I have no time to ask Hudson because Bill Anderson keeps talking. "At the end of the year, I will judge, along with the board of directors, which project has been the most successful." He gives us a stern look. "I will be monitoring both projects. If there's any hint of cheating or fraud, I have the authority to cancel the contest and put the company up for sale."

He turns to me. "Your father realized that he couldn't force you to participate," he says. "But he wanted to remind you that the livelihood of thousands of people was at stake. What do you think, Ms. Williams? Are you in?"

Everyone in the room is watching me. Some people look uncomfortable, but several wear thinly veiled sneers. *You don't belong here,* their expressions seem to say. *You're out of your league.*

They're right. I know nothing about construction. I have a job already, one I like. How can I pull this off?

I don't know what to do.

10

A man that studieth revenge keeps his own wounds green.

— Francis Bacon

Asher:

For an instant, I lose myself in a fantasy. Wendy agrees to Paul Hancock's insane conditions. Hudson designs the most beautiful building in the world, and I get the legal and regulatory hassles out of the way. The three of us get the Staten Island complex built, and Wendy inherits Hancock Construction.

And Thorne Hancock is left with nothing.

For ten years, I've waited for an opportunity like this. Thorne should be rotting in jail for raping Lauren, but that's never going to happen. Bankrupting him isn't as rewarding as sending him to prison, but it'll do.

All I have to do is convince Wendy to say yes.

"Gentlemen." I look around the room before making eye contact with Bill Anderson. "Before she makes any decisions, I'd like to talk to Ms. Williams, please. Bill, will you excuse us for a few minutes?"

"Of course." Anderson nods immediately. "Why don't you take my office? No one will disturb you there."

Wendy stares at me, puzzled by my request, but Hudson, who knows of my history with Thorne, understands at once. He levels a frown at me. *You can't do this,* his expression seems to say.

Anderson escorts the three of us to his office, and leaves us alone, shutting the door on his way out. As soon as he's out of the room, Wendy sinks into a chair and buries her face in her hands with a sigh. "What a mess."

"You didn't know what your father was planning?" I pull up a chair next to her.

"I knew Paul Hancock was my biological father," she replies stiffly. "I didn't know he was going to do this." She takes a deep breath. "We never even met. What on earth was he thinking? That I'd drop everything to run his company?" Her voice rises. "How dare he?"

"Thorne's not going to take this lying down," Hudson says, perching on Anderson's desk. "He's going to go on the offensive."

He's right. From bitter experience, I know Thorne fights dirty. Lauren killed herself because of his attacks. I can't expose Wendy to the same fate.

Wendy's chin lifts in a stubborn tilt. "I can take care of myself," she replies.

Hudson runs his hands through his hair. "You're seriously thinking about this?" he asks, sounding frustrated. "Is the money so damn important?"

"The money? You think I care about Paul Hancock's money?" Wendy laughs bitterly. "He gave my mother ten thousand dollars and told her to stay away from him. If I'd wanted to be rich, I could have approached him when he was alive. I'm sure he'd have paid a lot of cash to keep the truth from surfacing."

Her hands clench into fists. "My mother was laid off once when I was seven," she continues softly. "She couldn't pay her bills, and we were evicted from our apartment. Thankfully, it was summer. We spent two months living in her car until she found another job."

She fixes us with a fiery look. "I've kept up with the news on Hancock Construction. You know why Thorne's project is a highway build? Because that's the direction Thorne wants to take the company. But infrastructure is a lot more competitive and a lot riskier than residential and office construction, and guess who suffers if Hancock Construction fails? Not the business owners. No, it's the little people that'll bear the brunt of it. Should I stand by and watch it happen?"

I look at Wendy with new respect. She's no fool. She's smart and tough, and she has a good read on what's happening at her father's company.

She's sitting there, leaning forward, her eyes shining animatedly, her cheeks flushed with color. Looking at her, seeing her passion, her fire, her willingness to do the right thing for all the workers of Hancock Construction, I've never been more attracted to anyone in my entire life.

My voice softens. "You're used to doing things by yourself," I guess. "You don't like to ask for help, do you?"

Her lips curl into a wry smile. "I don't," she admits. "But I can't do this by myself. Bill Anderson was right; I need a team." Her voice lowers to almost a whisper. "Will you help me?"

I have to make one last-ditch attempt to dissuade her

from this. I don't want her hurt, damn it. "If you were my client, I'd advise you to reach a settlement with Thorne."

"I'm not going to do that."

Damn it. "Wendy, please. I know your half-brother. He's ruthless, and he's dangerous. I can't promise to keep you safe."

She puts her hand on my arm. "Did something happen?" she asks quietly. "Between you and Thorne?"

I can't think of Lauren now. My insides are too heavy with fear. I barely know the woman sitting next to me, but she makes me feel things that I thought I'd never feel again.

Tuesday night, I would have sworn that my interest in Wendy was purely physical. Today, watching her prepare to fight, I'm not so certain. "I can't tell you the details," I reply. "But please, Wendy, will you trust me? You don't want to do this."

It had been so cold by Lauren's grave. I feel the same chill now.

"I have to." She looks troubled. "I'm angry with Paul Hancock for disrupting my life. I want to be selfish; I want to walk away. But I can't." Her grip on my bicep tightens. "I hope you can understand that."

Hudson slants a look in my direction before nodding at Wendy. "You're going to need an architect," he says. "I'm in. Asher, in or out?"

Wendy's words echo in my ears. *I want to walk away, but I can't.* "I'm in too."

"Thank you." She smiles at us, warm and grateful, then her expression turns playful. "You both look really worried, but you shouldn't be. I've been taking boxing lessons, you know, and I even own a pair of gloves."

I flash a grin at her, but there's a dead weight in my stomach. I have to make sure that Wendy is protected.

Everyone's still in their seats when the three of us return to the conference room. "I'm in," Wendy announces without preamble.

To no one's surprise, Thorne does not take the news well. "You dumb bitch," he screams. "I will destroy you. I will bankrupt you. I will sue you into oblivion, do you hear me?" He glares at all of us. "I will make you regret this moment until you die."

"Is that a fucking threat?" My hands clench into fists. I will kill Thorne with my bare heads before I let him harm a hair on Wendy's head.

Wendy looks unfazed by Thorne's tirade. She straightens her shoulders and lifts her head high. "If that's the way you want to deal with this, I'll see you in court," she says calmly. She turns to Anderson, ignoring Thorne completely. Though I'm afraid for her, I have to admire her composure. She's as cool as a cucumber; I'll give her that.

"Excellent." Anderson shakes Wendy's hand vigorously. "Your father hoped you would step up. I'll make sure you have an office at Hancock Construction. It should be ready on Monday. There's a team waiting as well. Best of luck, Ms. Williams. I'll be in touch."

"Are you free sometime this weekend?" Wendy asks Hudson and me downstairs. "So we can figure out how to tackle this thing?"

Hudson laughs. "We're seeing you tonight," he reminds her. "I'm slightly heartbroken that you've forgotten our date."

She flushes. "I wasn't sure if you'd still want to go out," she mutters, not looking up. Her fingers worry at the hem of her gray jacket. "Now that we're going to be working together."

She's right. If I were being logical, I'd agree with her.

Wendy's now a client, and Thorne's gunning for her. This is Lauren all over again. If I had any sense, I'd protect my heart. But there's nothing logical about the sharp stab of disappointment that pierces me at the idea of canceling tonight's plans. I want her fire, her passion, and her softness.

"I'm sure," I reply. "I have to work for a couple of hours before our date, but we'll pick you up at seven?"

"Okay," she agrees. Then her smile disappears. "I just realized I have to tell the partners at my firm what I've just done."

"Are you going to be okay?"

She raises a shoulder in a shrug. "I guess I'll find out."

Once Wendy's gone, Hudson turns to me, a troubled look in his eyes. "What now?" he asks.

"I'm going to call Stone Bradley," I reply. "I need dirt on Thorne, and I need a guard on Wendy."

He looks up. "You think Thorne will resort to physical violence?"

"I can't take any chances."

"Fair enough," he agrees. He grimaces. "And I get to tell Nadja I signed up for yet another massive project."

"Can you manage the additional work?"

"Who needs sleep?" he asks dryly. "Still, my offer to help Wendy wasn't totally selfless. Staten Island was my father's dream project. If I get to build it for him..." His voice trails off.

"I understand." Hudson loved his father. He's going to want to work on this project to honor his memory.

And me? I went up against Thorne at the start of my career and lost. I can't lie. I want another go at the man, and this time, I want to win.

11

My great concern is not whether you have failed, but whether you are content with your failure.

— ABRAHAM LINCOLN

Wendy:

I've been avoiding talking to my mom ever since Derek Greene showed up at my door, but I can't put off the conversation any further. She deserves to know what's happening.

I'm not sure how she's going to react. Through my childhood, it was made clear to me that my mother didn't wanted to talk about my father. It was one of the very few things I was never allowed to ask questions about.

Then, on my eighteenth birthday, my mother told me the whole sordid story, and I understood why she preferred to forget Paul Hancock. The man who took her virginity had lied to her about being single when it turned out he was married. When he found out she was pregnant, he got her fired and paid her off, rather than deal with the consequences of his actions.

I don't blame her for wanting to forget him.

With shaking fingers, I dial her number.

"Wendy," she exclaims when she answers, her voice lighting up with pleasure. "You're a hard woman to reach. I've barely spoken to you this week."

"It's been a little crazy."

She goes instantly into protective-mom mode. "Those lawyers work you too hard," she says. "You need a vacation. How long has it been since you took one?"

"Too long." Before she can continue her pet peeve, I change the subject. "Mom, I have something important to tell you." I swallow hard. My mother is the most important person in the world. I don't want to cause her pain. "Paul Hancock died earlier this week."

"Oh."

That's not an encouraging response. I take a deep breath and continue. "I was asked to attend the reading of his will today."

"Did you go?" Her voice has cooled considerably.

I close my eyes. "Yes," I confess. "I went."

"And?"

I explain about the contest. "Mom," I finish at the end, my fingers gripping the phone hard enough that my knuckles whiten, "Paul Hancock played a role in my conception, but he's not my father. I don't care about the money. I just want to do the right thing."

"I know, sweetie," she says, sounding weary.

"Are you mad at me?"

Her reply is automatic. "No, of course not, honey. What are you going to do about your job? You've worked so hard to become a lawyer. Can you give that up?"

I don't want to worry my mother by telling her I'm getting a little tired of my job. "I'm going to talk to the partners today," I reply. "Hopefully, we can work something out."

She sighs. "Good luck, baby. I'll talk to you tomorrow, okay? But I'm working all day, so it might be six in the evening before I can call you."

I frown, puzzled. "You're calling me tomorrow?"

She chuckles. "It's your birthday, remember? Typical. The big 3-0 and it barely registers."

I shake my head. Of course I hadn't entirely forgotten about my birthday. *Until the events of this week pushed everything else aside.*

AFTER TALKING TO MY MOTHER, I head to Jeremy Nash's office. I'm dreading this conversation, but I know I need to talk to the partners at my firm before they find out what happened through the grapevine.

Muttering another curse at Paul Hancock, I knock on Mr. Nash's door. To my surprise, Pamela Adams, one of the three senior partners, opens the door with a pleasant smile. "Come on in, Wendy."

I enter the room and pause. All the senior partners are in Jeremy Nash's office. Shit. They've heard about the will already.

Sure enough, Mr. Nash waves me to a seat. "I got a call from a friend," he says directly. "You're Paul Hancock's daughter."

There's no point denying it. "Yes."

"And you're leading a construction project there?"

I nod.

Pamela Adams jumps in. "Let's cut to the chase, Wendy.

We're a law firm that specializes in divorces. There's no conflict of interest to worry about."

I exhale with relief, but my respite is short-lived. "However," she continues, "I'm going to be blunt. For the next year, your focus isn't going to be here."

I don't know how to reply. For the last six years, I've lived and breathed work. My life as a divorce lawyer was what I wanted. I earned it on my own. I studied for the LSATs while waiting tables, and I made my way through law school on a scholarship, eating ramen noodles to make my money stretch far enough.

Now, everything I worked for is at risk.

Chris Johnson, the senior-most partner, clears his throat. "You're one of our most promising lawyers, and we don't want to lose you. But," his voice hardens, "you can't be a divorce lawyer and work at Hancock at the same time. We've talked about it, and we've come to an agreement."

Pamela Adams' expression is sympathetic. "Lara and Helen will take over your current cases," she says.

I glance up at them in shock. "You're firing me."

Mr. Johnson meets my outraged gaze without blinking. "Yes," he confirms. "Security will escort you out."

There's a sick pit of failure in my gut. Damn it. I've busted my ass for this firm, and I'm being tossed aside. But it's not the partners I'm angriest with. It's my biological father.

This is Paul Hancock's fault.

I can feel the eyes of my fellow lawyers on me when I exit Nash's office. Most people look away, but Lara braves the looming presence of the security guard and follows me to the elevator. "Is it true?" she asks as we ride downstairs. "You've inherited a bunch of money?"

"Not exactly." I explain the details of my father's stupid contest.

"And the partners fired you?" She looks livid. "What a bunch of fools."

I'm struggling not to burst into tears. For six years, my goal has been to make partner, and it's been snatched away. Lara, who's just as ambitious as I am, understands what I'm going through. Her gaze softens as she looks at me. "You want to grab a drink?"

"I can't. I have dinner plans."

"With Asher Doyle and Hudson Fleming?" she asks astutely. "We saw you talk to them at *Nerve*."

"Yes," I admit, feeling the heat rise to my cheeks at her frank appraisal.

"Enjoy your date," Lara says with a sly grin. "And Wendy?" She holds her hands about ten inches apart. "Let me know if they measure up, will you?"

12

Life is really simple, but we insist on making it complicated.

— CONFUCIUS

Hudson:

As I expect, Nadja isn't happy about Staten Island. "Hudson, we can't handle this. Not on top of everything else we have going on. I can barely put together a plan for us to deliver on our current projects."

"This one's on me," I assure her. "I won't get anyone else involved."

She gives me an annoyed look. "How?" she asks bluntly. "Already, we're going to be working hundred-hour weeks all the way until Christmas. There's no extra time, Hudson. Why on earth did you agree to this job?"

Because Wendy asked for my help.

Guilt floods through me. I can work long hours without consequences, but unlike me, Nadja has a husband and three young children. I should be trying to take work off her plate, not add to it.

"This was my father's dream, Nadja. This was the project we were supposed to do together."

Her face softens a little, but the frustration remains. She leaves my office, her back ramrod straight. *Damn it.* As if things aren't already complicated enough, my second in command is pissed off at me.

Once she leaves, I pull the plans I made when my father died, and I spread them out on my table. They're just sketches; many hours of work need to happen before the drawings are transformed to usable plans. "But it's a starting point," I say out loud, trying to convince myself I'm doing the right thing. "I can make this work."

~

A COUPLE of minutes before seven, we knock on Wendy's front door. She flings it open almost immediately. "I wasn't sure what to wear," she says cheerfully. "Is this okay?"

She's dressed in a black t-shirt and matching yoga pants. As I take in the way the fabric clings to her curves, my dick perks up. She looks completely, utterly fuckable, and I have to suppress the urge to go caveman on her. Every single guy in the gym is going to be panting with lust.

"You look great," Asher replies. "Ready to learn how to box?"

"Absolutely," she replies with a radiant smile, holding up her gloves. "I can't wait. I've got a lot of aggression to take out on a punching bag."

"You're not the only one," I reply dryly. Wendy's excitement is palpable. When I saw her this afternoon, she'd looked weary and troubled. Not anymore. Her eyes sparkle and her entire body seems to dance in anticipation. "Shall we?"

I've elected to drive this time, my Land Rover being a lot more practical than Asher's sports car. "Did you talk to the partners at your firm?" Asher asks Wendy as we make our way uptown.

Her excitement seems to drain away. "They fired me," she says, with a heavy sigh. "I called Bill Anderson after talking to the partners. They've set up a budget for the Staten Island project, but it's going to be tight, and it really brought home to me what a risk I'm taking. I'm trying not to freak out."

I cover her hand with mine. Asher and I were afraid this might happen. "You can still change your mind," my friend says promptly from the back seat. "Your track record is excellent. You'll find another job in a second."

Wendy swivels in her seat and gives him an irritated look. "What's with you?" she asks crossly. "Are you going to tell me why you are so freaked out by Thorne?"

"I'm not freaked out by him," Asher replies, his expression hard. "I loathe the man."

"Why?" she repeats, her voice gentle. "What happened, Asher?"

She asked that same question earlier today, and Asher had blown her off with a non-answer. He ducks the question again, shaking his head. "That's a topic for another time," he replies evasively.

She exhales in a huff. "Fine, don't tell me." I pull into the underground garage of the building that houses our gym, and she jumps out before one of us can open the door for her. "Just tell me this. You think Thorne's dangerous, right? Why are you so certain I'll be his target? Why not either of you? Bill Anderson's going to be suspicious if something happens to me. If Thorne has any sense, his focus will be on you, not me. After all, I'm bound to fail without your help."

"You shouldn't be so hard on yourself," I tell her. "You're perfectly capable of pulling this off."

"Oh come on, Hudson," she scoffs. "I'm way out of my league here. I don't know anything about construction."

"Don't sell yourself short." Asher gives her an intense, probing look. "It doesn't suit you. You're a fighter, Wendy. Don't ever pretend to be anything else. You'll take on this challenge, the way you've taken on every other challenge that life has thrown at you. And you'll win, the way you always do."

"Do I always win?" Her voice is so low I barely hear her. "It doesn't always feel like it."

I smile widely. "In that case," I tell her, "a couple of hours in the ring is exactly what you need."

As soon as we walk into the gym, Dimitri, the guy who runs the place, comes up to us, giving Wendy a speculative look. "I reserved a ring for you like you asked," he says to Asher. "You learning how to box?" he asks Wendy.

She nods. "Hudson and Asher have volunteered to teach me," she says with a wicked smile. "Are they any good?"

"Hey," I say indignantly. "I resent that."

Dimitri laughs. "I like you," he says to Wendy. "These two are too used to having it easy. It's time they started working for it." He winks at her. "They're good enough for the basics, but if you want a real expert, you come and find me, okay?"

"Dimitri, stop flirting with our girl." He's just pulling our leg, and Asher and I have no cause to be jealous, but that doesn't stop the surge of possessiveness I feel.

Wendy raises an eyebrow at my words, but she doesn't say anything. The three of us step into the corner ring, and she puts her gloves on. I help her with the strap on her right boxing glove; Asher steps close to help her with her left.

Her breathing catches. "I can do that," she says, her voice shaky.

"Or you could let us." Asher trails his fingers up her forearm. Her skin breaks out into goosebumps as he touches her, and my groin tightens almost painfully. All I want to do is tear off her clothes and feast on her. I want to palm her breasts and suck her perky nipples. I want to hear her moan, and when she's writhing with need, begging for our dicks, I want to plunge my cock into her sweet pussy.

Unfortunately for my cock, we're in a public gym, and we promised her we'd show her the basics. Once again, I struggle to clear my head, and Asher gives me an amused look. "Hudson's mind isn't on boxing at the moment," he says mockingly. "While he's pulling himself together, why don't I show you the basics? Let's start with your stance."

Her forehead wrinkles. "What do you mean?" she asks, then she catches sight of my dick tenting my shorts, and her cheeks flush a fiery red. "Oh."

"Part your legs," Asher instructs Wendy with a grin.

Wendy's lips twitch. "I think you should buy me dinner first," she quips.

I chuckle. "He's talking about your boxing stance and you know it," I accuse her. "Now, pay attention."

She's a quick student. In less than ten minutes, she has the stance and the foot movement down. "Don't cross your feet," I tell her with a grin. "Always keep them shoulder-width apart. Knees slightly bent."

"I never realized how dirty boxing could be," she jokes, but she replicates the movement we're showing her perfectly. "Can I punch now?" she asks, swinging her gloves in a move that leaves her face completely exposed. "Pow."

"Pow?" Asher asks, laughing at her pleased expression. "Don't leave yourself open," he says, correcting her hand placement, "and you should probably lose the sound effects."

"So boring."

We're hot and sweaty by the time we're done. Wendy's shirt is plastered to her body, and I have a hard time tearing my gaze away from her. Asher's just as affected. "Dinner?" I ask, my voice rough with need. "At my place?"

She swallows. "Just dinner?"

"It's your call, Wendy," Asher replies quietly. "Hudson makes a mean stir-fry, and his refrigerator is always stocked with cold beer."

"And if we sleep together," she asks softly. "What happens tomorrow?"

I have no desire to lie to Wendy. Even if we weren't going to be working together, it's not my style. "I was married once," I reply. "I'm not interested in a relationship. When Asher and I share women, it's always casual." I take a deep breath. "We're going to be spending a lot of time on the Staten Island project. I'm an adult; I can handle the situation. But if it's going to complicate things for you, we shouldn't do this."

"I don't date multiple women at once," Asher elaborates. "I don't make any promises. But while we're together, it's just you." His voice lowers. "In or out?"

She tilts her chin up and surveys us for a long moment. Finally, she breaks the silence. "In."

I release the breath I didn't realize I was holding, and offer her my arm. "Let's go."

13

Be happy for this moment. This moment is your life.

— OMAR KHAYYAM

Wendy:

We get to Hudson's penthouse condo in a hurry. As soon as we're through the door, Hudson and Asher are on me, kissing, stroking, and touching me. Their mouths are demanding, their hands possessive.

Desire pools in my body. I tremble between them, caught in desperate lust. I wanted them at *Residence,* and I want them now.

Except I've spent the last hour and a half in a boxing ring. I'm sweaty, and not in a sexy way. "Bathroom," I pant. "I need to shower."

Hudson growls in frustration but pulls away. "This way." He grabs my hand and tugs me down a short corridor, Asher bringing up the rear, his eyes glued to my ass.

I add a sashay to my strut when I notice his gaze. Judging from the grin that forms at the corner of his lips, Asher appreciates the gesture.

The room we enter is obviously a guest bedroom. The bed is made, and there are no photos or personal touches anywhere. "There's a bathroom through that door," Hudson says. He pauses for an instant. "If you'd like, Asher and I can get started on the stir-fry while you shower."

Is that what I'd like? A moment to gather my thoughts, to take stock and ask myself if I'm prepared for this?

Not tonight. Tonight I want to be reckless with abandon, wild with passion.

"Or you could join me." I hold their gazes as I pull my t-shirt over my head. I shimmy the yoga pants down my hips and peel my underwear off my body. In less than thirty seconds, I'm completely naked.

"You're beautiful." Asher's voice is hoarse.

My heartbeat quickens at the raw hunger in their eyes. "You're wearing too many clothes," I retort.

Hudson stalks toward me. His fingertips swirl on my skin and caress the curve of my shoulder, before sliding down to cup my ass. Asher moves in front of me. His hot gaze moves slowly down my body before his thumbs caress my nipples.

I stop breathing.

He brushes against my aching peaks once more, and I moan and arch my back into Hudson's broad and powerful chest. This is crazy. *So crazy.* I want more.

I'm naked, and they're fully clothed, and this imbalance must be corrected before we step into the shower. I need to feel them, skin against skin. Grabbing the hem of Asher's t-shirt, I yank it above his head, inhaling sharply as his sculpted chest comes into view. He smirks at my expression. "Like what you see, Wendy?"

Hell yes. A sprinkling of chest hair covers the rock hard muscles, and my gaze follows the happy trail lower and lower. His cock is tenting in his gym pants. Unable to help myself, I reach out and graze my hand against that thick length, rubbing as he hardens at my touch.

He groans, his head thrown back.

I marvel at that sound. Asher Doyle is always in control, always calm, always composed. Now, he looks like he's unraveling with lust. Because of me. *Because I touched him.*

Out of the corner of my eye, I see Hudson's t-shirt fly across the room. His pants follow. "Shower," he says harshly. "Now."

We move to the bathroom, bodies entwined and touching. I'm awash in lust, though the magnificence of Hudson's shower jerks me out of my pleasure-befuddled trance for a moment.

"Wow," I gape, taking in the jets embedded on three sides of the stall. I do well for myself as a divorce lawyer— *well, I did until I got fired today*—but this is a completely different level. This is billionaire territory. "This is a guest bathroom? What does yours look like? Is your tub made of solid gold?"

Hudson's lips curl into a smile that doesn't reach his eyes. I've stumbled on another forbidden topic. But before I have time to wonder exactly what caused the change in his expression, Asher flicks a switch, and the jets come to life.

The water pulses against my naked skin, but I don't have time to compose an ode to high pressure shower heads. Asher moves behind me, his thick cock bobbing in a way that has me licking my lips, aching to taste him. He pours some shampoo into his palm and gently massages it into my hair.

In front of me, Hudson picks up a bar of soap and teases my nipples with it, making me moan with pleasure. I wrap my arms around his body, and press my breasts into his chest, tilting my head up for a kiss.

Hudson's mouth covers mine hungrily. He trails his hand down my body, outlining the curve of my breasts with a light, teasing touch. Before I can beg for more, he moves to the cleft between my legs. I make a sound of need as his fingers part my lips, flicking at my clitoris.

I'm soaked. When Hudson touches me, his eyes gleam. "So wet," he says with a cocky grin. He plunges two fingers into my pussy, and for an instant, I lose the ability to think.

"So hard," I retort when I can form words again. I close my fist around his fat cock and slowly slide my hand up his length. He clenches his eyes shut, his face taut with desire.

"So much fucking conversation." Asher's voice breathes into my ear. "Part your legs wider for me, Wendy, and give me your hands."

I follow his instructions. Asher holds my wrists behind my back with one hand, and he thrusts the other between my legs. His fingers join Hudson's as they both explore my aching pussy, caressing my lips and teasing my nub until I'm writhing between their bodies, mindless with pleasure.

Hudson's expression is hot with desire as he gets on his knees in front of me. He trails slow kisses up my thighs. I hold my breath, my insides twisting in anticipation of the moment when his mouth meets my core. When his tongue touches my cleft, I gasp and spread my legs wider. "Please," I beg, desperate for more contact, more pressure.

My head falls back against Asher's broad shoulder. "Do you like that?" he whispers, his breath hot against my skin.

He cups my breasts and pinches my nipples, and I gasp once again in pleasure. "Do you like what we're doing to you?"

Hudson's tongue flicks my clitoris. His fingers pump in and out of my slick channel as he devours my pussy.

Hot water rains down on us; I barely notice. I'm moaning almost continuously, overloaded by sensation. It's almost too much to bear—Asher tugging and pulling at my nipples, kneading them between his thumb and forefinger, Hudson's mouth feasting on me, his thick cock erect with his desire—this is better than anything I could have imagined.

They are relentless, and I feel my orgasm start to build. My insides tighten and clench. My body stiffens as my release approaches, and then as Hudson presses down on my clitoris with the tip of his tongue, I explode.

That's only the beginning.

They towel me off and push me back onto the bed. Asher parts my legs and bends my knees, positioning himself in the space between them. His lips are on mine, pressing my mouth open and capturing my tongue with his.

Hudson moves to my side. He squeezes my breast and lowers his mouth over my nipple. He nibbles and sucks the pebble-hard nub. I grab the silky-soft sheets as a shiver wracks my body.

"Please," I groan. I reach for Hudson's thick cock and slide my hand along his length. I take Asher's hard dick in my other hand and luxuriate in the feeling of holding both these men in the palm of my hand.

Asher's demanding lips caress mine. I pump their hard cocks, hearing their moans of need, watching their faces contort with lust, loving the way their cocks grow even harder as I touch them.

This is better than my wildest fantasies.

"Enough." Asher's voice is low and smooth. He straddles

my chest, and I open my mouth gladly, eager to taste him. His eyes burn into me. His cock bobs in my face, but he holds himself steady. "Want this?" His eyebrow quirks wickedly.

In response, I tilt my head forward and poke my tongue out, flicking at his length. "Want this?"

He laughs and thrusts his hips forward. I suck greedily, swirling my tongue around his head. I feast on him, feeling him tremble, hearing him groan. His eyes are closed, and his hands grip the headboard so hard that his knuckles turn white. His breath comes faster and faster as I explore the velvet-soft steel of him.

I hear the sound of a condom wrapper tear, and Hudson parts my legs. His huge cock rubs at my entrance, then he plunges into me in one smooth stroke.

My pussy clamps around him like a vise. "Fuck, you're so tight." He pulls his cock halfway out of my pussy and slides back in again, and the delicious friction sets me panting around Asher's cock.

It takes me a few minutes to get used to the unfamiliar rhythm, but once I do, Hudson and Asher pick up the pace. Hudson pounds into my tight channel while his fingers trace light circles against my clitoris.

Each forceful stroke makes me ache for more. My body starts to tense, clenching around his cock, quivering in response to his steady thrusts. I'm close. I reach for Asher, putting my arms around his hips and drawing him deeper into my mouth, my movements frantic as my orgasm approaches.

Then Hudson's fingers move just a little faster, strum just a little harder, and I erupt. My muscles clench around Hudson's cock, milking him. Wave after wave of pleasure washes over me.

Hudson's fingers dig into my thighs. He grunts loudly, then his body jerks as he climaxes, and a moment later, Asher erupts in my throat.

The three of us collapse in a heap on the bed. We lie in silence for about ten minutes. I feel boneless, drained, and sated.

Until Asher's fingers snake down and fondle me between my legs.

"Ready for round two?" he asks. Hudson nuzzles my neck, his mouth kissing my sensitive flesh until my body starts to spark again.

I'm shocked to see that their dicks are already hard. "How is this possible?"

"You're very hot," Asher says solemnly, rolling a condom over his cock. "So, *are* you ready?"

I smile widely and part my legs for him. "Absolutely."

After three rounds of intense sex, I fall asleep. It's dark when I wake up, and the clock at the side of the bed tells me it's four in the morning. Hudson and Asher are sound asleep on either side of me, their eyes closed and their breathing deep and steady.

My mouth curls into a grin as I realize it's now officially my birthday. *What a good start,* I congratulate myself, rolling out of bed. *Happy birthday to me.*

I tiptoe around the room, trying to find my clothes. A light flickers on. "Where are you going?" Hudson asks me.

Asher's still asleep, but when the light fills the room, he stirs, and his eyes blink open. "Sorry," I whisper. "I didn't mean to wake you. I was just leaving."

Hudson frowns. "You don't have to go," he says. "You're welcome to spend the night."

I shake my head. "Casual, remember?" I say lightly,

pulling my t-shirt over my head and tugging my pants over my hips. "I'll catch a cab home."

Asher sits up. "What are you doing tomorrow? Would you like to get dinner with us again?"

My heart beats faster at his question, but then I remember I already have plans. "I can't. I'm going out for drinks with my girlfriends." I don't want them to think I'm blowing them off, so I add, "It's my birthday."

"Is it?" Hudson gets to his feet. "Hang on for a second." He takes off in the direction of the kitchen.

I give Asher a puzzled look. "What's that about?"

He shrugs. "I have no idea." He glances at the clock, then smiles at me. "Happy birthday."

"It's a big one," I tell him, though I'm not sure why I'm chatty at four in the morning. "The big 3 - 0."

Hudson calls us from the kitchen. "You two, come here for a second."

Asher gets to his feet, comfortable in his nakedness. "Where did I put my pants?" he mutters, looking around the room, then he finds them and tugs them on.

Pity. I was enjoying the view.

We make our way to the kitchen in silence. I'm a little uncomfortable, but this situation isn't anywhere near as awkward as I feared. Thank heavens for that.

"I thought I had one left," Hudson says with a wide smile. He gestures to the counter, and I look down to see a large cupcake on a plate, with a candle in the center. "Happy birthday. It's pineapple carrot. The bakery across the street makes them, and they're delicious."

"You found a cake for me?" I don't think I've ever dated someone who even wished me happy birthday, let alone light a candle on a cake. Of course, that might be because I've never told anyone I've been involved with when my birthday was. I have no idea why I mentioned it to Hudson and Asher.

"Well, I would have got a real cake," he replies, "but you did just tell us, so we'll have to make do with the contents of my kitchen."

Asher laughs. "Let us take you out for dinner for your birthday," he says persuasively. "Thirty is a milestone year. You should celebrate it. If you can't make tomorrow, how about the day after? Have you eaten at *Tent*?"

Tent, a small pop-up restaurant in the Village, is the hottest table in town right now. Their three chefs engage in a nightly competition to see who can serve the most delicious tasting menu in the city. Reservations are almost impossible to come by.

I gape at Asher. "You can get into *Tent*?"

He grins. "Hudson can. He designed the space. So, is that a yes for dinner?"

I shouldn't see them socially again; things will get complicated. Except, I really want to.

"That sounds great."

"We'll pick you up at seven," Hudson replies. He nudges me toward the cupcake. "Make a wish, Wendy."

I blow out the candle. *If this is a dream, I don't want to wake up.*

14

Keep your face to the sunshine and you cannot see a shadow.

— HELEN KELLER

Asher:

We have dinner with Wendy on Sunday at *Tent*, and end up back at Hudson's place afterward. Again, she refuses to spend the night. Though I don't want her to leave, she's probably making the right call. Casual sex is one thing. Getting involved is another.

Monday morning, Hudson and I accompany Wendy to her office at Hancock Construction. It turns out to be no larger than a closet, and it contains exactly one table and one chair.

"Seriously?" Hudson shakes his head. "How petty can Thorne get?"

"Is that a rhetorical question?" Wendy asks dryly. She tosses her handbag on the table and turns to the woman who accompanied us. "I'm supposed to meet with Jeff Choi at nine," she says. "Can you let me know when he arrives?"

The woman, whose name is Amanda, flushes. "Mr. Choi was here earlier," she says. "He suggested moving the meeting to his office. I can show you there?"

We follow her up three flights of stairs and through a set of glass double doors. On this floor, the dove-gray carpet is thicker and more luxurious, and the offices are large and expensively furnished. Jeff Choi, the Vice-President of Strategy of Hancock Construction, and our point person on the Staten Island project, is in one of them. "You must be Wendy Williams," he says, giving her an appraising look as he shakes her hand. "Welcome to Hancock."

"Thank you," Wendy replies. I shut the door, and the three of us sit in front of Jeff's massive walnut desk. "These are my associates, Hudson Fleming and Asher Doyle."

Choi nods in greeting. "Ms. Williams," he says, once we're done with the pleasantries, "I'm going to speak frankly. When Paul died, I was ready to resign. I had no interest in working for his son. Then I heard about the contest, and I changed my mind."

"Why don't you want to work for Thorne?" I probe. I talked to Stone Bradley over the weekend, who promised to dig up dirt on the man, but this is a chance to hear about Wendy's half-brother from someone who's worked with him on a daily basis.

"Let me tell you a story." Jeff Choi leans back in his chair and steeples his fingers. "Three years back, Thorne wanted to bid on a bridge project in Barbados. Paul didn't like the idea at all, but Thorne kept at it, and the old man eventually relented. The bidding process took almost a year, but we won."

He sighs. "Thorne was secretive of the details, with good

reason. He'd severely underbid the project, and the time-lines he agreed to..." He shakes his head. "Insane. Of course, everything started falling apart. We were losing money, hand over fist. Or so I thought."

"What do you mean?"

Choi fixes me with a piercing look. "When the numbers were finalized, it turned out that the project didn't lose money, after all."

The confusion I'm feeling is echoed in Wendy and Hudson's faces. "That's good, isn't it?" Hudson asks.

"One week before that report came out," Choi continues, "the Head of Finance, Jean Nakashima died and Stuart Fischer, one of Thorne's golf buddies, was chosen to be her replacement. And one of the first things that Fischer did was run the numbers on Barbados and claim that the project had eked out a small profit."

"How did she die?" I hone in on the most important detail. I don't think Thorne is capable of murder, but the timing seems far too coincidental. What if I'm wrong?

He looks sober. "Her boat was found capsized a few miles off the coast of Nantucket." He's visibly upset. "She was an avid sailor," he says. "But the storm came out of nowhere, and it must have caught her by surprise. They never found her body."

"I'm so sorry." Wendy's voice is soft. "That must have been difficult for everyone here."

Jeff Choi bobs his head in agreement. "Still, that's in the past," he says, making a determined effort to dispel the cloud of gloom in the office. "In the present, we have the Staten Island project and a team that's ready to push forward."

"I'm trying to get my bearings here," Wendy says. She smiles at him warmly as she speaks, and he crumbles against her charm. "Can you tell me what's been done so far?"

"We have a construction permit," he says. "We'd hired a firm to lay the roads when Thorne halted the project. This was just before Paul went into the hospital."

"The permit's done?" Hudson looks relieved. "Good, that's the most time-consuming part."

Wendy gives the executive a puzzled look. "I don't know anything about construction," she says, "but if you don't know what the buildings are going to look like and where they're going to go, how can you lay roads? Am I missing something?"

"You aren't." Jeff Choi looks pleased with Wendy's question. "Brad Pankratz's crew is busy. We paid a deposit to get on his schedule."

"Have you canceled the road crew?" Hudson asks Jeff Choi. "Officially?"

He shakes his head. "Call it wishful thinking," he says, "but I hoped that Thorne might change his mind. Staten Island is a good project. It isn't as flashy as building bridges and highways, but Hancock has always made its money in the commercial space."

"Hudson," Wendy asks, leaning forward. "If we get a rough design together, we can still get the roads built on schedule. That makes sense, doesn't it?"

"It does." Hudson smiles at Wendy's excitement. "Is that our next step, boss?"

She blushes a little, but nods. "Mr. Choi, can you verify that Brad Pankratz is holding our spot?"

Choi's impressed, as am I. He rises to his feet as we prepare to leave. "Call me Jeff," he says, smiling at Wendy for the first time. "Welcome to the team, Ms. Williams. I have a feeling that we're going to do great things."

She looks faintly embarrassed but smiles back. "I hope so too," she replies. "Thank you, Jeff. And please, call me Wendy."

We meet with a couple of other people in the morning. The guy heading up Legal, Mark Allen, is openly hostile. "I told Choi a million times," he gripes. "Your project schedule is too aggressive. My team is already operating at peak capacity. We can't take on any more work."

I survey Allen coolly. I don't have to look too hard to see who is going to cooperate and who isn't. Mark Allen is clearly on Team Thorne. "That's fine," I tell him. "My firm will handle the additional legal tasks."

"You can't do that," he blusters.

"I don't see what the problem is, Mr. Allen." Wendy sounds implacable. "You said you couldn't handle the workload. Asher's firm can."

The man stalks out of Wendy's office without another word. "Well, that went well," I say with a shrug. "You two want to break for lunch?"

"What do you have in mind?" Wendy asks.

"Well," I lower my voice suggestively. "My office isn't too far away. If you're starving, we can pick up some Italian food on the way."

She gives me a coy look. "And if I'm hungry for something else?"

We'd made love on Friday night. She was busy on Saturday, but we went to dinner on Sunday and ended up tangled in Hudson's sheets afterward, sweaty and sated. I still can't get enough. She's like a drug in my veins, sweet and powerful, totally irresistible.

"I want to hear you say it." My fingers trail over her breasts. "Tell me what you want."

She bites her lower lip. "We're at work."

"So what?" Hudson grins wickedly and cups her ass. "The door is shut. No one can hear you."

She hesitates. "This is so weird," she mumbles. "I've never mixed business with pleasure this way. It feels so strange to be thinking sexual thoughts about my colleagues."

I smirk openly. "Let's go to my office, and you can tell me all about your sexual thoughts."

We leave Hancock Construction and head to the downtown skyscraper that houses Doyle and Miller. Once we're in my office, I shut the door and lock it, and turn to Wendy. "My office," I tell her, "my rules. Understand?"

Her eyes sparkle with amusement. "Yes, Asher," she says meekly, spoiling the effect by winking at me.

Hudson chuckles. "Asher's assistant is right outside these doors. Unless you want her to hear everything, you should keep your voice down."

She lifts her chin up. "Challenge accepted."

Good. I have her exactly where I want her. I survey Wendy openly. Her black blazer is buttoned up, and her narrow pencil skirt skims the curve of her ass and ends just above her knees. Underneath the jacket, she's wearing a pale pink blouse. She looks like a sexy librarian, prim, proper, very much in control. I can't wait to watch her unravel with desire.

Hudson sits down and leans back in his chair. I lean against my desk. "Stand in the center of the room," I order, my cock hardening as she obeys.

Every teenage fantasy of mine is coming true in this moment.

"Unbutton your jacket."

She bites her lower lip, her white teeth indenting the soft pink flesh. My cock immediately takes note. Hudson shifts in his seat, adjusting himself openly. "Is there a problem, Ms. Williams?" he asks sternly as she hesitates.

Her lips twitch. "No problem, Mr. Fleming," she replies, giving Hudson a coy look from under her lashes. *The little minx.* We can pretend that we're in charge here, but she knows we're putty in her hands, and I wouldn't have it any other way.

She starts taking off the jacket, but I stop her with a lift of my hand. "Did I tell you to take it off?"

"No, Mr. Doyle." She flutters her eyelashes at me. "I'm sorry, Mr. Doyle."

Fuck me. I've never done something like this in my office. My cock is a steel shaft of rock-hard need. I ache to end this silly game, throw her over my desk and plunge my dick into her. I want to feel her slick heat around me, to touch her silky soft flesh and watch goosebumps break out on her skin. I want to hear her moan, her head thrown back, her need overcoming her fear of Vivian overhearing us.

You're not an out-of-control teenager, Doyle. Pull yourself together.

She's standing there, her fingers clutching the fabric, waiting patiently for the next instruction. Hudson gets to his feet, his expression hungry. He moves behind Wendy and eases the jacket from her shoulders. He hangs it up on a hook behind my door before stalking back to his seat. "Very nice," he says appreciatively. "Very sexy, Ms. Williams."

I have to agree. I can see the outline of Wendy's bra under her blouse. White lace, if I'm not mistaken. My prim librarian has a naughty edge, but I knew that already.

"Now the top," I say hoarsely.

"Not my skirt?" Her eyebrow rises as she pulls the hem of her shirt free. "I thought you'd want the skirt next."

"Perhaps you're focusing on the wrong thing, Ms. Fleming," Hudson says silkily. "Shouldn't you be thinking instead of how you're going to keep quiet when Asher and I lay you back on the desk, spread you open and feast on you? Shouldn't you be wondering how you're going to bite back your screams of pleasure?"

She squirms in response, her legs rubbing together. She pulls the shirt over her head and tosses it on a chair next to Hudson.

I inhale sharply as I see her breasts, covered in creamy lace. God, she's a tasty treat. Her lush curves spill out of her bra, and her pink-tipped nipples are clearly visible underneath the lace. I can't decide if I want her to lose the bra or keep it.

Keeping it wins out. "Now," I instruct, "pull your panties down."

Her eyes glaze with need. She bends down, and the view of her bountiful cleavage makes me dizzy.

Hudson growls deep in his throat as she wriggles her hips and her fingers emerge with her panties. "Where should I put these?" she asks, every syllable coated with desire.

"Come here," I say gruffly, my self-control snapping when I see the tiny scrap of white lace she holds in her hand. "Sit on the desk."

She sits down on the edge, demurely, smoothing her skirt, so it doesn't ride too high over her thighs. Hudson is having none of it. "Oh no you don't," he breathes. He yanks the skirt up to her waist, and tips her back so she's lying on my desk, her legs spread, her pussy already slick with her juices. My heart almost stops at the sight, and the blood leaves my head and rushes to my cock.

Hudson doesn't waste any time. He slides his fingers into her slick channel and bends his head over her clitoris, sucking at that erect nub until she's gasping and biting her knuckles to keep from screaming out.

I unzip my trousers and pull my dick out in my fist, stroking it as I watch her respond to Hudson. Her face is flushed, and her eyes are hazy and unfocused.

I have to touch her. I pull her breasts out of the cups of her bra, kneading the soft flesh in my palms. I thumb her pink nipples and watch them swell in response. "Asher," she groans. "This is crazy. We're in your office. What will people think?"

"The advantage of being the boss," I tell her, "is that I don't care."

She writhes and wriggles under our combined onslaught. Hudson's hands move to her knees, parting her legs wide. My fingers tweak her nipples, pinching them and watching the rosy nubs darken to a deeper hue.

"Oh my God," she cries out, grasping Hudson's hair between her fingers and pressing his head into her pussy. "Don't stop, please... whatever you do, don't stop."

Fuck. I've never been this hard in my life. I'm aching for release. My hand flies over my cock, pumping.

She notices. "Come here," she breathes, her mouth falling open in invitation. I think I've died and gone to heaven as she envelops me in her warm wet heat. Her tongue swirls over my head in little teasing strokes and her hand fists the base of my cock.

I groan, louder than intended, as she slides her palm over my length. She removes her lips from my dick long enough to sass me. "Finding it hard to keep silent?" she asks mockingly. "Not so easy, is it?"

I bite back my smile. I love her attitude. "That's it," I tell her, hoisting her up by the waist and flipping her over so she's on her hands and knees on the desktop. Hudson gives me a *'what the fuck, dude'* look, before recognizing the undeniable advantages of her new position.

"Here's what you're going to do," I tell her. "You're going to wrap those pretty pink lips around my cock while Hudson slides his dick into your sweet, slick pussy. And you're not going to have any time for smart ass remarks, Wendy because you're going to be busy giving me the best fucking blow job you can."

She grins. "You're hot when you're bossy," she quips. Though her words are joking, her lips are half-parted, and her eyes are glued to my cock.

I grab a condom from my desk drawer. Though I've never had sex in my office, I believe in being prepared. Just like a Scout.

Okay, maybe not exactly like a Scout.

I throw the condom to Hudson, who catches it and tears it open. He yanks at Wendy's creamy thighs and buries himself in her to the hilt. "Oh fuck," he groans. "You are so fucking wet for me, aren't you, Wendy?"

Her mouth falls open, and I ease my cock into it, almost blowing my load when I see her pretty lips wrapped around my shaft. "You like being naughty, don't you? You like knowing that Vivian can walk in at any moment."

I locked the door, and Viv's probably at lunch, but Wendy must have a minor exhibitionist streak because she shivers at my words and sucks my cock deeper into her mouth. Her tongue laps the underside of my shaft, and I just about lose it. Oh God, her mouth. Her mouth is fucking amazing.

Her body trembles and her muscles quiver as Hudson pounds into her, forcing her mouth deeper onto my cock. When he drives into her, her perfect tits jiggle and I have to think about tort reform to keep from exploding in her mouth. I'm not going to last very much longer. "I'm going to come," I warn her.

She nods, her expression almost wild with need. Hudson grunts as he plows into her, gripping her creamy round ass with his fingers. "Touch yourself," he orders. "Rub your clit. Make yourself come. I want to feel your muscles clench around my cock."

She presses her finger against her nub. Her tongue still works its magic on my cock, and I watch her, transfixed by how wild and crazy and perfect this moment is.

We're all close. The rhythm builds up; desire pulses like electricity, binding us together. I try to hold back, but I can't pause now. I grab her hair, thrust my hips into her face, and I explode into her throat. Through the fog that fills me, I register that Wendy goes over the edge, her fingernails sinking into my hips. Hudson shouts as he reaches the brink, his face contorted with pleasure.

I'm having sex at work. *On my goddamn desk, for fuck's sake.* What is this woman doing to me?

15

Life is like riding a bicycle. To keep your balance, you must keep moving.

— ALBERT EINSTEIN

Wendy:

My girlfriends and I used to hang out on Thursday night, but life happened and we moved it to Mondays. We kept the old name though, because it was funnier that way. By the time Monday evening rolls around, I'm more than ready for the Thursday Night Drinking Pack. I'm not the only one.

"What a week." Piper flops on the couch dramatically, and her cat Jasper immediately jumps on her lap.

"Tell me about it," Katie agrees with a grimace. "I had a pregnancy scare last Tuesday."

There's only three of us at Piper's apartment. Miki's Skyped in, grinning at us from the screen mounted on top of the fireplace, but the rest of the crew is missing. Bailey left this week to go to Argentina for a research project, and Gabby, who lives in Atlantic City, texted us earlier to tell us she wouldn't be able to make it.

"You did?" I look up, happy to focus on someone else's problems for a while. "What happened?"

"I missed my period," Katie replies. "I was freaking out. You guys, I love my twins, but Adam and I have decided we're done being parents." She shudders. "I've finally forgotten the horrors of the three A.M. feedings. Adam and I used to keep score about whose turn it was to wake up." She drains her glass of wine and pours herself another.

"I'm assuming from the copious wine consumption that you aren't pregnant," I tell her dryly. "Congratulations. Happy non-motherhood to you."

She laughs. "Don't be so quick to judge," she says. "There were two of them. One of them would fall asleep; then the other would wake up. All night long. I didn't sleep for a year."

"Fair enough." I clink my glass against hers.

On the screen, Miki toasts to Katie before throwing back her drink. "What's going on with you?" she asks Piper. "Why was your week crazy?"

Piper looks exasperated. "A customer forgot to tell us she was allergic to shellfish when she ordered the gumbo."

"Oh dear."

"Yup," Piper nods. "It wasn't pretty. Her tongue swelled up; her skin turned blue and hives started breaking out on her body. Then she threw up everywhere. We spent hours cleaning the mess. Still, she's alright. It wouldn't look good if I killed a customer."

I know it isn't a laughing matter, but I have to chuckle at Piper's morose expression. My friend is almost never disgruntled. "What about you two?" Piper asks Miki and me. "Tell me your week was better than mine."

Well, let's see. On Monday a guy almost punched me at a bar, but two hot men saved me before offering to help me explore a ménage fantasy. There's my father's will, because of which I'm leading a construction project for the next year. Plus I got fired on Friday. Where do I even start?

My inclination is to say nothing, my wariness of people inherited from my mother, but I'm trying to change that. I would trust the women in this room with my life; they're like the sisters I never had. "Have I ever told you about my father?" I ask.

Piper's the only one who nods. The rest of them shake their heads. "I've always assumed you didn't know who he was," Katie says carefully. "You've never mentioned him, and I know your mom raised you on her own."

"No, I've known his identity since my eighteenth birthday," I reply quietly. "He died on Monday. And there's more." I fill them in on the whole story, starting with Derek Greene knocking on my door and ending with today's conversation with Jeff Choi. I mention Asher and Hudson, but I deliberately leave out that I slept with them. That bit is too embarrassing to mention.

When I finish, there's complete silence. Finally, Piper breaks it, her face etched with sympathy. "Oh Wendy," she says, leaning forward to put a comforting arm around my shoulder, "I can't believe they fired you. I'm so sorry."

"I don't know what to do," I tell them. "I keep second guessing my decision to work on this project. I don't know anything about construction. Of course Thorne is going to do better than I am."

"Will he?" Katie asks me, a skeptical expression on her face. "What's his record so far?"

"Pretty spotty," I reply honestly. "According to Jeff Choi, his last venture lost a ton of money. Still, Thorne's spent his entire career at Hancock Construction. I'm an interloper."

"Paul Hancock must have set up the contest for a reason," Piper says staunchly. "Maybe he believed you would be a better owner than Thorne."

"I can look into their financials for you," Miki offers.

I lean forward to snag some chips and salsa. "If you're not too busy, I'd appreciate it."

Miki gives me a thumbs-up. "I'll call you tomorrow to discuss the details."

"So, what are you going to do?" Piper asks. "Are you going to look for a job at another law firm?"

I take a deep breath. "Hancock Construction employs ten thousand people. All those people are going to work, wondering what's going to happen to their jobs because Paul Hancock died."

I munch on my chips and salsa. "I've been there, Piper. Growing up, we lived paycheck to paycheck. If my mother's car needed fixing, we ate canned pasta all month. If she fell sick, we lived in fear that she'd lose her job. My instincts tell me that Thorne isn't good for the company."

Sipping my wine, I continue. "I don't care what my father wanted," I tell my friends. "He chose not to be a part of my life; I owe him nothing. But my mom taught me to care for people, to be responsible."

Katie gets up for another bottle of wine and tops up my glass. "It looks like you've made up your mind."

"Yes." I sip at my drink, finally feeling the rightness of my decision in my heart. "If I think Thorne is going to be a good CEO, I won't get in his way, but until then, I'm going to become a fixture at Hancock Construction."

16

He will win who knows when to fight and when not to fight.

— SUN TZU

Asher:

Two weeks pass. I spend one of those weeks in Seoul, working on a merger. Though I normally enjoy traveling for work, this time around, I can't wait to get back to Manhattan.

It was supposed to be casual, but I can't get Wendy out of my mind.

I thought that my attraction to her could be sated in a few hours, but I was wrong. She's lodged in my thoughts. Even when I'm working, I see her in the back of my mind, her eyes hazy with desire, her red lips wrapped around my cock, her clever tongue stroking me to the point of wildness...

It's driving me nuts. A few nights with Wendy Williams, and I'm like an addict, looking for my next fix.

I dial her number as soon as I land. It's Thursday evening, but knowing Wendy, she's probably at work. "Are you at Hancock?" I ask without preamble when she answers.

"Asher," she exclaims, sounding delighted to hear from me. "Are you back in town? Hang on, Hudson's here. I'm going to put you on speaker."

"I just got in," I reply. "Listen, I've spent fourteen hours on a plane. I'm going to head to my place and shower, and then I'll meet you at Hudson's condo, okay? Do you want me to bring pizza?"

"Not for me," Wendy replies instantly. "My stomach's been acting up. I'm trying to stick to salads until this bug passes."

"Okay, salad it'll be." Hanging up, I reach for my luggage and navigate the absolute mess that's JFK. It's raining, and it takes me forever to find a cab. By the time I get home, I'm cranky as hell.

Levi's watching something on TV when I walk in. "Hey buddy," he greets me. "You look like a drowned rat."

My lips twitch reluctantly at Levi's bracing assessment. "It's raining," I point out. "As you'd know if you looked outside. How've you been?"

He shrugs. "I'm good," he replies. "By the way, some suit was looking for you earlier today. He left this for you." He hands me a large official-looking manila envelope.

"Thanks, buddy." Taking it, I head to my bedroom. When I'm alone, I rip it open and extract the contents, and my heart stops.

There's a note, but that's not what catches my attention. I'm transfixed by the five large eight-by-eleven photos that have fallen out of the envelope. Photos of Hudson, Wendy and I, in her shoebox-like office, laughing and kissing. In one photo, Hudson's palm cups her ass possessively. In another, my fingers graze the side of her breast.

Fuck. I'm a fool. I should have known Thorne would have cameras in her office.

Already, there's gossip about the three of us. Hudson and I have a reputation; we've never been particularly invested in keeping our sexual preferences a secret. Jeff Choi's curious about our relationship, but he's too professional to ask for the details. Amanda, the woman acting as our liaison at Hancock, is more openly inquisitive.

These photos will pour fuel on the fire.

This is how things started with Lauren. Thorne raped her; there was DNA evidence. I foolishly assumed we had an open-and-shut case.

Then the first shot was fired. An article in the campus paper, accusing Lauren of faking the whole thing. A 'friend' came forward, swearing that Lauren had planned the entire sordid affair, hoping that Thorne would pay her off for her silence. Countless interviews were conducted with her former boyfriend Mike, who claimed that Lauren was desperate for money.

Lauren lost her scholarship. She spiraled into a depression from which she never recovered. Losing faith in the system, she dropped the charges against Thorne Hancock.

The note has fluttered to my bed. I pick it up and scan it. It's short and to the point.

Remember Lauren Bainbridge? It'd be a shame to see history repeat itself. If you don't want these photos to go public, both Hudson Fleming and you need to walk away from the Staten Island project.

It's unsigned.

I don't need a signature to know that Thorne's behind this. A feeling of helplessness sweeps over me, one I remember well from ten years ago. Lost in our burgeoning relationship with Wendy, I've become complacent. I've let myself forget how ruthless Thorne Hancock can be.

Lauren is dead. I couldn't protect her, but I can protect Wendy. All I need to do is walk away from her project. All I need to do is let her fail.

Even if she ends up hating me.

17

We sail within a vast sphere, ever drifting in uncertainty, driven from end to end.

— BLAISE PASCAL

Wendy:

For the last ten days, my stomach's been acting up. I haven't been sleeping well; I've been waking up nauseous. I've bailed on the Thursday Night Drinking Pack more than once. The only thing I seem to do is work.

I should be miserable, but I've never been happier, and it's all because of Asher and Hudson.

I'd accepted their help reluctantly; I'm still hesitant to trust them completely. But I'm changing; I can feel it. The caution built up over a lifetime is slowly slipping away, and a new me is emerging. I like it.

Then there's my amazing sex life. *Meow.* Let's just say I

now understand why Bailey glows when Daniel and Sebastian are around; why Piper positively radiates joy in Wyatt and Owen's presence. *It's only casual,* I keep reminding myself. *We aren't in a relationship. Hold on to your heart, because Hudson Fleming and Asher Doyle have the power to shatter it.*

"You look exhausted," Hudson says in the cab, looking at me with concern. "You have dark circles under your eyes, and you're far too pale."

I snuggle into his side. "Some sleep would be nice," I admit.

His fingers stroke my hair. "Want to skip tonight?" he asks.

Out of some unspoken agreement, the two of us haven't made love while Asher's been away. It doesn't feel right without him. Eight days without sex and my need has grown, inflating like a balloon that's ready to pop at the slightest touch. Sleep can wait. "Hell, no," I say indignantly. "Don't even think about it."

He chuckles softly and presses his lips down on my hair. "Ah, Wendy," he says appreciatively, "you're so fucking amazing. Asher and I are the luckiest guys in the world."

Does that mean you want to be in a relationship? Those insecure words almost pop out of my mouth, but I push them back. An instinct warns me that the time isn't right for that question.

As soon as Asher walks in, he tosses his coat across the room, sets the pizza and salad down on the table, and pushes me against the wall. "I want you," he growls, raw, carnal heat glittering in his eyes. "Now."

I can feel the weight of Asher's hand on the back of my neck. His fingers entwine in my hair. At his rough touch, need builds in me.

He tightens his fingers and pulls my neck to his lips. My breathing shortens. He's just walked in the door, and I'm already wet for him.

His fingers trail a path down the nape of my neck. "I'm not in the mood for gentle," he growls. "I'm not in the mood for sweet and soft."

I lift my head up and meet his eyes squarely. I'm as hungry for him as he is for me. I want everything they've got. "Bring it on."

His lips lift in an involuntary smile, and he takes a step back. He undresses me with his eyes, slowly, deliberately. "Would you like me to take off my clothes?" I offer, eager to feel his naked body against mine.

He shakes his head. "Did I ask for help?" he demands. He continues to stand in front of me, letting the heat build up in the small gap between us. I lean back against the cool wall and wait, shivering at his scrutiny. Asher's often dominant, but this feels more intense.

"Are you attached to this blouse?" he asks.

I glance down at the shirt I bought on sale at the Gap. Hancock Construction's offices aren't anywhere as formal as the law firm I used to work for. My conservative suits languish at the back of my closet, and I spend my days dressed in casual shirts and slacks. Except for today. Today, in anticipation of sex, I've worn a skirt. "No," I reply.

"Good." He brings his hands up to the collar of my blouse and tugs hard. Buttons fly all over the foyer, and the fabric rips.

Hudson stalks toward me, tugging me forward, and he positions himself behind me, never letting his hands leave my body. As he grips my waist, I feel his hard cock against my ass.

We're not hungry for each other. *We're starved.*

My breasts push against the confines of my bra. The anticipation is unbearable. Desire pools in my pussy, and I clench my thighs together.

Asher notices. "In a hurry?" he asks mockingly. He traces the outline of my nipple through my bra, and then he tweaks the bud hard.

Behind me, Hudson's hands loosen from around my waist. One hand pushes me against Asher's strong chest, while another lightly caresses my back, cupping my ass, then trailing down the back of my thigh.

My breathing hitches as Hudson's fingers move up my skirt. Asher bends forward and brushes his lips against my neck.

"No," I whisper harshly. "Enough with the foreplay. Take off your clothes, both of you."

"Bossy," Asher chides, but I'm not cowed. I reach for his belt and undo it. I unzip his fly and let his pants fall to the floor.

He's hard. Really hard. His cock jumps at me, thick and erect, and I lick my lips. I'm ready for him, for them. My pussy is slick, and I'm rubbing my legs together, trapping Hudson's hand between my thighs.

Speaking of Hudson, his hand slides further up my thighs until his thumb meets my wet panties. "Tell us who makes you this wet," he orders, his tone possessive. "Tell us who your pussy is dripping for."

"You," I pant out immediately. *If he just moves that thumb an inch higher.* I try to grind my hips down on his hand, desperate to feel his touch against my clitoris, but Asher stops me, his hands grabbing my hips. He holds me immobile, while continuing to brush his lips against my neck, nibbling and nipping at my tender flesh with his teeth.

"No," I protest again. This is unbearable. Damn it. Hudson's still clothed and I'm about to combust.

Hudson finally moves the gusset of my panties aside. His fingers slide over my swollen lips, making their way to my clitoris.

He lets the anticipation build, moving with agonizing slowness. *Faster*, I want to scream. *More.*

Hudson grazes my clitoris just once, then his hands drop from my pussy, ignoring my whimper of protest. He grabs hold of the waistband of my panties and tugs them down my legs, then he gets undressed too. *Finally.*

Asher pushes my skirt up so it bunches at my waist. He fishes a condom out of his pants and rolls it on. Pressing me against Hudson's chest, he lifts my knees in the air and thrusts his hard cock into me. His eyes burn into mine, his palms gripping my thighs. "Tell me what you want."

"You," I gasp. "Both of you. Now."

Hudson's finger teases the tight bud of my ass, and I inhale sharply. Asher fucks me with deep, steady strokes. Every time he plunges into me, my ass is pushed onto Hudson's dick and from the harshness of his breathing, he likes it.

My pussy clenches and spasms against Asher's cock. "I can't hold on," I whimper. It's too much. "I'm going to come."

"Not yet," Hudson orders. He grabs a handful of my hair and yanks my head back. "You don't come until we give you permission, you understand?"

"I'm too close," I gasp out. Hudson's thumb is rubbing over my clitoris, and Asher's dick pounds into me, and my pussy feels so swollen that I don't think I can hold back my orgasm for another second.

"Now," Asher orders, slamming into me, his face contorted with desire. "Come for us now."

I let myself fall off the edge with a sob, Asher only a half-thrust behind. I collapse on the floor, leaning against Hudson's tightly muscled chest. "Your turn now?" I ask him, stroking his thick cock.

He grins, and he kisses the back of my neck. "I thought you'd never ask."

THREE HOURS LATER, we're finally done. "You don't have to leave," Hudson says to me as I button up my coat. There's a slight smile on his lips, but his eyes are serious. "You could spend the night."

"I'll make you pancakes in the morning," Asher adds. He doesn't look at me as he makes the offer, and I get the sense he doesn't mean it. *He's probably exhausted from his flight.* "With chocolate chips, if you like."

"Oh, that's a low blow. You know I'm a chocolate fiend." It's an appealing offer. I'd love to wake up between them, pressed against their hard bodies. I want to shower with them in the morning, and maybe sneak in a quickie before we run off for work. But it's just casual, this thing between us. We've been together for less than three weeks. It's too much, too soon. *Perhaps if we survive the one-month mark.*

"Tempting though it is, I'm going to pass," I decline, keeping my voice light. "I snore, and I'll keep you up all night."

I hug them both before I leave. Hudson clasps me against his body, his touch warm and lingering, but Asher's hug is almost perfunctory, and I'm not the only one that notices. Hudson's eyebrow rises as he takes in Asher's stiffness.

He's just jet-lagged, I tell myself. I decline their offer to drive me home, and hail a cab instead, but as I lean back in the taxi and close my eyes, I can't shake off a feeling that something is seriously wrong.

18

We are afraid to care too much, for fear that the other person does not care at all.

— ELEANOR ROOSEVELT

Hudson:

Once she leaves, I turn to Asher. He's acting a little weird. "What's the matter with you?" I ask.

In reply, he pulls an envelope out of his laptop bag and hands it to me. "This."

My heart beats faster as I look at the photos. My hands tremble as I read the note. I'm silent for a long time, then I lift my head up and look at my friend. "Are you going to give up?"

Poor choice of words. "Give up?" Asher explodes. "You think I'm giving up? Fuck you, Hudson." He jumps to his feet, pacing in front of the window. "Read the note. *'Remember Lauren?'* Thorne's figured out who I am and he's figured out the best way to attack." He takes a deep breath and calms himself. "I can't let history repeat itself," he says quietly. "I can't let what happened to Lauren happen to Wendy."

"I don't want that to happen either," I respond, "but Wendy is a grown woman. I don't think you should make this decision for her. Show her the note. Thorne's obviously trying to pull us apart—let's not walk into his trap. We should work together to beat him."

"You don't think that it occurred to me to show this to Wendy?" Asher glares at me. "Tell me, Hudson, what do you think is going to happen if Wendy finds out? Do you think she's going to quit the Staten Island Project?"

Damn it. Wendy's not a quitter. Thorne's thrown down the gauntlet—Wendy won't walk away. "She's going to fight harder."

He nods. "Exactly. And Thorne's not going to fight fair. There's too much money on the line. The situation is just going to escalate until someone gets hurt."

I go cold at the thought of physical harm befalling Wendy. It's been three short weeks, but already, she's more important to me than my ex-wife ever was. On the surface, she's sarcastic and funny, but that's a mask, her way of protecting herself from being hurt. Scratch the surface, and there's sweetness underneath, a sweetness mixed with a fiery passion that makes her irresistible.

I wanted her to stay with us. I wanted to spend the entire night with her curled up between Asher and me, and I wanted to watch her wake up in the morning. Fuck, I even wanted to make her breakfast.

It had taken effort to play it cool, to hug her goodbye and watch her leave. Had I known it was the last time, I'd have held on tighter. I'd have put my pride aside and begged her to stay with me.

"I don't want to quit this project."

"You think I do?" Asher's hands ball into fists. His voice is tight with frustration. "You think I haven't been searching for any way out?" He sinks onto the couch and gazes blankly at the wall. "When Lauren killed herself," he says, so quietly that I can barely hear him, "my world shattered. It took months before I could function, years before I could think of her without pain. I'd see someone with red hair on the street and my heart would beat faster." He lifts his head up and stares at me. "My infatuation with Lauren was one-sided," he says flatly. "And it still broke me. With Wendy..." His voice trails off. "What we have is real. If something happens to her, I don't think I'd be able to live with the guilt."

The anguish in his tone distracts me from my own misery. "So we let Thorne get away with blackmail?"

"No." The look on Asher's face chills me. "Thorne Hancock is not getting away with anything. I let him win once. That won't happen again."

"What are you planning to do?" Asher sounds as if he has a plan, or at least the beginnings of one.

"We need something on Thorne," he replies. "Jeff Choi hinted that Thorne cooked the books in our first meeting with him, remember?"

I nod. I'd been hopeful that we'd uncover something criminal on Thorne, but unfortunately, that trail had led nowhere. "You looked into it and couldn't find any evidence to back Jeff up," I respond.

"Yes, but what if I was wrong? I'm not an expert on financial fraud. Stone Bradley is a competent investigator, but this is beyond his skill set. We need someone who specializes in this kind of thing. Someone we can trust."

The memory hits me like a thunderbolt from the sky. "What about her friend Miki?" I ask. "Wendy mentioned her when she was talking about the Lippman divorce, remember? She said Miki was responsible for finding the money he'd hidden away."

His expression brightens. "Hudson, you're a genius. Do you know Miki's last name?"

I search my memories, but I draw a blank. "We can ask Wendy."

"I'll get Stone to find it for us," he replies grimly. "Once we walk away from Wendy's project, I'll be shocked if she wants to talk to us again."

He's right. Wendy's going to believe that we betrayed her, and our fledgling relationship won't survive. I can only hope that one day, we will be able to tell her the whole truth, and she'll find it in her heart to forgive us.

∼

THE NEXT MORNING, I pull Nadja aside and explain what I need her to do.

I have a bad feeling in my gut. All night, I've been thinking about Thorne's blackmail attempt. Yes, Stone Bradley's men are watching Wendy, but because she doesn't know about her bodyguards, they can't be with her twenty-four seven. I've poured over the news articles on Jean Nakashima's death. From all accounts, she was an expert sailor. She was in her college sailing team; she was even in contention for the Olympic team at one time. There was a storm the night she disappeared, but it wasn't severe. I can't shake off my suspicion that Thorne caused the woman's death.

To keep Wendy safe, we need to sever ties with her. For good.

"I don't like it," my second in command says once she's heard me out.

"Please, Nadja. I really need your help."

She gives me an unreadable look. In the last three weeks, we've been treading carefully around each other, avoiding talk of anything other than work. She still hasn't forgiven me for taking on Staten Island. This discussion is about the longest conversation we've had on a topic that isn't work. "Fine," she agrees at last. "But I think you're making a mistake."

I GET to Hancock Construction at half-past eleven. Walking in, I see Amanda chatting with another assistant, Lucy. Good. Amanda is a nosy gossip, and we need witnesses for what we've planned. The more, the better.

There's a hot ball of shame in my throat. *I like Wendy.* What the two of us are planning to do will devastate her. She doesn't have a high opinion of men because of her mother's history with her father. She's just beginning to trust us, and we're going to let her down.

"Hey, Hudson." Wendy looks up as I walk in. Her face is pinched, her expression drawn. My heart immediately lurches with concern.

"Are you okay?" I ask her.

"I think I have the flu," she admits. "I've been sick all morning."

"You should have taken the day off."

She rolls her eyes. "That's not feasible," she says. "I have meetings all afternoon. Jeff Choi thinks we're spending too much money; Brad Pankratz thinks he should get paid more, and Bill Anderson wants a status update." She smiles at me. "I'm counting on your ability to haggle with Brad to keep us on track."

"Right."

Asher walks into the room at that moment, looking grim. "Wendy," he says without preamble. "We need to talk to you."

She looks at Asher's face, then at mine, and her smile fades. "What's going on?" she asks quietly.

I feel like scum. "We're quitting the Staten Island project." My voice comes out louder than I intended. Outside the open door, Amanda's conversation with Lucy trails off as she tries to listen to us.

Her face turns white. "You are?"

One quick tug, just like a band-aid, I tell myself. *It'll hurt less this way.*

"Yes," Asher confirms. He smiles at her tightly. "And I think it's best that we don't see each other anymore. No hard feelings, okay?"

Nadja makes her appearance at that moment, her timing impeccable. Exactly the way I've planned it. "Hey you two," she greets us, fluttering her eyelashes at Asher and lacing her arm in mine. "I got tired of waiting downstairs. I thought you said this would only take a minute."

"Sorry, Nadja." I kiss her cheek affectionately. "We're almost done here."

For an instant, there's a flash of pain in Wendy's eyes, and then her face hardens. "I'm afraid I delayed them," she says, her voice cool and polite. "It won't happen again." Her lips lift in a bitter smile. "Just casual, right? Have a nice life, guys."

Just like that, it's over.

Amanda watches us leave, her mouth hanging open. Lucy's eyes are wide with shock. *This is necessary,* I repeat to myself, trying to convince myself of the truth of my words. *We have to keep Wendy safe.* But I can't get Wendy's stricken expression out of my mind.

19

In three words I can sum up everything I've learned about
life: it goes on.

— Robert Frost

Wendy:

Three hours later, I'm still reeling. I've been trying
not to think about Asher and Hudson, but my
mind keeps circling back to them. And I grow
angrier and angrier.

Last night, they'd put on the act of a lifetime. They'd
pretended they wanted me. Hudson had even asked me to
spend the night, and I'd come so close to agreeing. And to
think, they were seeing someone else at the same time. They
had to be—there was too much familiarity in the way the
dark-haired woman had greeted them. It was obvious that
she knew them well.

There's a sick pit in my stomach, and it's not because of
the damn bug. Everything was a lie—their willingness to

help me, their spiel about how they didn't date more than one woman at once.

My phone rings and I pick it up. It's Miki. "Do you have a minute?" she asks.

I frown when I hear her voice. She sounds like she's been crying. The last time I talked to her, she hadn't sounded happy either. "For you, anytime," I reply immediately. "Is everything alright?"

"No," she confesses. "I might as well tell you. Everyone's going to know soon enough anyway. Aaron's been working long hours. Friday evening, I thought I might surprise him at work and drag him away to watch a movie." Her voice trembles. "When I walked in, his secretary was giving him a blowjob."

"Oh, Miki." I forget about Asher and Hudson's betrayal in the face of Miki's troubles. If Aaron were here, I'd fucking *Bobbit* the asshole. Miki moved to Texas for this jerk. They've only been married for a year. "That sucks."

"Yeah, it does," she says bleakly. "All week, I've been trying to figure out if my marriage is worth saving."

Leave him, I want to shout, but this isn't my decision to make. "What are you going to do?"

"I don't know," she says bleakly. "Enough about me. I'm still looking through Hancock Construction's books, but it's tough going."

"That's okay," I reply tonelessly. The mention of Hancock Construction reminds me of this morning's events. "It's not urgent."

Her voice sharpens. "What's wrong with you?" she demands. "You sound awful."

I blink my eyelashes rapidly, trying to hold back the tears that threaten to overflow. "Nothing," I say, but the shakiness of my reply gives me away.

"Don't lie to me, Wendy," she says at once. "Is it work? You're driving yourself to the point of exhaustion."

"I think I'm falling sick," I admit, "but that's not the problem." I tell her about Hudson and Asher. "I thought they were different," I whisper, "but I'm the stupidest person on earth. They totally played me, and I don't even know why." My tears spill over my cheeks. "They didn't have to pretend to care. I'd have slept with them anyway."

Miki swears into the phone. "The fuckers," she snarls. "Wendy, don't cry. They're two jerks who don't deserve you. You're better off without them."

"I'm not crying," I lie, wiping my cheeks with the back of my hand. "I just don't know how I'm going to manage; that's all. I have to find a new architect and a new lawyer." I take a deep breath. "I don't get it, Miki," I confess. "We made no promises to each other." My heart hurts as I say those words, but it's the truth. "If they wanted to sleep with someone else, all they had to do was say so. Why did they quit the project?"

Amanda pokes her head into my office at that moment, holding a cup of coffee. "Wendy," she says, sounding forcedly cheerful, "I needed a coffee break. You like caramel lattes, don't you?" She steps into the room and notices I'm on the phone. "Sorry," she mouths.

It's a kind gesture. I reach for the steaming beverage, but as soon as the smell of the caffeine wafts over me, my stomach roils, and I'm overtaken by a wave of nausea. "Thank you," I mumble, trying not to breathe in the warm-caramel smell of the latte. What the heck is wrong with me?

Mouthing another apology for interrupting me, she leaves, shutting the door behind her. I resume my conversation with Miki, struggling not to throw up all over my desk. This bug is getting worse, not better. "God, I wish this stomach bug would go away. I don't have time to be sick right now."

"Is your stomach still bothering you? Wendy, you've been fighting this thing for two weeks. Go to a doctor."

"I don't have time for that." There's too much to do here, especially with Hudson and Asher's departure.

"Do you have time to listen to me nag?" she asks pointedly. "Because I will. What's more, I'll call the others. Do you want to get Gabby mad at you? Or have Piper smile sweetly while marching you off to bed?"

Hell no. "I'll call the doctor this week," I say meekly.

"Today. Right after we hang up."

$\sim$

MY DOCTOR HAS an unexpected opening on her schedule, so at five, I make my way to her office. Once I check in, I barely have time to flip through the selection of magazines before a nurse calls my name. "Wendy Williams?"

I rise to my feet and follow her into a quiet examining room. She takes my blood pressure and jots the readings on a screen, then she leaves. I perch on the chair next to the examining table and play Angry Birds on my phone until Dr. Dittmar bustles in.

"Hello, Wendy," she greets me warmly. "How are you today?"

"I have a lingering stomach bug," I reply. "I've been throwing up a lot in the last two weeks. It's probably stress."

"Hmm." The doctor finishes reading my chart and turns to me. "I noticed you're a month overdue on your birth-control shot. Is there any chance you could be pregnant?"

My blood runs cold. I feel the color drain from my cheeks, and I shiver instinctively. "No," I reply automatically. It can't be true. "They..." I bite back the sentence I was going to utter. *They used condoms.* I don't want my doctor judging me for my threesome. "We used condoms," I say instead.

"Condoms aren't foolproof," she replies. She opens a drawer and pulls out a syringe. "Before I write you a prescription for your stomach, I'm going to do a blood test as a precaution, okay?"

"Sure."

She quickly draws blood. "It'll take ten minutes to analyze the sample. I'll be back as soon as I have your results."

"Okay."

As I wait, my palms sweat and my heart races. Time passes with excruciating slowness. My mind churns with a thousand anxious thoughts. What if I'm pregnant? How will Hudson and Asher react? One of them has to be the father —I haven't been with anyone else in almost a year.

My father rejected me. Is that what Asher and Hudson will do to my baby? Already, they walked away from me this morning. What will happen when they find out?

You can't be pregnant, I reassure myself. *We used condoms.*

But Dr. Dittmar's suspicions make sense. My stomach has been queasy. I've barely been able to eat in the morning; my appetite doesn't return until the afternoon. I've been puking my brains out. Today, a whiff of Amanda's caramel latte sent me running to the toilet.

If I'm pregnant, which one of them is the father? Hudson never speaks of his ex-wife; maybe he still has feelings for her. Asher wants to keep everything casual; work is the most important thing in his life. How will fatherhood change these men?

A thought strikes me, one that has my insides clawing

with panic. What if they want custody? What if they try to take my baby away from me?

You're being silly, Wendy. Asher and Hudson might have screwed you over today, but that's no reason to assume the worst-case scenario. But once the thought occurs to me, I can't banish it from my mind. I've learned one thing from my painful history. Rich and powerful men do what they want without consequences. My father hid his marriage from my mother and had her fired from her job when she found out the truth and confronted him with it.

I should have resisted the sweet temptation that was Asher and Hudson. I shouldn't have allowed my resolve to weaken. I shouldn't have let desire overcome my innate caution.

And now, I'm waiting to find out if I'm pregnant.

The sun streams in through the window. Everyone in Manhattan seems to be out early this Friday afternoon, enjoying the good weather before winter sets in. I'd normally be at my desk, envying them their freedom. Not today.

There's a knock on the door, and Gloria Dittmar enters, holding a clipboard. "The blood test results are in," she says. "You're definitely pregnant."

I'm in a fog. Vaguely, I'm aware that she's saying something about pre-natal vitamins, about refraining from smoking, drinking, and drug use. She asks me some questions about my health; I answer her on auto-pilot. She warns me to take it easy at work and to listen to my body, and I mutely agree.

I stumble out of her office in a complete daze.

I'm going to have a baby.

I can't conceal this news from Asher and Hudson. I'm

going to have to tell them, and when I do, they're going to freak out.

My hands cover my still-flat belly protectively. "Don't worry, monkey," I say aloud, talking to my little impossible bean for the first time. "No matter what, you'll always have me."

20

The secret of getting ahead is getting started.

— MARK TWAIN

Asher:

I go through the next few days in a daze. Everything reminds me of Wendy. I watch some kind of legal drama on TV, but the lead protagonist is a smart, funny woman and I can't watch it without being overwhelmed by sadness. I bury myself in work and avoid both Hudson and the boxing gym. I keep telling myself that I'm doing this to keep Wendy safe, but after three days of misery, even that feels hollow.

Stone Bradley calls me on Tuesday. "You wanted me to track down a phone number," he says. "You have a pen handy?"

It takes me a few seconds to realize he's talking about Wendy's friend Miki. "You can't email it to me?"

"This chick's a hacker," he replies. "I'm not putting anything on the internet."

Rolling my eyes, I rummage through the sheets of paper on my desk, looking for something to write on. Stone's a good guy, but sometimes, he's a little too paranoid for his own good.

"TELL me why I should talk to you." Miki sounds hostile, as I'd known she would be.

"I know it sounds difficult to believe, but I'm trying to help Wendy."

"Not difficult to believe," she says tightly. "Impossible. I don't like you very much, Mr. Doyle. You hurt my friend. So if you don't want me to hang up, stop giving me vague assurances that you mean well. It's not going to work. I want facts. You have sixty seconds."

Wendy's friend is angry and protective, and I need her help. "Fine." I take a deep breath and tell her everything. Thorne's history with Lauren, the photos in the mail and the blackmailing letter, and Jeff Choi's suspicions about financial fraud.

There's a moment of silence when I'm done, then Miki says, "Well, you're right about the money. I've been looking into Hancock's books. They've definitely been tampered with."

"Who did it?" I ask urgently.

"Not so fast," she replies. "Tell me why you didn't just talk to Wendy."

I heave a sigh of frustration. "She's your friend," I say, keeping a tight hold of my emotions, trying to keep the pain and the rage I've felt in the last four days under control. "You know that she doesn't walk away from dangerous situations. The first time I met her, she was taking on a two-hundred pound drunk guy at a bar. If she finds out that Thorne's blackmailing me, she'll call his bluff. And if Thorne believes there's a real chance she might win this fucking contest, he's not just going to be content with blackmailing me. He's going to target her."

"You're probably right," she concedes. "What do you want from me?"

"Wendy's not going to be safe until Thorne's in jail. If there's proof that Thorne committed fraud, we can alert the authorities."

"It's not much of a plan," Miki says skeptically.

"It's all I have at the moment."

"Fair enough." She seems to reach a conclusion. "Here's what I've found so far," she says. "The project in Barbados was hemorrhaging money. There are multiple emails between the Head of Finance and Thorne about the project. She kept asking for information; Thorne rebuffed her repeatedly. The week before she died, she spent hours in the accounting system." Miki's voice is grim. "Once she died, her emails were deleted, and her concerns swept under the rug. Thorne dumped sixty million dollars into Hancock Construction's bank accounts, and they made it look like the money had been there all along."

I focus on the obvious flaw. "Thorne doesn't have sixty million dollars. His father set up a trust fund for him that pays five million dollars every year. He spends most of it."

"I know," she replies. "Someone loaned Thorne the money. Jean Nakashima was trying to find out who that was when she drowned."

I feel chilled. There's another player in the mix, someone who loaned Thorne sixty million dollars, someone who might have made Jean Nakashima disappear.

The situation has just got a thousand times more dangerous. I need to call Bradley and double the guards on Wendy.

Miki reaches the same conclusion as I do. "I'm searching for a name," she says. I'll call you as soon as I have it. And Asher?"

"Yeah?"

"Keep Wendy safe."

21

With the new day comes new strength and new thoughts.

— ELEANOR ROOSEVELT

Hudson:

Idon't reach out to Asher for the next few weeks. I don't want to talk to him; I'm angry with my friend. I understand why he acted the way he did; I'd have made the same decision in his place. But as I spend weekend after weekend alone, I feel Wendy's absence keenly, and I resent Asher for it.

October slips into November. The Monday before Thanksgiving, Nadja and I have a meeting with Brian Dobson. Dobson's building a mega-mall on the outskirts of Houston, and Nadja is spearheading the project. She presents the design confidently, and I can tell Dobson is blown away. Once she's done, Brian applauds enthusiastically, then turns to me. "I'm surprised to see you here," he says. "I thought you'd be putting out the fire at Hancock

Construction. I guess the rumors are true—you guys have pulled out of the Staten Island project?"

"What are you talking about?"

"I golfed with Jeff Parsons over the weekend," Brian says. "He said that Thorne Hancock came to the board of directors and complained that the Staten Island project is at serious risk of failure. The board has called an emergency meeting today. If their concerns aren't addressed, they're going to stop construction." He gives me a speculative look. "You don't know what I'm talking about," he guesses. "So it's true? You're not involved anymore?"

An emergency board meeting. Thorne planned this. He got rid of Asher and me, and now he's shifted his attention to Wendy.

I think of Wendy, alone, ambushed by the board. They'll ask her pointed questions about the design, and I won't be there to answer them. They'll nitpick about contract details, and Asher won't be there to assure them that things are under control. Wendy is doing a great job managing the project, but she's neither an architect nor a corporate lawyer.

It's probably for the best. If the board halts the Staten Island project, Thorne will cease his attacks on Wendy. For a brief second, I even fantasize that the three of us will resume our relationship.

Then cold reality intrudes, and I think about Wendy. She got fired from her law firm because of Paul Hancock's stupid contest, and instead of complaining about it, she rolled up her sleeves and got to work. She's hammered away at the Staten Island project, familiarizing herself with the construction industry, spending long hours at work absorbing every single detail so her project can be successful.

She'll be shattered if the board shuts her down.

And I can't stand by and let that happen. I don't care what Asher thinks. I don't care about the danger; we'll handle it together. Right now, the only thought on my mind is that I want to be there for Wendy. "I am involved," I tell Brian, glancing at my watch. "I'm heading to Hancock Construction now, as a matter of fact. See you later, Brian, Nadja."

I expect Nadja to react with displeasure, but instead, there's a half-smile on her face.

In the hallway, as I reach for my coat, my assistant Clarisse stops me. "Mr. Doyle called," she says. "He said it was urgent."

I shrug. I have no intention of calling Asher back. Not until I've helped Wendy.

∼

SHE'S SEATED in the middle of the long conference table, facing the door. Jeff Choi is at her right; the seat to her left is occupied by Mark Allen, who scowls at the papers in front of him.

I haven't seen Wendy for more than a month. I pause at the doorway, drinking in the sight of her. Her blonde hair is scraped back into a tight topknot. She's wearing her gray suit, her blouse buttoned up to her throat. I know that outfit. Wendy's dressing for battle.

Thorne's seated himself at the head of the table. Pompous ass. He's addressing the gathering. "They don't have an architect," he says accusingly. "They don't have a lawyer—Mark hasn't even seen the contracts they're signing. I think we have a right to know what's going on in Staten Island."

Bill Richardson is seated next to Thorne. "Is Thorne right, Ms. Williams?" he asks Wendy. "Is Fleming Architecture no longer working on your project?"

That's my cue. "Sorry I'm late, Wendy," I say, stepping into the room. "I had a meeting that ran over."

For a second, Wendy's expression is shocked, then her face goes blank again. "I wasn't expecting you, Hudson," she says neutrally.

I move a chair from the back and position it next to Wendy, edging Mark Allen out of the way. "You know me," I say, nodding at Thorne, feeling deeply satisfied at the stupefied look on his face. Asshole. "I don't miss client briefings."

Bill Richardson smiles at me, relief in his eyes. Next to him, Thorne tries to recover his composure. "Fine, Fleming's here," he sneers. "But that doesn't address Mark's questions about the contracts." He looks at the Head of Legal. "Mark, do you want to explain your concerns to the Board of Directors?"

"Please do," a voice interjects from the doorway. Asher walks into the conference room. "I worked on them personally. I'm curious to know what Allen thinks is wrong."

Thorne's face grows pale, then he glares at Wendy, an unpleasant scowl on his face. I hope we haven't made things worse.

HALF AN HOUR LATER, the Board of Directors has been satisfied that the Staten Island project is on track. "I'm not sure what the urgency was, Thorne," Andrea Sommers, one of the board members, and a long-time friend of Paul Hancock chides. "Why couldn't this update have waited until after Thanksgiving? Wendy appears to have everything under control."

Thorne mutters something and stalks away. Ms. Sommers turns to me with a warm smile and shakes my hand. "We've never met, but I knew your father quite well. I'm so glad you're working on this project."

"Indeed." Michael Berry, the Chairman of the Board, nods vigorously. "Wendy, do you have Thanksgiving plans?"

I wonder if these people know how Paul Hancock treated Wendy's mother. Everyone seems to be happy to gloss over the uncomfortable fact that Hancock waited until after his death to acknowledge his daughter. They all appear content to treat Wendy like a colleague, sweeping the whole sordid family history under the carpet. I'm suddenly furious with all of them.

"I normally spend Thanksgiving with my *mother*," Wendy replies, placing pointed emphasis on the word. "But she has to work this year, so I'll be spending the holiday with my friends."

"Ah." Berry, realizing that he's broached an awkward topic, looks uncomfortable and avoids her gaze. "That's good." He directs his next question at Asher and me. "What about the two of you? Are you spending the holiday with family?"

What family? My parents are dead, and so are Asher's. Megan never cooked; she was always on a diet. Since my dad passed away, there hasn't been much to be grateful for around the holidays.

For an instant, I imagine what the holiday would be like if Wendy were around. Asher would cook dinner. Wendy would make jokes about my incompetence in the kitchen, and rope me into helping out. I'd light the fireplace and open a bottle of wine, and after our meal, the three of us would relax on the couch. *And we'd make love...*

"Every year, Hudson and I order pizza and watch football," Asher replies. "And the four-day weekend will give me a chance to catch up on work."

Andrea Sommers gives us a sympathetic smile. Out of the corner of my eye, I notice that Wendy is listening to our conversation, an unreadable look on her face. I wonder what she's thinking.

22

There is only one happiness in this life, to love and be loved.

— George Sand

Wendy:

Piper's is packed. The restaurant is officially closed for the holiday, but you wouldn't know it from the number of people there.

The tables are loaded with food. A giant turkey takes center stage, and it appears that Piper and Sebastian, the two chefs in the room, have made a hundred side dishes. There are potatoes: mashed, roasted and scalloped. There are yams and squash. Cranberry sauce, brussels sprouts, steamed broccoli, roasted mushrooms, three kinds of stuffing, Piper's special recipe macaroni and cheese, Gabby's cucumber and cheese sandwiches, and so much more.

Thank heavens I'm eating for two.

Miki called me a week ago and told me she was flying

back to New York for Thanksgiving. "I'm staying through Christmas," she'd said. "I just can't deal with Aaron over the holidays." Understanding completely, I'd told her she could crash at my place, and she'd gratefully accepted.

She arrives just in time for the meal. "My flight was delayed," she explains, giving me a warm hug. "Thank you so much for letting me stay."

"No worries," I tell her. My friend looks about as good as can be expected under the circumstances. "Prepare for the inquisition. You didn't tell Piper, Gabby, and Katie you were coming, and they're going to want to know why Aaron isn't with you."

"Crap on a cracker," she groans, and though the situation is serious, I have to laugh. Miki's curses are always so colorful. "Please Wendy, would you just tell them the truth if they ask? Tonight, all I want to do is eat some food, hang out with my friends and drink myself silly."

"Done." I know exactly how Miki feels.

Katie and Adam walk up at that moment. "Miki," Katie squeals in pleasure, flinging her arms around her. "I didn't know you were coming."

The three of them start to catch up, and I leave them to it. I wander away to a corner, wanting to be alone with my thoughts. I hadn't expected Hudson and Asher to show up yesterday. After the board meeting, I'd avoided talking to them; I didn't know what to say. The only thought running through my brain was that I was pregnant and one of them was the father.

Though I'm still angry about the way they'd left, I can't deny that I'm grateful for their help yesterday. Without their presence at the meeting, Thorne would have almost certainly succeeded in stopping my project.

No one should be alone for Thanksgiving, yet that's

exactly how Hudson and Asher will be spending the day. *Pizza and football,* Asher had said. *And time to catch up on work.*

As I look around the restaurant, packed with my friends, I feel a prickle of guilt. I could have invited them here. There's certainly no shortage of food.

AFTER DINNER, Piper drifts toward me. "Where's Aaron?" she asks me. "How come he's not here?"

Since I promised Miki I'd spread the word, I tell Piper the truth. When I'm done, she gapes at me. "Why didn't she say anything?"

So much has happened in the last few months. Bailey broke up with the asshole she was dating and started seeing Daniel and Sebastian. Gabby reunited with Dominic and Carter, the two men she'd had a one-night stand with, and the three of them decided to make a go of it. They're even helping raise Noah, Carter's young nephew. Most recently, Piper's two investors, Owen and Wyatt fell in love with her. The last few months have transformed our little group into one large, happy family.

I don't blame Miki for keeping her marriage troubles to herself. As silly as it sounds, when all your friends are happy, you don't want to bring them down. "You know Miki. She doesn't really say much at the best of times."

"She's not the only one," Piper states. "I haven't seen much of you either. What's going on?"

I avoid looking at her. "Work," I say vaguely. "You know how it is."

I'm lying. I've been using the Staten Island project as a way to avoid the Thursday Night Drinking Pack. If my friends notice I'm not drinking, they'll guess why in a heartbeat.

It shouldn't be this hard to tell them about the upheaval in my life. They're the most supportive group of women I've ever met. But the words lodge in my throat. I haven't told anyone about the baby. Not even my mother.

Piper's boyfriend Wyatt walks up to us carrying a couple of flutes of champagne. "Ladies," he says gallantly. "You need drinks."

Piper gives him a dazzling smile as she takes the offered glass. I hesitate for an instant before reaching for the champagne, and Piper looks exasperated. "Aren't the two of you friends yet?"

That's what she thinks this is about? Early in Piper's relationship with Wyatt and Owen, I'd warned them against breaking my friend's heart, but my caution was misplaced. Wyatt and Owen adore Piper, and they treat her like a queen.

"Of course we are." I grin at Wyatt, punching him lightly on his arm. "Unless you hurt Piper..."

"At which point you'll chop my balls off and use them in a stir-fry," Wyatt quips. "Don't worry," he says, winking at my blushing friend. "I take very good care of Piper."

I pretend to chuckle. Piper's obvious happiness is making me wistful. If Piper were to tell Wyatt and Owen she was pregnant, they'd be overjoyed. Asher and Hudson? I have no idea what their reaction is going to be.

Just then, Owen raises his glass in a toast. "It's time for thanks," he says to the crowded room. "And I have many things to be thankful for. Let's drink. To laughter, to love, and happily ever after."

Everyone takes a sip of their champagne. I lift the glass to my lips, trying to figure out a plan to dump the beverage when Piper catches sight of me. Her gaze sharpens, and her mouth falls open. "Excuse us," she tells Wyatt, grabbing me by my wrist and dragging me through the kitchen doors. "You're not drinking," she accuses me once we're alone. "What's going on?"

I take a deep breath and set my champagne glass down on the spotless stainless-steel kitchen counter. I'm somewhat relieved that Piper's guessed my secret. Perhaps if I tell her, it'll give me the practice I need to tell Asher and Hudson. "Almost two months ago, the day before my birthday, I decided to have a one-night stand with two men. I thought it was just one night, no strings attached. What could possibly go wrong?"

Piper waits for me to continue. I force the words out through my dry throat. "Except the condom failed. I was in a ménage, and there were two of them, and now I'm pregnant. And I don't know which one of them is the father."

My friend stares at me, shock written clearly on her face. "I'm going to be a mother," I whisper. "And Piper, I'm terrified."

"You're pregnant?" Miki's voice slices through the quiet. She's standing in the doorway. "I didn't mean to overhear," she adds apologetically. "I came to find Piper to tell her I was leaving."

I smile weakly at her. "I was going to tell everyone anyway. Piper just happened to guess. How much did you hear?"

She gives me a careful look. "Ménage. Pregnant."

"I'd say that about sums up the pertinent facts."

Piper finds her tongue. "Do you know them? The guys you slept with?"

"Yeah. It's Asher and Hudson."

Awareness dawns on Piper's face. Miki, who already

knows about my relationship with them, looks unsurprised. "Are you happy about the baby? You said you were terrified."

"I am terrified," I admit. "I'm also thrilled about the little monkey."

Piper's face softens, and she pulls me into her arms. "I'm so happy for you, Wendy," she says, choking up a little. "You're going to be a great mom. And your little monkey will have five adoring aunts who are going to spoil him or her rotten."

Miki asks the question I'm dreading. "How did Hudson and Asher react to your news?"

I flush. "I haven't told them," I confess. "I don't even know which one of them is the father. What if they hate me?"

"You need to tell them, Wendy," Piper says gently. "They're going to want to know, and it's the right thing to do."

"Will they want to know?" My voice is bitter. "They quit my project. They're seeing some other woman now. I don't think they're going to care, to be honest."

Miki flushes. "I have a confession to make," she admits. "They only walked away because Thorne blackmailed Asher."

Piper and I gape at her. "What are you talking about?" I finally ask my friend.

Miki sighs. "Asher called me," she says. "Thorne had pictures of the three of you making out in your office. He threatened to make them public if Asher and Hudson didn't stop working with you."

Shock courses through me. That's why they walked away? Then I remember the woman they left with and my heart sinks again. "It doesn't matter anyway," I mumble. "They're seeing someone."

"Who?" Piper asks.

"I don't know. I think her name was Nadia."

Miki pulls up something on her phone. "This woman?" she asks, showing me the screen. "Nadja Breton? She's an architect at Hudson's firm. I'm pretty sure she's married." She puts her arm around my shoulder. "I don't think Asher and Hudson wanted to leave, Wendy," she says quietly. "They did it to protect you."

"I think you should talk to them," Piper says.

I'm completely confused. First, they walk away, then they reappear at the board meeting, and now I find out they've been on my side the entire time? I don't know what to do.

In my heart, I feel the truth. I can trust Asher and Hudson.

It's only eight. With any luck, they haven't eaten. "Piper, can you pack me some leftovers?" I ask my friend. "They were planning on eating pizza for dinner. Somebody should stop that."

A wide smile breaks out on her face. Piper's such a romantic. "Somebody like you, you mean?" she teases. "Sure. I'll get you some food."

Once Piper leaves, Miki gives me a serious look. "I want you to be happy," she says. "But I also want you to be careful."

I'm always careful. My mother's wariness of men has rubbed off on me. My instincts tell me it's time to be brave.

23

Keep your face always toward the sunshine - and shadows will fall behind you.

— WALT WHITMAN

Asher:

Levi's been living at my place for the last two months. He's been to hundreds of job interviews, but he's yet to find an employer that's prepared to take a chance on him. He's been doing odd construction jobs here and there for money. As for me, while I'd prefer having my place to myself, Patrick Sullivan's warning reminds me that there's far more at stake than my privacy.

"Do you have Thanksgiving plans?" I ask Levi on Thursday morning. "I'm heading over to Hudson's place to watch football if you'd like to join us."

He makes a face. "Hudson's the architect, right? No thanks. Your billionaire friend doesn't approve of me. I'm heading to Lloyd's mother's house."

"Lloyd Beecham? Are you hanging out with him now?"

He shrugs. "It's just a meal, buddy. His mom makes the most amazing pecan pie you've ever tasted. Stop worrying about me. I'm on the straight and narrow."

I wish I could believe Levi's assurances, but I don't. Levi's gone two months without finding a decent job. Soon enough, Beecham's going to dangle one in front of him, and he's going to take the bait.

"Are you sure?" I try again. "The Lions are competitive this year. It'll be a good game this afternoon."

"Ash, I've been dreaming about Lori's pecan pie for weeks, not to mention the turkey and all the trimmings. What are you two going to eat? Pizza? Thanks. I'll pass."

I don't blame Levi. Thanksgiving is a time for family, friends, and feasting. Why would Levi trade that for hanging out with Hudson and me? "Have fun," I tell him.

An evening spent watching football has never felt as unappealing as it does right now.

~

THERE'S tension between Hudson and me, but that doesn't stop us from hanging out, drinking beer and watching football. Our friendship goes back too far for us to stay mad at each other. We're watching the Lions defensive line crumble against the Packers offense when there's a knock on the door. "Expecting company?" I ask my friend, who shakes his head and gets up to see who it is.

It's Wendy. Her hands are laden with bags, and her cheeks are pink with cold. "I just had a very interesting talk with Miki," she says. "Let's make a deal. I'll trade you a Thanksgiving meal made by two of New York's finest chefs in exchange for some answers."

My heart does a funny pitter-patter in my chest as she marches into Hudson's living room. I can't believe she's here. After everything we've done.

"What are you talking about?" Hudson asks carefully. He gets her coat and tosses it on the couch.

She rolls her eyes. "Please," she scoffs. "Miki is my friend. You had to know she'd tell me about the photos eventually."

To be honest, I'm surprised Wendy's friend has kept silent as long as she has. I thought she'd have told Wendy the whole story *weeks* ago. I wonder what's changed now.

I clear my throat. "Sit," I tell her. "You look like you're freezing."

She sinks down on the couch in front of the fireplace with a look of pleasure, which vanishes when she turns toward me. "The truth, Asher, or I walk. And I take the food with me."

I reach a decision. Hell, I made my choice yesterday, when I showed up at the board meeting. Wendy deserves to succeed, and I can't let a fear of what Thorne might do rule our lives forever. I won't cower before Hancock. "Okay," I respond, "I'll tell you everything."

I gaze into the flames. "When I graduated from law school, I had my pick of offers, but like you, I wanted to make a difference."

Wendy's listening with rapt attention. "You already know I grew up in a bunch of foster homes," I continue. "When I was sixteen, I was arrested and almost sent to jail."

I'm a little concerned about her reaction when she learns the truth about my past, but I have nothing to be worried about. Her eyes never leave my face. "What happened?"

Hudson snorts from his spot on the couch. "Levi *fucking*

Engels happened," he growls. "His buddy beat his ex's boyfriend to a pulp. Asher was arrested because he was in the wrong place at the wrong time."

"It's not quite as simple," I tell Wendy. "Anyway, Levi and I were arrested for assault, but I got lucky. I was a minor, and the district attorney decided not to prosecute me. He mentored me, made sure I got a high school diploma and he helped me with college applications. Naturally, I wanted to emulate him. I became a district attorney too. Then Lauren happened."

I draw a deep breath. "This is going to be difficult to hear," I warn her. "Thorne is your half-brother; Paul Hancock is your father. Are you sure you want to learn the truth?"

She nods. "Blood doesn't make family, Asher," she says quietly. "I grew up learning that lesson. Paul Hancock was never my father. My mother raised me. She's the only family that matters to me."

"My first case concerned a young woman called Lauren Bainbridge. Thorne Hancock plied her with alcohol at a fraternity party and raped her. We had DNA evidence. I thought we'd have no trouble convicting him."

A look of comprehension flashes on her face. "That night at Residence," she whispers. "When I had too much champagne. That's why you sent me home?"

"Partly," I reply, tracing the contours of her cheek with my finger. As I touch her, goosebumps rise on her skin. "Though I don't need to get women drunk to get them in my bed."

Her breathing quickens. Then she shakes her head and seems to gather herself. "The rest of the story," she says firmly. "That's the deal."

"Thorne started a whisper campaign to discredit

Lauren. Ex-boyfriends came out of the woodwork, accusing her of being a sex-hungry nymphomaniac. Photos of her drinking and dancing at parties were circulated on the campus. Thorne couldn't deny he'd slept with her; the DNA evidence would make a liar of him. But he could ruin her credibility."

The flames flicker and dance; heat washes through the room in waves, but it doesn't warm the cold in me as I relive the past. "Lauren couldn't take it. She dropped out of school and spiraled into a deep depression. Three years later, she committed suicide."

"Oh, Asher." Wendy's eyes are filled with understanding. She moves next to me and puts her arms around my shoulders. "I'm so sorry."

For ten years, ice has shrouded my heart, but when Wendy nestles next to me, I feel it crack. "I was in love with Lauren," I admit. "It was one-sided and futile, but I couldn't change the way I felt."

"That's why you switched to corporate law?"

"Yes. Thorne showed me that money matters more than the truth."

The expression on her face shows that she understands far more than I'm ready to reveal. "You chose a field where you didn't have to watch people suffer," she says quietly. "And you thought that if you walked away from Staten Island, I wouldn't get hurt."

"I didn't want your name in the tabloids."

"And yesterday?" she asks. "Why did you change your mind?"

"I thought about you facing the board alone, and I couldn't do it." I lace my fingers in hers. "I thought it was enough to keep you safe, but I realized that safe isn't the only thing that counts. You want this project to succeed; you want to protect the people that work at Hancock from Thorne's irresponsible gambles. And that matters too."

"What about Nadja?" Wendy sounds tentative. "Are you dating her?"

"That was my idea," Hudson replies, looking shame-faced. "I'm sorry; I shouldn't have done it, but I thought that if you believed we were seeing someone else, it would be a cleaner break. We've never dated Nadja; she works for me. For the record, she thought it was a stupid idea."

"It was," Wendy agrees. "Are you guys hungry?"

I exchange a look with Hudson. I can't read Wendy's reaction, but the fact that she's still here gives me hope. "I'm starving," I reply, getting to my feet and making my way to the kitchen for plates and forks.

Hudson follows me and reaches for a bottle of a Cabernet Sauvignon from the rack. "Wendy, would you prefer beer?" he asks her.

A look of hesitation crosses over her face. "Umm, could I have a cup of tea instead?" she asks. "I'm still a little cold."

The fireplace is radiating heat. I shoot her a concerned look. "Are you coming down with something? It's a furnace in here."

She looks uncomfortable. "I'm fine, really," she mutters. "I'm cold, not sick."

I fill the kettle with water and plug it in. Once the tea is ready, we make our way to the table, and Hudson and I dig into the food. Wendy sips on her tea in silence. Something's on her mind. I still don't know what she's thinking.

Here's what I *do* know. Wendy's in my thoughts all the time. I need to know what she wants from us, because if it's casual sex, I want out. I want more than that from her.

After pie and ice cream, we migrate back to the couch and watch the game. After football, we switch to Netflix and watch Breaking Bad, but before the first episode is done, Wendy's fast asleep, her head on my shoulder.

Neither Hudson nor I have the heart to wake her. We watch episode after episode in silence, but my attention isn't on the screen. It's on Wendy, on the warmth of her presence.

Things feel different between us. They feel more real.

After four episodes, Hudson turns off the TV. I tap Wendy gently on her shoulder, and she opens her eyes. As soon as she figures out where she is, she stiffens. "Sorry I dozed off. I'll call a cab."

Hudson leans forward. "You brought us dinner," he says intently. "Will you let us make you breakfast?"

I hold my breath as I wait for her answer. *Say yes. Please say yes.*

She thinks about it, and then she gives us a sleepy nod. "Okay."

I exhale in relief. We've been given a second chance. *This time,* I vow silently, *I won't screw it up.*

24

Find a place inside where there's joy, and the joy will burn
out the pain.

— JOSEPH CAMPBELL

Wendy:

I know I should tell them that I'm pregnant, but I'm
selfish. After almost two months without Asher and
Hudson, I just want to savor the moment. I don't want
anything to change.

"Do you want the guest room?" Hudson asks me, almost
tentatively.

I gape at him. I'm so used to their assertiveness and their
dominance that his hesitation takes me by surprise. "What?"

"After what we did," he says, "I'll understand if you don't
want to be with us again."

Have I misread the signals? "Do you want me in the
guest room?"

Asher rolls his eyes. "Oh, for fuck's sake," he growls.

"Wendy, I want to sleep with you. I'm pretty sure Hudson wants to sleep with you. In or out?"

Joy spreads through me. They want me. I stifle a laugh at Asher's disgruntled look. "In."

"Excellent." Asher and Hudson sink on the couch, on either side of me. Their hands move to my shoulders and they tip me back. Hudson's fingers make quick work of my shirt, while Asher tugs my pants down my hips.

"God, you're beautiful." Hudson's voice is reverent. "I thought I remembered how gorgeous you were, but the memories do not do you justice."

My cheeks heat under their scrutiny. I'd tried to forget them. I'd tried to use my anger as a shield, but it didn't work. I've been dreaming about them, waking up with my body aching in desire. Now they're actually here, looking at me with need in their eyes, and I don't want this moment to end.

Asher trails his finger over my shoulder. He slides my bra strap aside, and his lips kiss my skin, warm and soft. My body tingles where he touches me, and my breath hitches.

"I can't stop thinking of you," he says into my ear. "About how it feels when I slide into your tight pussy. The soft sighs you make when I touch you." His hands caress my midriff and brush over my stomach. I freeze for a second, before forcing myself to relax. *I'm not showing yet. They won't be able to tell.*

Hudson's hands cup my breasts, then he unclasps my bra and lowers his mouth over my nipple. I bite my lip in pleasure, leaning back against the couch. My brain is starting to short-circuit. I run my hands over their broad chests, savoring the feeling of them, the taut firmness of each tight muscle, the warmth of their skin.

I've missed this. I've missed them.

In normal circumstances, they would delight in tormenting me until I'm whimpering with need, alight with desire. These aren't normal circumstances. It's been months since I've felt them against me. All I want to do right now is rip their clothes off, and thankfully, from the predatory gleam in Hudson's and Asher's eyes, they're just as impatient as I am.

We get naked. Asher pushes me back so I'm lying on the couch, my head near Hudson's thick hard cock. His head lowers between my legs and his mouth descends on my pussy. He licks my slit, and his tongue flicks over my nub.

Groaning, I arch my hips into Asher's face. I grope around for Hudson's cock, and sigh with satisfaction when my fist closes around his steel shaft.

Hudson loosens my fingers and gets on his knees. His strong thighs straddle my face, and his cock rests against my lips. Yum. I reach out and swirl my tongue around his head, rewarded when he groans in abandon.

"God, I love the way you taste," Asher says, spreading my legs wider and intensifying his attack on my pussy. He plunges his middle finger into me, twisting and pressing down on my g-spot. Whimpering with need, I take Hudson's cock all the way into my mouth.

It's in the middle of the night. The air is quiet, punctured only by the sounds of our harsh breathing, my breathy moans and Hudson's gasps of pleasure. While Manhattan sleeps, my body is brought to orgasm, again and again.

Afterward, for the first time, I let myself sleep between their bodies, burying my face in Hudson's shoulder, while Asher presses against my back.

There's part of me that feels like I'm jumping off a high bridge without a safety net. I never stay the night. I always take cabs back home and sleep in the safety of my own bed, because unlike sex, cuddling is intimacy.

I've feared intimacy all my life.

But this time, I stay, sandwiched between them. And for the first time, I let myself hope that the three of us can make our relationship work.

As PROMISED, Hudson and Asher make me breakfast the next day. Thankfully, my morning sickness has abated somewhat, so I can eat the eggs and bacon without heaving. "What do you have planned for the day?" Hudson asks me once we're done eating. "It's Black Friday. Are you going shopping?"

I give him a quizzical look. "I didn't think billionaires bothered with Black Friday."

He snorts. "Megan shopped all the time," he says, referring to his ex-wife. "She used Black Friday as an excuse to spend the entire day in the stores."

"Can I ask a personal question?" I'm a little hesitant to broach the subject, but especially now that I'm pregnant, it's important for me to know why Hudson divorced his wife. "Why did you and Megan break up?"

"She was only with me for my money," he says dismissively.

His tone warns me that I should change the topic, but I persist. "You married her, right?" I ask him. "You must have been in love with her at some point. What changed?"

Asher watches us from the top of his newspaper. Hudson shakes his head. "The only reason we got married," he says quietly, "was because Megan told me she was going to have our baby. Of course," he adds bitterly, "like everything else she said, it was a lie."

Oh dear. I know I have to tell them I'm pregnant, but given Hudson's revelation, I'm fairly sure that his reaction isn't going to be good.

Everything is going to change when they find out.

25

Friends show their love in times of trouble, not in happiness.

— EURIPIDES

Asher:

Friday morning, I level with Wendy about Stone Bradley's bodyguards. She takes the news better than I expect. "I'm not stupid, Asher," she says with a roll of her eyes when I tell her I'm surprised that she's not mad at me. "I'm a fan of safety too. I just don't think it should limit what I do."

I don't argue. I'm too busy enjoying my time with her.

The three of us spend all weekend together. After Wendy confesses that she hasn't had time to visit the Statue of Liberty, we take a ferry to Ellis Island and see the iconic monument. We take in a Broadway show and spend a lazy afternoon at the Met. And we have sex. A lot of it.

I don't get back to my place until late evening on Sunday.

It's after nine when I push open the door of my apartment, but when I get in, Levi's not around. The door to his bedroom is wide open, and there's no one inside.

I grab a bottle of water from my refrigerator and collapse on the couch. The coffee table is strewn with papers, and I start to move them aside so I can prop my feet up. Then I catch sight of their contents, and all the euphoria I'm feeling from my weekend with Wendy drains away.

They are surveillance photos of a warehouse by the docks. Mikhail Vasiliev's warehouse, if I'm to believe Levi's parole officer. Notes are scribbled next to them, but I don't register what's written because I'm in shock. How could Levi be so stupid? How could he let Beecham drag him into trouble once again?

The door swings open, and Levi lurches into the room, swaying on his feet. Even from my spot on the couch, I can smell the alcohol on his breath. He steps closer, and then he sees the papers on the coffee table and freezes.

"Did you read any of it?" His voice is uncharacteristically nervous.

Fuck. If the Bar Association finds out I know what Levi's planning, they will not hesitate to strip me of my license to practice law. I should call Levi's parole officer.

But if I do, there's enough evidence here for the DA to press charges. I don't think I have it in me to send my friend to jail again.

"Asher?" Levi prompts. "Did you see anything?"

Loyalty wins out. "Did I see what?" I ask blandly.

He exhales in a loud sigh of relief. "Thanks, buddy," he replies. "I knew I could count on you."

I shouldn't say anything, but I can't resist trying to dissuade him. "Who are you working with?" I ask. "Is it

Beecham's crowd? The cops are onto his crew, Levi. For fuck's sake, don't be a fool. Walk away from this job."

"Listen to you," he sneers. "It's so easy for you. Do you know how hard it is for an ex-con to make an honest living? I don't have any other choice."

"I will loan you money," I reply, desperate to change his mind. "I will *give* you money. Whatever you need. Don't get sucked back in, Levi."

He walks past me to the bedroom. "I don't need your money or your pity, Ash," he says. "I can take care of myself."

I wish I could believe him.

26

If ignorant both of your enemy and yourself, you are certain to be in peril.

— Sᴜɴ Tᴢᴜ

Hudson:

When we get to work Monday morning, the first thing we do is make our way to Thorne's office. We've planned this over the weekend. Thorne was furious when Asher and I showed up to the board meeting on Wednesday, and Wendy insists we tell him we're not going to back down.

He's sitting behind his desk, reading something on his computer. He looks up in outrage as we march in. "What do you want?" he spits at Wendy.

She's not cowed. "To tell you this," she replies coolly. She tosses the photos of the three us on the table. "I don't care what other people think about me." Her eyes glint with anger. "I grew up in a small town. For eighteen years, everyone in Fredonia gossiped about who my father was. Kids would mock me. Adults would look at my mother and me with pity, and guess what, Thorne?" She gives him a steely look. "I have really thick skin. I don't care if these pictures get leaked to the tabloids. I don't care if everyone in the company knows that Hudson, Asher, and I are sleeping together."

Thorne's only reaction is a clenched jaw. "I don't know what you are talking about," he says.

Wendy rolls her eyes. "We aren't going to back down," she warns him. "So if you know what's good for you, you'll stay out of our way. Unless you want me to talk to Bill Anderson?"

Asher shakes his head on the way out. "Anderson will want proof and we have none," he says, stating the obvious. "I better call Stone Bradley and have him double his guards on you. *Again.*" He gives Wendy a fondly exasperated look. "Did you *have* to threaten him?"

"You have to stand up to bullies, Asher," Wendy replies. We get into the elevator and the doors close.

"I agree," he says quietly. "Unless you are protecting someone very precious." His thumb brushes over Wendy's lower lip. "When you are responsible for someone you cherish, some battles aren't worth fighting."

Her breath catches. "I can take care of myself."

THE NEXT BIG milestone on the Staten Island project is a presentation to the retailers that we're hoping will lease space from us. Jeff Choi has set up a meeting on the fifteenth of December with eight key players in the industry. "You know what would wow them, Hudson?" he says to me when we meet on Monday afternoon. "A model of the whole complex. Is there any way you can pull that together?"

"I'll give it a shot."

Jeff frowns. "This meeting is critical," he insists. "Thorne's team has, against all odds, started construction on their South Carolina highway. If we don't keep up, Thorne's going to win this contest."

Wendy jumps to my defense. "I'm sure Hudson's doing everything he can, Jeff," she says quietly. "We all are. We'll get this done."

My heart warms at her support, but I don't deserve it. Thorne's blackmail attempt caused Asher and I to pull away from her project. *It won't happen again,* I vow silently. Whatever happens this time, we're in it together.

Not just on the Staten Island project. I was foolish enough to let Wendy go once, but after the four days we've spent together, I realize what a mistake that was. I really like Wendy. I don't want to lose her again.

"I THINK WE'VE GOT IT." Wendy shuts her laptop, looking tired.

Two weeks have passed. In that time, Thorne, mindful of our warning, doesn't move openly against us, but he orchestrates a thousand petty irritants. Our computers are mysteriously infected by viruses that the IT guys can't remove. Wendy's office is scheduled to be renovated, so we're moved to a cube just outside a busy conference room. It's impossible to work when we are constantly distracted by the conversations happening around us, but we persist. We're determined to beat Thorne.

It's six in the evening, and the big presentation is tomorrow. We've just finished rehearsing our pitch. Wendy will lead the discussion, but as the architect on the project, I will introduce the design of the space, and Asher will cover the highlights of the legal agreements.

I get to my feet and stretch, feeling the muscles in my neck burn from the hours I've spent hunched over a keyboard. For the last two weeks, I've been working fifteen hour days. It's been exhausting juggling everything on my plate—keeping on top of the projects I'm responsible for, trying to hire new architects as well as complete the Staten Island design. But it's worth it. I feel really good about what we've achieved. Any moment now, Raul and Alyssa should show up with the model of the complex, and when the retailers see it, I'm convinced they'll be lining up to sign on the dotted line.

There's a knock on the conference room door. Asher opens it, and Raul and Alyssa enter with the building model. "God, this thing is heavy," Alyssa huffs.

I grab her end and Raul and I set it down on the table in the middle of the room. "Is this where it's going to go?" Raul asks me. "We promised Nadja we'd deliver it safe and sound."

Alyssa sinks down on a chair. "We were terrified every time the van went over a bump," she agrees. "Nadja will kill us if something happens to it."

I laugh. "You guys did great." The model is unharmed, and it looks amazing. Built the old-fashioned way by a team of model-makers in a workshop, constructed with wood and cardboard and glue, it's the kind of painstaking work that takes days to do. This one took ten days, and Dave's team worked around the clock on it.

"This isn't where you're doing your presentation, are you?" Alyssa looks around the small, shabby conference room that we're using as an office.

"No," I reply. "We'll be presenting in the main board-room on the eighteenth floor. Asher and I can set it up tomorrow morning."

Raul and Alyssa leave, and Wendy looks at me with shining eyes. "This is beautiful, Hudson," she says, throwing her arms around me and hugging me tight. "Thank you."

I kiss her forehead. "Anything for you, baby." With a start, I realize I mean it. When my marriage with Megan ended, I thought I'd never allow myself to be vulnerable again. I thought I'd never allow myself to trust a woman. But Wendy's shattered my defenses. I'd do anything for her.

Asher's phone beeps. He glances at the display and his expression tightens. "I need to head to my office," he says. He gives Wendy a stern look. "Don't wait for me to eat dinner."

Something in his face causes me to pause. "Is everything okay?" I ask my friend.

He nods tightly. "I'll meet up with you two later. Save me a slice of pizza."

Once he leaves, I turn to Wendy. We've been eating junk food too many nights in a row, and I'm sick of it. "We're in good shape here. Want to go eat a real meal at an actual restaurant?"

"Yes please," she replies at once with a grin. "I'm ready to take a break from this room."

I help her with her coat, and we head downstairs. "Where do you want to go?"

"*Piper's.*" She gives me an amused look. "My friends are dying to meet Asher and you. Piper threatened to drop by at work if I didn't show up at her restaurant this week."

I laugh. "We've met Miki," I point out. Wendy's hacker friend has given us a couple of updates on her progress, but unfortunately, she isn't making much headway. I don't blame her. She's got a lot on her mind at the moment as she navigates the end of her marriage.

"True," she agrees. "And now you're going to meet Piper. Gabby's going to visit New York for Christmas, and Bailey's done in Argentina at the end of the year, so you'll get to meet them on New Year's Eve." She hesitates. "Assuming we'll be together then."

New Year's Eve is two weeks away. "Count on it," I assure her, looking into her light blue eyes. I want to say more, to tell her that I want to be in a real relationship with her, to tell her I can't see a future without her in it, but now's not the right time. *At Christmas,* I promise myself. *When we have a moment to think about something that isn't work.*

Wendy's obviously a regular at Piper's. The hostess seats us quickly, and the waiter arrives in a minute to take our drink order. I survey the small but thoughtfully chosen wine list. "Should we get a bottle?" I ask Wendy. "I'm ready to unwind, and I'm assuming that Asher will join us at some point."

She shakes her head. "I don't want to drink tonight," she says, her head bent, and her attention focused on her menu. "I want to keep a clear head for tomorrow's meeting."

After the first night, when the three of us polished off four bottles of champagne between us, I've rarely seen Wendy drink. Come to think of it, she hasn't touched a glass of wine in weeks. "Fair enough." I lower my voice. "If you don't want wine to help you relax, I'm happy to think of other ways."

Blushing, she orders a sparkling water. I ask for a glass of the house red. The waiter leaves to fill our order, and Wendy clears her throat. "Hudson," she says, her fingers playing with the edges of her napkin, creasing and uncreasing the linen, "Can I ask you a personal question?"

Her tone places me on alert. "Of course," I reply.

Before she can continue, a blonde woman in a white apron winds her way through the tables, a big smile on her face. "Wendy," she exclaims, giving her friend a hug. "You made it. I haven't seen you in weeks." She turns to me, holding out her hand. "You must be Hudson," she says. "It's good to meet you at last."

I get to my feet. "Likewise," I reply. "Thank you for the feast on Thanksgiving."

Piper is about to reply when the waiter reappears with our drinks. Her smile fades. "You aren't drinking?" she asks Wendy pointedly.

"No," Wendy replies. "I have meetings all day tomorrow."

Piper bites her lip, her expression neutral. "I better get back to the kitchen before one of my sous-chefs sets something on fire," she says. "Hudson, I hope to see you again."

I watch Piper leave, then turn to Wendy, who seems lost in thought. "Are you stressing about tomorrow?" I ask her gently. Wendy doesn't know how to give less than one hundred percent. She's been refining this presentation for days, looking for the perfect words to pitch our project to the retailers who might become our tenants.

She shakes her head. "You never talk about your marriage," she says hesitantly. "Did it make you stop trusting women?"

Three months ago, thinking of Megan would have made me bitter and angry. Of course, that was before Wendy entered my life. Now, when I remember Megan, all I feel is indifference. "Somewhat," I answer honestly. "It made me better at putting up shields. Not letting people in close." *Until now,* I think. *Until I met you.*

"You said the other day that she was only with you for

your money," Wendy says, her voice barely a whisper, her eyes glued on her empty plate. "How do you know that? Because she liked to shop?"

I take a sip of the excellent Shiraz. The waiter shows up again to take our food orders. We both choose the meat special, and when we're alone again, I tell Wendy the ugly truth. "My father left me a lot of money when he died. I make a very comfortable living; I didn't need it. So I set up a foundation with his money, dedicated to the causes he cared about when he was alive. Accessible housing, senior housing and education. Megan didn't know about the foundation, and she was very unhappy when she found out." My lips twist into a grimace. "She wrote a long email to her sister, bitching about the amount of money I gave to charity. Unfortunately, she accidentally sent that email to me, not Hailey."

"Ouch." She toys with her napkin. "I'm sorry."

"Don't be. It was a relief to end the marriage. It was based on a lie. I mean, come on. We only date three weeks, and a condom fails and she gets pregnant? What are the odds of that happening? I should have guessed that it was just about the money."

Wendy goes very still, and the color drains from her face. "I guess so," she says.

"Anyway, that's ancient history." I lean back in my seat, relaxing for the first time in weeks. Good food, good wine, and a perfect woman. I can't ask for more. Megan is a distant and unimportant blur in the past. "I'm really looking forward to next week. The design is mostly done, and we can't start construction until winter has passed. Once we're done with tomorrow's meeting, things will get much quieter."

She nods, not meeting my gaze. We finish our meal in

relative silence. Asher doesn't join us, and when I try to call him, his phone goes straight to voicemail. I feel a prickle of worry but dismiss it. I'm probably just nervous about the upcoming meeting.

"Want to go to my place?" I ask Wendy when we're ready to leave. With Levi staying at Asher's apartment and Miki crashing with Wendy until her divorce is finalized, my penthouse has ended up where the three of us spend all our time. I'm not complaining. Wendy and Asher make the condo feel like home.

"I left my laptop at the office," she replies. "Can we pick it up on the way?"

"Are you going to do another dry run of your presentation tonight, Wendy?" I scold her. "You have dark circles under your eyes. You look exhausted."

"The words every woman dreams of hearing," she quips. "Would it make you feel better if I lie to you?" She wraps her scarf around her neck and pulls her leather gloves on her hands. "Is Asher at your place?"

"Bored of me already?" I tease.

She doesn't smile back. Her expression is serious. "I need to tell you guys something."

I feel another flicker of worry, more insistent this time, warning me that something's not quite right. "What is it?"

"Both of you need to be around."

Damn it. I don't like surprises, but Wendy's expression is resolute, and I know she's not going to tell us what's on her mind until both of us are around. Shaking my head, I hail a taxi. When we get to the conference room that houses her laptop, Wendy turns the handle with a frown. "I could have sworn I locked this door before I left." Then she enters the room and comes to a dead halt. "Oh my God," she says faintly.

I'm a half-step behind her, so I don't see the cause of her outburst right away.

Our scale model—the one that took ten days of work to build—lies in ruins. Someone's taken a hammer to it and has smashed it to pieces.

We'd grown complacent. We'd grown accustomed to Thorne's petty acts of aggression. Now, as I take in the wreckage of the building model, I realize how wrong we were to assume that we had Thorne beat.

·

27

The trouble with having an open mind, of course, is that people will insist on coming along and trying to put things in it.

— TERRY PRATCHETT

Asher:

A couple of Hudson's architects have just delivered the model when my phone buzzes with a text message from Miki.

Call me back ASAP, she writes. *Don't let Wendy overhear.*

That sounds ominous. I decide to head to my office before I return her call. I make my excuses to Hudson and Wendy and head out. When I'm seated at my desk, I dial Miki's number. "What's the matter?" I ask her. I'm hoping against hope that Miki's found something we can pin on

Thorne. Time's running out. Already, almost three months have elapsed.

"For weeks, I've been poring over individual invoices," Miki says. "I've been searching for patterns, see if I can spot anything that looks fraudulent."

"I know."

"I found something peculiar. Every year for Christmas, Jean Nakashima used to send flowers to her employees as a thank you present. She ordered the arrangements from a florist in Lower Manhattan. Well, the same transaction just went through three days ago. Flowers for the entire team."

"She could have just set it up as a recurring transaction," I point out. "We do that at Doyle and Miller. I send my assistant something for her birthday that way."

"That's what I thought, especially when the transaction was reversed. I assumed the new Head of Finance doesn't believe in Christmas presents."

It wouldn't surprise me. Stuart Fischer is a cheap SOB, and there's no love lost between him and his team. From conversations with people in Finance, I've learned that the team adored their former boss. They barely tolerate Fischer.

"But you found something," I guess. "You wouldn't have texted me otherwise."

"The transaction was canceled, but the flowers were still delivered. And when I hacked into the florist's system, I found out that they'd been paid for with a personal credit card." She clears her throat. "Jean Nakashima's credit card."

I sit up in my seat. "What are you saying, Miki?"

"That there's a very good chance that Ms. Nakashima is still alive. And if she's alive, then I can only believe…"

I finish the sentence. "That she faked her own death."

"Exactly." There's a tremor in Miki's voice. "Why would she do something like that?"

"I don't know," I reply grimly. "But I'm going to find out. Is there any chance you have an address?"

"No." She pauses and I hear keys click in the background. "But there's one other transaction on the same credit card around the same time. A pizza place in Hoboken."

I glance at my watch. It's a little before seven. If I leave now, with any luck, I can be at that pizza place in an hour. Someone has to know something, and I intend to find out what it is. "I'm heading there now."

"Be careful, Asher," Miki says. "We don't understand what's going on here, but whatever it is, it caused this woman to fake her death. Jean Nakashima has a daughter who believes her mother drowned. She has a grandson who thinks his grandmother died two years ago."

Miki's right. Something spooked the Head of Finance. It can't be Thorne. The Hancock heir is rich, spoiled and entitled, but he shouldn't inspire this level of fear. There are wheels within wheels here, and I'm not going to stop until I solve this puzzle.

When I first met Wendy, I found her fascinating, but I wasn't interested in a real relationship. Things are different now. I can't get Wendy out of my mind. Her fire and passion. Her warmth and softness. I can't look at another woman without thinking of her. I can't sleep at night because when I close her eyes, all I see is her. Not just her beautiful body. It's more than that, and the intensity of my need terrifies me.

I think I'm falling in love with her.

It's raining outside, and the streets are heavy with traffic. I speed toward Hoboken, weaving in and out of traffic like a lunatic. The wipers move back and forth, clearing the water drops from the windshield the movement hypnotic. There's an accident on the Hudson River Greenway, so I'm forced to take the Lincoln Tunnel, which is, as usual, illuminated by a sea of brake lights. Eventually, an hour and twenty minutes after I set out, I arrive in front of a small cheerful-looking pizza parlor with black and white awnings.

I push open the door, and a bell chimes to mark my arrival. The young man behind the counter looks up with a smile. "Hell of a night," he says conversationally. "Have you been here before?"

I shake my head. There are no tables in the place, just a wooden counter along the front windows, with half a dozen barstools where customers can sit and eat their slices. There are a million places like this in New York.

"The specials are on the board," he says. "I'll give you a moment."

I decide on the direct approach. "I'm not here for food," I tell the guy. "I'm looking for someone that ordered a pizza here three days ago. She paid with a credit card." At the same time, I withdraw a hundred dollar note from my wallet and slide it across the battered countertop.

The kid looks around to make sure there's no one within sight, and he grabs the bill. "I don't want any trouble," he mutters.

"Of course not," I soothe. "I just need her address. She's an old friend."

He looks nervous. "You're not a stalker, are you?"

I roll my eyes and fish another hundred out of my wallet. This time, I don't give it to him; I hold it between my fingertips where the guy can see it. "Do I look like a stalker?" I ask him. I incline my head toward the window, through which he can see the Bugatti parked outside.

He whistles when he catches sight of the car and seems to reach a decision. "Three days ago, you said?"

"Yes." I give him the credit card number and the time it

was used, to help him narrow down his search. A couple of minutes later, he finds what he's looking for. "Oh, that's Mrs. Sato," he says. "She comes in once a week, though she normally pays cash. She lives in one of the apartment buildings on Jefferson Street."

He writes the address on a post-it note, and I give him the hundred dollar note in my hand. "She's not in trouble, is she?" he asks, his conscience making a rather belated appearance.

"Not at all." I just want some answers. I nod at the guy. "Merry Christmas."

THERE'S a cheap plastic wreath on the door of Jean Nakashima's apartment. I knock and wait. A dog begins to bark, and when a middle-aged Japanese woman opens the door, the small beagle almost bowls me over. "Settle down, Mollie," the woman says, patting the excited pet. She gives me a cautious look. "Can I help you?"

I've seen photos of Jean Nakashima. It's definitely her. I wedge my foot in the doorway so she can't shut the door on me. "Ms. Nakashima, my name is Asher Doyle. I need to talk to you about Hancock Construction."

She pales. "My name is Aiko Sato," she stammers. "You must have me confused with someone else."

"I don't think I do." My voice holds an edge of desperation. Miki hasn't been able to find Thorne's mysterious backer. Without a name, we don't have a case against Thorne. The former Finance executive *has* to tell me what happened. I *have* to keep Wendy safe. "Please," I beg. "This is important."

She searches my face. "Who are you?" she asks.

"My name is Asher Doyle," I repeat. "I'm a corporate

lawyer." I pull a business card out of my wallet and hand it to her. She takes it from me and checks it, and then her gaze returns to my face. "I recognize the name," she says slowly. "You tried to prosecute Thorne once, didn't you? For the rape of that poor girl? Laura something?"

"Lauren," I reply tightly. "Her name was Lauren Bainbridge."

"Yes." Her eyes are sad. "Come on in, Mr. Doyle."

I enter the apartment, which is small but well-furnished. Two overstuffed couches dominate the living room, and the side tables are covered with photo frames. Most of the pictures are of a happy-looking toddler. "My grandson Hiro," she explains, noticing my gaze. "He turns five in February." Her tone turns harder. "What do you want from me?"

"I want to know what you found." I don't try and hide the reason I'm here. "A woman I care about very much has been dragged into Hancock Construction."

The beagle jumps on one of the couches and promptly falls asleep. Ms. Nakashima sits down next to the dog. "Wendy Williams," she replies. "I have internet access in Hoboken," she clarifies, seeing my startled look. "Paul's will has set many people gossiping."

"You know about the contest." I lean forward. "You know about Thorne's highway project and Wendy's Staten Island build. And more than that, you know the truth about Barbados."

Her fingers flex, curling and uncurling, fidgeting with the hem of her paisley skirt. "Barbados," she whispers.

I lay my cards on the table. I have no other choice. "We know someone gave Thorne sixty million dollars. We don't know who it was."

"This is a hornet's nest," she replies. "Don't stir it."

"That's not an option," I snap.

The beagle sits up, alerted by the tension in the air, and the woman strokes her head. "There's no need to take that tone with me, Doyle. I'm not your enemy." She looks troubled. "I knew Paul Hancock for over thirty years," she says. "He wasn't a perfect person, but he was a good owner. He ran the company well, and he treated his employees fairly." She sighs. "But he had one gigantic blind spot."

"Thorne."

She nods. "When Paul got sick, Thorne started taking a more active role in choosing projects," she says. "And he screwed up, but he didn't want his father to find out. I pressed him for details, but he was evasive. So I went looking for the truth."

The truth. Whatever she found, it had terrified her enough that she'd faked her death, even to her loved ones. From the pictures in the room, it's clear that Ms. Nakashima cares about her family. Why the elaborate charade?

"And I found more than I wanted. The person who loaned Thorne the money was Mikhail Vasiliev."

My head jerks up. Vasiliev. Thorne's beholden to the most feared man in New York, the head of the ruthless Russian Mafia.

"Then an FBI agent made contact with me," she whispers. "They were building a case against Vasiliev for money laundering. They were going to subpoena me. And I knew that if I testified against the Russian mob, my life was forfeit. The *mafiya* would kill me, and they would kill every member of my family as an example." She looks up. "I was caught between a rock and a hard place," she says quietly. "I had no choice. I had to disappear."

She rises to her feet. "Thorne is desperate to become the CEO," she says. "If he doesn't, there's no way to pay the

Russians back. And Vasiliev *always* collects." She gives me a somber look. "Wendy Williams is now in the line of fire. That's why I let you in. If something happens to her, it'll be on my conscience. I couldn't let that happen."

"Thorne won't resort to violence," I say, desperate to believe my words.

"Not at first," she replies. "The boy isn't a killer. He'll look for other ways. But if they don't work, and if Vasiliev himself gets involved..." Her voice trails off.

My heart hammers in my chest. I can't fight the Russian mob. This time, we've bitten off more than we can chew.

There's a sick feeling in my gut. Once again, it looks like I'm not going to be able to keep someone I love safe.

28

Honesty is the first chapter in the book of wisdom.

— THOMAS JEFFERSON

Wendy:

I'm in shock.

Hudson's still bitter about his ex-wife. My heart had stopped at his words. *We only dated three weeks, and a condom fails, and she gets pregnant? What are the odds of that happening?*

What are the odds? Better than you'd think, apparently. My life feels like an M.C. Escher painting. Everything is upside down and inside out, and I don't know what to do.

I should have told them earlier about the baby, I know. I was going to tell them at Thanksgiving, but then Hudson had revealed that Megan had pretended to be pregnant to get him to marry her, and I'd bitten my tongue. I should have told them sometime in the last two weeks, but for the first time in my life, I seemed to be in a relationship that made me happy. So I'd hesitated, my desire for them winning out over the need for truth and honesty.

I was going to tell them today, but then Asher left abruptly before dinner, and he still hasn't returned.

Now the model's smashed to pieces, and we have nothing to present to the retailers tomorrow. Thorne's struck a body blow this time, one I can't recover from. He's going to win, and I'm going to be unemployed and pregnant.

And Hudson is going to think that it's because of his money that I'm telling them about the baby.

A wave of dizziness overtakes me, and I slump to a seat. Hudson gives me a sharply concerned look. "Are you sure you're okay? You've been strange all evening."

"Forget me." I wave my hand at the carnage in front of me. "What about this?"

Hudson looks bleak. "This is my fault," he grinds out. "I should have anticipated Thorne's actions. I should have stored it at my office until the last possible minute."

"It's not your fault." My voice is tired. I'm tired, too tired to fight back, too exhausted to think of a plan to combat this. I can't even reassure Hudson properly. He's blaming himself for something that Thorne did. Just like Asher does with the woman that Thorne raped.

Ultimately, there's only one person responsible for these actions, and it's my half-brother.

"I can't think in this room," Hudson says savagely. "Do you want to get out of this fucking place?"

"Sure," I agree. I can't bear to look at the crushed wreckage in front of us. The model had been so beautiful, so perfect, and now it's in shambles. It could be a metaphor for my life. "Where to? Your apartment?"

Hudson shakes his head. "There might be something I can use at the office," he says.

The situation is hopeless, I want to tell him, but I can't bring myself to admit defeat by saying those words out loud. "Sure," I agree, "let's go to your office. You never know what we might find."

It's late. I expect the place to be empty, but though the office corridors are dim, a sliver of light shines from under a closed door. "Nadja's still at work," Hudson notes. He doesn't look particularly surprised.

"Hudson, is that you?" The door opens, and Nadja gives us a surprised look, then flushes as she realizes who I am. "I thought you'd gone for the day," she says. "I was just catching up on emails."

"Seth at home with the kids?" he asks.

She shakes her head. "They're visiting his parents," she says. "We made a deal. Seth disappears with the kids for a couple of weeks, and I catch up on work, and I do all the Christmas shopping in return." She grins easily. "I think Seth got the better bargain. Mara loves having her grandchildren around. What are you doing here? I thought you'd be at Hancock Construction. Raul said they'd dropped off the model earlier without any problems."

Hudson's face darkens. He quickly fills Nadja in on what happened while we were at dinner, and her mouth falls open. "That's terrible," she says, sounding horrified. "So you thought you'd use the 3D printer?"

I'm guessing from Hudson's stupefied expression that the thought has never even occurred to him. "Of course," he exclaims, hugging her tight. "Nadja, you're a genius. Do you know how to use it?"

I push back the reflexive jealousy I feel. From the smile on her face when Hudson's coworker talked about her husband, she's obviously in love with him. I have nothing to feel insecure about. Besides, judging from Hudson's reaction, I think Nadja has just saved our bacon.

She disentangles herself with a chuckle. "I've been playing with it in my spare time," she admits.

"What free time?" Hudson asks dryly. "You've been working non-stop the last couple of months."

"I fiddle with it when I need a break," she replies. "Come on. I'll load your design into it." She leads the way down another dimly lit corridor. "You'll have to print it in stages," she warns over her shoulder. "You're going to be here all night."

"Not a problem," Hudson replies. "Even a rudimentary model seems like a miracle at this point."

JUST THEN, my phone beeps. I glance at it, expecting it to be Asher, but the display shows my mother's number. "Hey, I have to take this," I tell Hudson.

"You should go home," he says, looking at me with a frown. "You look exhausted. You need rest."

"And you don't?" I ask pointedly. "I'm not going anywhere, but I do need to talk to my mom."

Hudson realizes there's no point arguing with me. "Fine," he concedes. He flashes his key card at the door just opposite the printer room. "My office. Make yourself comfortable."

I bite my lip. I've been avoiding telling my mom about the baby, but I'm running out of time. She's visiting me in a couple of days. She'll be staying with me for two weeks over Christmas, and the truth is bound to come out then. I'd much rather tell her about the baby on the phone now, than risk seeing her disappointed expression in person. Yes, I'm a coward.

However, even with the door shut, there's a chance that Hudson will be able to overhear my conversation. He's in the room opposite me, after all. "Where's the washroom?" I ask him.

Nadja points down the hallway. "The ladies room is the third door on the right," she says with a friendly smile. "The code on the door is one-two-three-four."

"That's very secure," I snark, unable to help myself.

She laughs. "I changed it when I was pregnant," she says. "I needed to pee all the time in my final trimester, and I didn't want to fuss with a complicated password. This guy here," she says, looking at Hudson with fond exasperation, "insists on codes for every single door. Including the washroom."

"Basic precautions," Hudson explains to me. "Design plans are easily stolen."

She snorts. "Please," she says with a roll of her eyes. "You're just paranoid."

This sounds like an old argument, and they're both looking at me as if they're expecting me to play referee. "I need to go," I say hastily, and make a run for safety.

I BARRICADE myself in a bathroom stall in the ladies room and call my mother. "Hey sweetie," she says in greeting. "My call went to voicemail, so I figured you were busy." She takes a deep breath. "Do you have a moment? There's something I need to tell you."

Her tone is almost diffident. "What's wrong, mom?"

"I've been hiding something from you," she confesses

with a sigh. "Please don't be angry. Ten months ago, Paul came to see me."

"What?" I squeak out. "Why?"

"He'd learned he was dying. He told me he was trying to make amends for all the things he'd screwed up." She sounds sad. "As you can imagine, I wasn't exactly thrilled to see him. I hadn't seen him in thirty years, and I didn't have good memories of him. But he stayed for hours, looking at all your baby photos. I think he really regretted not knowing you."

"He had a choice about that," I snap. *He looked at my baby pictures?* "He could have contacted me."

"I know," she whispers. "I didn't want to tell you about his visit; there was no point getting your hopes up. Paul Hancock was not good at having difficult conversations. He preferred to avoid them, to throw money at the problem rather than deal with it in a straightforward manner."

"I don't want to hear this," I say flatly. "I don't want to hear any excuses. Paul Hancock made his choices."

"Wendy, wait," my mom says urgently. "I agree with you. When Paul showed up, I almost shut the door in his face. In the end, I listened to him, not for his sake, but for mine." Her voice falters. "For more than thirty years, I've refused to trust anyone because of what Paul did. But listening to him gave me some closure."

Her voice falters. "I'm afraid I've let my bitterness corrode you. You turned thirty a few weeks ago, yet you've never dated someone for longer than a few months. I taught you to mistrust men, Wendy. I shouldn't have. Not all men are like Paul."

An image of Hudson and Asher flashes in my mind. They've been at my side from the start. They've watched out for me. They've held me when I've been down. They've done nothing but provide solid, unwavering support, and because I'm afraid of their reaction to my pregnancy, I've hidden the truth from them.

My mom is right. There are good guys out there. And I'm doing Asher and Hudson an injustice by not telling them about the baby.

"Umm, mom?" I grip the phone tight and hope she doesn't take the news too badly. "I've been meaning to tell you something too." I swallow hard. "I'm pregnant."

"Oh, Wendy." My mom sounds like she's tearing up. "I'm so happy for you, sweetie." She clears her throat. "Are you dating someone?" she asks carefully. "I haven't heard you mention a boyfriend."

I grimace. Time to blurt out the truth. "I had a three-some," I mutter, my cheeks hot with embarrassment. "One of them is the father. I haven't told them yet."

I hear the phone clatter to the floor. Shit. My mom's so shocked she's dropped the phone. Somebody just kill me now.

"Mom?" I sound desperate when the silence stretches. "Say something. Anything. Tell me you're ashamed of me. Call me a slut. Just speak to me."

"Of course you aren't a slut," she replies at once, her voice sharp. "And I could never be ashamed of you." She gives a strained laugh. "You're a grown woman, but you'll always be a little girl to me. I guess that I prefer to think of you as a virgin."

"Yeah. That ship sailed a long time ago."

"Wendy," she says. "You know you can't keep something like this a secret. You have to tell them."

"I'm going to," I tell her. "Soon."

WHEN I OPEN the bathroom stall, Nadja is outside, her eyes wide with shock. "Before you ask," she whispers, "I overheard everything. You're pregnant, and either Hudson or Asher is the father."

Fuck, fuck and fuck again.

"I'm going to tell them," I beg Nadja, desperate for understanding. "But Hudson keeps talking about his ex-wife, and I lose courage..." My voice trails off.

A brief look of understanding flashes across her face, then her expression hardens. "You haven't told them yet," she accuses.

I shake my head. "I will," I whisper. "I just need some time."

"No," she replies at once. "Hudson is my friend. I can't keep this from him. Tell him today, Wendy, or I'll have to tell him myself."

29

Courage is resistance to fear, mastery of fear, not absence of fear.

— MARK TWAIN

Asher:

I want to act. I need to take the fight to Thorne but I can't. I'm paralyzed by fear. This isn't about a spoiled trust fund millionaire anymore. This isn't a fight about who's going to be the CEO of Hancock Construction.

This is about the Russian Mafia. And I know how to fight Thorne Hancock, but I don't have weapons big enough to take on Mikhail Vasiliev. The NYPD can't touch him—how can I? I haven't felt this helpless in ten years.

Then I arrive at Hudson's penthouse, and the two of them aren't there. I feel a moment of pure unadulterated fear until I call my friend, who fills me in on his evening. "I think the 3D printer is going to work though," he says.

I don't feel comfortable leaving them alone. "I'm heading to your office," I tell him. "I'll see you soon."

I OVERHEAR Wendy talking to Hudson when I walk in. "I bet you wish you hadn't agreed to help me," she's saying. "Tell me you don't think that your life was more peaceful before you met me." She sounds distressed, at the point of tears. "Asher gets blackmailed. Your model gets ruined. What a waste."

"Hey." I enter the room and give Hudson a questioning look. Why is she so upset? Hudson appears to have the 3D printing under control. Things aren't as bad as they appear. Well, based on what Jean Nakashima said, they're a lot worse, but Wendy doesn't know that.

I put my arm around her waist, drawing her near, and I kiss her forehead. "The time we've spent with you isn't a waste." My lips find hers fleetingly. "Our lives are better because of you." I run my fingers through her hair, breathing in the scent of her shampoo, feeling the warmth of her body. "If I had to choose again," I whisper in her ear. "I'll choose you. I'll choose you every time."

Her hand wraps around my neck. "Kiss me," she demands, a ragged edge in her voice. "Both of you. Please?"

Hudson's office is empty except for the three of us. I lift her up and set her on the couch in the corner, then I kiss her softly. Pushing aside my fear, I focus on Wendy. My fingers trail down her body and I try to memorize the way she feels. Soft, warm. Alive.

I can't let anything happen to her. My thoughts swirl like angry bees trapped in a glass jar. I will protect her with my life, if that's what it takes, because I don't want to exist without her.

She kisses me back, her need just as fierce as mine. She reaches out for Hudson, who kneels on the floor and parts her legs.

Our lovemaking is hurried, desperate and feverish. When we're done, I cling to her, unable to let go, even for a moment.

What am I going to do?

30

If you could kick the person in the pants responsible for most of your trouble, you wouldn't sit for a month.

— THEODORE ROOSEVELT

Wendy:

Guilt floods me the next morning when I wake up in Hudson's bed.

Asher's words from last night echo in my heart. *Our lives are better because of you.*

I love them. I've known that for a while now, though I've shied away from acknowledging the way I feel. But I can't hide from the truth anymore. I've delayed telling Hudson and Asher about my baby because I'm afraid I'm going to lose them.

Now, Nadja has forced my hand.

I don't blame her. In her place, I'd do the same thing. Her loyalty is to her friend. I respect that.

And she's right.

You've blown it, Wendy. Admit it. You should have told them at Thanksgiving.

I remember Piper's horrified look last night when she realized Hudson still didn't know I was pregnant. My mother's gentle admonishment. Nadja's implacable glare. They've all been united in one thing. I must tell Asher and Hudson the truth.

Do it now, Wendy, I urge myself. *You told your mother. Can this be any worse?*

I DRESS in the clothes I was wearing last night, and head to the kitchen. Asher's perched on a barstool at the kitchen island, reading the Wall Street Journal, while Hudson's frying something on the stove. Unexpectedly, my stomach roils at the scent of bacon.

"You're up." Hudson smiles in my direction. "How are you doing on two hours of sleep?" He lowers the heat and walks toward the coffeepot. Pouring some coffee into a mug, he offers it to me.

Too late, I breathe in the scent of the beverage, and my stomach goes into full-fledged rebellion. Before I heave in their presence, I clasp my hand over my mouth and make a mad dash for the washroom, where I retch out the contents of my gut.

I thought I was done with morning sickness. Clearly, I was wrong.

I do my best to throw up silently and pray that the bathroom fan muffles the sound. When I return to the kitchen, feeling like someone sent my insides through the wringer, Asher eyes me with concern.

Hudson, on the other hand, looks at me sharply. He's on the verge of figuring it out—I can tell. I'm not drinking. I can't keep food down. Had the three of us not been so busy with work, they'd have worked it out a long time ago.

Looking at them, my courage fails me. My news is too big. Too monumental. The moment I tell them the truth, everything will change. I'm not ready.

But it's time.

"I have to tell you something." My voice comes out in a quiver. "I'm pregnant."

My news is greeted by complete silence.

"One of you," I continue nervously, "is the father."

Neither of them responds.

"I think it was the first night," I babble. I swallow back the lump in my throat. "I don't want anything from you. This isn't about that."

Say something, damn it.

Hudson finally breaks the silence. He's gripping the frying pan so tightly that his knuckles are white. "How long have you known?"

I close my eyes. The one question I don't want to answer, and that's the question he asks. "Since the middle of October."

"You knew two months ago that you were pregnant and you didn't tell us?" Asher looks shell-shocked, but Hudson's eyes are so hard, and his expression is colder than I've ever seen. "You hid something this big, this important from us?"

"I'm sorry," I whisper. Tears well up in my eyes and I brush them away with the back of my hand. "I wasn't sure how you'd react."

"For two months," Hudson says slowly, "you've lied to us." He finally looks me in the eye. "There's a lot I can forgive, but lying to me? Deceiving me?" He shakes his head. His voice drops so low I can barely hear the words. "I'm so angry with you that I don't even know how to react."

He loosens his grip on the pan. Giving me one last, cold look, he walks out of the kitchen. I hear the sound of a door slam.

Asher still doesn't say anything. He just stands there, staring at me.

I can't breathe. I can't feel. I have to get out of here. I grab my coat, my hat, and scarf. "I'm sorry about everything," I choke out, then I run, as fast as I can, out of there.

I was right to be afraid.

Now, I have to figure out what comes next.

31

Doubt thou the stars are fire, Doubt that the sun doth move. Doubt truth to be a liar, But never doubt I love.

— William Shakespeare

Hudson:

I 'm still furious when I get into work. My anger doesn't abate when I see the fully constructed model sitting in our conference room.

"Isn't it gorgeous?" Nadja looks up when I walk in.

"You look like hell," I respond. "What on earth are you doing here so early? You should have taken the morning off."

She shrugs. "I'm going to be completely unavailable between Christmas and New Year," she replies. "I want to get everything done before I leave." She dabs a 3D tree with some green paint. "That's the girl you're dating?"

I think of Wendy's bombshell this morning with savage intensity. "If you can call it that," I say bitterly.

She crooks an eyebrow in my direction. "What's the matter, Hudson?"

"Nothing." I grab another paintbrush and dab a tree angrily. I don't even know why I'm working on the damn model. I'm not taking it to Hancock Construction. I'm done. Wendy betrayed me; I'm through with her and her damn project. I'll be happy never to see her again. I'm better off never hearing her soft laugh again, never seeing her warm smile.

And the baby? My conscience prods me. *Can you wash your hands of a baby as well?*

Nadja shakes her head as she looks at the mess I've made. "Perhaps you should let me finish this up," she suggests.

The intercom buzzes before I can tell her where she can put her suggestion. "Hudson, Jack Price is here. He says it's urgent."

I snort; Nadja rolls her eyes. "I thought he'd make it to the three-month mark with Kent before he gave up," she mutters, her attention on the trees she's artfully decorating. "Want to bet he's going to hire us back?"

"No bet." Good. I'm glad Jack Price is here. I feel like yelling at someone today; Jack's a worthy target. I lean over the intercom. "I'll meet him in my office, Clarisse."

"You still haven't told me why you're acting like a surly bear this morning," Nadja says. "Come back here when you're done and tell me what's wrong."

"You work for me, you know," I retort. "Not the other way around."

She gives me a withering look, and my lips curl up in an involuntary grin. "Fine."

"Hudson, we need you back on Clark Towers." To his credit, Jack Price doesn't beat about the bush. "I made a mistake. Kent is a fucking disaster. The architects on his team are fresh out of school. They have no idea what they're doing."

I frown at him. "George Kent poached half my team. They know what they're doing."

"Cartwright was one of yours, wasn't he?" Price sighs heavily. "He quit two weeks ago."

"Why?" I ask sharply.

He lifts his shoulder in a shrug. "Something about unpaid bonuses," he says. "He didn't get into the details with me."

So Colin's out of work. Good, I think harshly. He deserves it for lying to me. As does Wendy.

I'm having trouble focusing on Price. My thoughts are on Wendy. *She lied to you,* I tell myself, trying to hold onto my rage, but then I remember her expression, tight and tense, when she told us she was pregnant.

She's going to have a baby. Maybe a little girl with blonde hair and light blue eyes. A little girl who'll grow up to be a superhero like her mother, with a ferocious belief in right and wrong.

"So will you?" Price asks hopefully.

I have to jerk myself back to this stupid conversation. "Will I what?"

"Work on Clark Towers again?"

"Oh. That." I shake my head to clear the image of Wendy from my mind. "No, of course not." I get to my feet. "Your loyalty can be bought by a set of tickets to a Knicks game. Why on earth would I want to work with you?"

His face goes red. "You're making a mistake," he says, his voice taut with anger. "You can't afford to be this picky. One day, the clients will dry up if you keep up this attitude."

"Maybe," I tell him, indifferent to his threat. "Goodbye, Jack. You know your way out."

"So?" Nadja looks up expectantly when I return to the conference room. She's painted all the trees in my absence and has moved to gluing miniature people on the grounds. I debate telling her that her work is wasted, since I'm not going to the damn meeting, but that'll open up a can of worms, and I have no energy to get into a fight with her.

"I told him to go away."

"Good." She steps back from the model, surveying it carefully before setting the figure she's holding down on the central walkway.

"Price told me Colin's quit his job at Kent."

Her expression is surprised. "Why?"

"From the sound of it, George lied about the bonuses he was going to pay."

"Asshole," she remarks. "Colin will be approaching you for a second chance."

"No second chances, Nadja. Colin lied. I'm done with people that can't be straightforward with me."

She looks up. "Okay, what really happened?" she demands. "Last night, you were happy as a clam. What changed?"

Nadja won't stop nagging until I answer, so I tell her the truth. "Wendy told me she was pregnant this morning. She's known for two months, and she hid it from me."

"Shit." Nadja looks sheepish. "I wouldn't have pressured her to tell you if I'd known you were going to get crazy."

"You knew?" I give her an outraged look, and she returns my stare steadily, unfazed.

"I overheard her talk to her mother on the phone last night. So what's bothering you?" She gives me a searching look. "You can't be sure if you're the father, is that the problem?"

I've known Nadja since graduate school; she's aware that Asher and I share women. "No, that's not it," I reply at once. I couldn't care less whose sperm made the baby; that's biology. Fatherhood is much more than that.

"Okay, if this isn't some caveman possessive thing, what is it?"

"She had a thousand opportunities to tell us the truth and she didn't."

"Get over it," Nadja snaps. "Put yourself in Wendy's shoes for a minute. You and Asher said you only wanted something casual. You pretended you were dating me and walked away from her project. You kept telling her how Megan pretended to be pregnant to trap you into marriage. Of course she's going to be nervous about telling you. Who wouldn't be?"

I stare at Nadja. "Wendy isn't anything like Megan."

"Did you tell her that?" she asks pointedly. "I've known you for years, so I can see you're crazy about her, but did you tell Wendy how you felt? Did you ever tell Wendy you wanted a real relationship?"

Crap. "We made plans for New Year's Eve," I murmur, fully aware of how incredibly lame I sound right now.

She snorts in disgust. "So you committed to an event that's two weeks away," she scoffs. "Hudson, she's pregnant. She thinks she's going to be a single mother. She's probably terrified."

"And I yelled at her." I sink into a chair and cover my face with my hands. "Oh God, I'm such a fucking idiot."

"Yes you are," Nadja says, unrelenting. "But you can fix

this. Take this model to Hancock Construction, help her with her presentation, *and then tell her how you feel.*"

Tell her how I feel.

Tell her that my life is incomplete without her.

Tell her I've been the biggest fool in the world.

Tell her I love her.

Because it's true. I love Wendy Williams.

32

The only thing we have to fear is fear itself.

— Franklin D. Roosevelt

Asher:

Hudson slams the door to his bedroom. Wendy mutters something and slips out. I stand in the center of Hudson's living room, frozen.

Wendy is going to have a baby. One of us is the father.

Shit has suddenly got very, *very* real.

Underneath the fear, I feel a dawning sense of joy. *A baby.* A little girl as beautiful and stubborn as her mother, with the same ability to charm the pants off anyone with her smile.

I can't predict exactly how it's all going to work out. I don't know what Wendy wants. Hudson's too angry right now to think calmly, but once his temper abates, the three of us are going to have to sit down and discuss how to proceed.

But I know what I want. I don't want anything to change

between Hudson, Wendy, and I. Our relationship is unconventional, I know, but it works for us, and we'll make it work with a baby.

I want us to be a family. I want the three of us to live together and raise the baby together. I want to be a better parent to our child than my parents ever were.

I thought I was in love with Lauren, but it's nothing compared to the way I feel about Wendy. She's smart, sassy, and incredibly passionate, and I'm crazy about her.

It's time for action. I can't sit on the sidelines anymore. Not when there's a baby involved. I need to talk to Mikhail Vasiliev, but before that, I need to do something else.

LEVI ISN'T ANYWHERE to be seen when I get to my apartment. Good. He's not going to like what I'm about to do.

Taking a deep breath, I reach for the card that Patrick Sullivan left me, and dial the parole officer. On the drive back from Jean Nakashima's place, I made a decision. The former Head of Finance was so afraid of the Russian mafia that she faked her death and went into hiding.

Ms. Nakashima is not a fool. If Levi robs Vasiliev, he's writing his death sentence. I can't allow that. Even if it means that my friend heads back to jail, and even if it means that he discovers it was me that sent him there. If he hates me for my betrayal, so be it. I was at Lauren's graveside. I cannot be one of Levi's pallbearers.

"It's Asher Doyle," I say when he answers. "I want to cut a deal with you."

"What kind of deal?" he asks warily.

"The kind where you arrest Levi for a minor parole violation." I wonder if Sullivan will cooperate with me.

"There's a bar in Brooklyn that he's been spending a lot of time at. Isn't that against the rules?"

"Doyle, I don't arrest people for drinking. Do you know what that'll do to my workload? Cut the bullshit. What do you know?"

I'm not telling Patrick Sullivan about the surveillance photos of the warehouse by the docks. I don't know the parole officer, and I can't trust that he won't arrest Levi for planning a robbery. "I know that Levi had Thanksgiving dinner with Lloyd Beecham. I know that he's been spending a lot of time with his crew." I take a deep breath and play what I hope is my trump card. "And I know you don't want Engels' blood on your hands."

He exhales. "Drinking at a bar, you say?"

"That's a minor violation, isn't it?" I ask, already knowing the answer. "A maximum of six months in a minimum security prison."

"Don't get cute with me, Doyle. I'm only cooperating with you because Levi's a good guy."

"Fair enough," I agree. "One more thing. Once Levi gets out of jail again, you're going to suggest that he applies for a job at a company called Carreras Entertainment."

"Friends of yours?"

"Client of mine." Miguel owes me a favor, and he runs several bars in the city apart from *Nerve*. Levi is smart and tough and will fit in perfectly in his organization.

"But you don't want your friend to know the job came from you?" His voice is shrewd.

"Levi is going to know that I clued you in on the drinking, Mr. Sullivan," I reply. "I'm fairly sure he's going to want nothing to do with me."

"Yeah." He hesitates. "You're doing a good thing, Doyle. I'll pick Levi up tonight."

I hang up and stare out of my window. The call with Patrick Sullivan went as well as I could have expected. Now for the harder conversation. I need to talk to Mikhail Vasiliev, but first, I need to head to Hancock Construction. It's almost time for our meeting with the retailers, and Wendy's going to need my help, especially if Hudson decides not to show up.

33

Keep love in your heart. A life without it is like a sunless garden when the flowers are dead.

— OSCAR WILDE

Wendy:

On auto-pilot, I manage to get home. I should go to Hancock Construction, though I don't see the point. Thorne smashed the model of the Staten Island complex, and even though Hudson managed to make a replacement, he wants nothing to do with me.

It's over. My career is over, and more importantly, my relationship with Asher and Hudson lies in ruins. I shiver when I think of the harshness of Hudson's tone, the shocked expression on Asher's face.

You've managed to screw everything up pretty well, haven't you? I think bitterly. It's all my fault. For the first time in my life, I wanted to be in a relationship. For the first time in my life, I fell in love. I was afraid because I had something to lose.

And now I've lost everything.

Miki's typing something on her computer at my kitchen table. She looks up in surprise when she sees me, and then she catches sight of my expression. "Oh dear," she says, getting up at once and enveloping me in a warm hug. "What happened, Wendy?"

Tears well in my eyes and fall to my cheeks. "I told Hudson and Asher about the baby," I sniff, rubbing my nose with the back of my hand. Miki scrunches her face and hands me a tissue, and I dab the tears off my cheeks. "They were furious, especially Hudson." My breath catches in a hitch. "He said he could never forgive me for lying to him."

"Oh, sweetie." Miki's voice is kind. "I'm sure he didn't mean it. He was probably just in shock."

"You weren't there." I can't forget the anger etched on Hudson's face. "You didn't hear him."

"You're right," she replies. "But I also know that Hudson loves you, and so does Asher. You don't see the way they look at you. Their eyes light up when you walk into the room, Wen. They'll come around."

I shake my head, and her expression tightens. "You're upset right now; I get that," she says. "But I won't let you screw this up. You have something really great with Asher and Hudson. It's rare, and it's precious, and I won't let you throw it away because you're afraid."

Hope stirs in my heart. Stupidly optimistic hope. "You think they love me?"

"I know they do," she replies. "Look, put yourself in their shoes. They find out you're pregnant, and that hits every single one of Hudson's triggers, doesn't it?"

I nod. "Yes, his ex-wife pretended she was pregnant to force him to marry her."

"Right. Of course he's going to take the news badly. But once he stops to think, he'll come to his senses, and he'll realize what an idiot he's being. What did Asher say?"

Ouch. Asher had barely said two words. "I didn't try to talk to him," I confess with a wince. "After Hudson's reaction, I just ran away."

She frowns at me. "You think all men leave," she says. "Your father left your mother, and you're convinced that's what guys do. And to protect yourself, you leave first, before you can get hurt."

I'd like to dispute her assessment, but I can't.

"Except this time," she continues softly, "it's real. And Wendy, this time, you can't run away. You have to fight."

She's right. I grew up without my father's presence in my life. I don't want my little monkey to grow up without Hudson and Asher.

My heart skips a beat. "I want both of them." I give Miki an uncertain look.

"So go get them."

I gulp. "You don't think it's weird? I mean, we're a threesome. Don't you think a baby should have one mother and one father? People will gossip, won't they?"

She squeezes my hand. "I think babies should be surrounded by people that love them," she replies. "So what if people gossip? You've never struck me as the sort that cared what other people thought."

She's right; I don't care. The only people whose opinion matters are Hudson and Asher. I have to talk to them again.

"Don't you have a meeting today?" Miki asks suddenly.

"Right." I tell her what happened with the model. I'm

expecting her to frown, but she's smiling. "Why are you grinning?" I demand.

"Because you're a fool," she says fondly. "Of course Hudson's going to be there with the model, and of course Asher's going to be there to talk through the legalese. They won't let you fail, Wendy. They're always going to be there for you."

Her expression is wistful. She's going through the ending of her marriage, and it has to be painful for her, but she's giving me her full support because that's who she is. I'm really lucky; I have great friends.

Now, I just have to hold onto hope that I still have two boyfriends.

JEFF CHOI IS in my office-slash-conference room, looking at the wreckage with horrified eyes. "What happened?" he asks, and I tell him the story. I leave out the part where Hudson and I spent all night making another model using his 3D printer. Miki might be certain that Hudson's going to show up, but I'm not as sure as she is. There's no point in getting Jeff's hopes up.

He visibly deflates when I'm done talking. "We're screwed," he says quietly. "We can still go through a presentation, but without something to show them..." His voice trails away.

"Who says you won't have anything to show them?" Hudson's voice sounds from across the hallway. I look up to see Asher and Hudson carrying the model between them. The damn thing even has green trees and little people in the walkways. "Jeff, can you open the executive boardroom for us? This is a lot heavier than it looks."

"Oh thank heavens," Jeff breathes, looking intensely

relieved. "You had a spare." He hurries off to the elevators with a wide smile on his face.

"You're here," I whisper. Damn it. I think I'm going to cry again.

Hudson looks ashamed. "Can you forgive me?" he asks. "I completely overreacted. I'm so sorry, Wendy. I was a fool."

"As was I," Asher replies. "I should have run after you. Stopped you from leaving. Told you how important you are to us."

My heart swells. "Tell me all of these things," I say softly, "after the meeting?"

OUR PRESENTATION IS A RESOUNDING SUCCESS. The retailers are blown away by Hudson's model and the clever lease terms that Asher has come up with, and they cluster around us at the end of the meeting, eager to sign on the dotted line. By the time we're done, we've sold over ninety percent of our available retail space. "That's an industry record," Jeff says, his eyes wide with shock. "We've never done better than seventy percent before this."

Thorne's passing by as Jeff says this. He comes to a halt and pokes his head inside the boardroom. He turns pale when he sees the model sitting in the middle of the table. "Where did that come from?" he asks.

You just gave yourself away, Thorne.

Hudson gives my half-brother a disgusted look. "What are you really trying to say, Hancock?" he asks coolly. "Are you wondering how we managed to get a replacement model ready so quickly? Did you think that smashing our display would kill Wendy's project?"

"I don't know what you're talking about," Thorne blusters. "It sounds like you're accusing me of something, Fleming. You better watch it. We take these kinds of incidents very seriously in this company."

My eyes narrow. We won't have any proof; from the incident with the photos from the security cameras, I know that Thorne has the people in charge of facilities firmly in his pocket. *We'll get you one day,* I vow silently. *You won't get away with your crimes.*

JEFF LEAVES. The three of us leave Hancock Construction and adjourn to Asher's office. When we are finally alone, I look at the two men that I've fallen in love with. "I'm sorry," I blurt out, my words coming out in a rush. "I should have told you about the baby as soon as I knew. I didn't mean to keep it from you. I was just afraid..."

Hudson's shaking his head. "No," he interrupts. "I'm sorry. Nadja yelled sense into me. How could you tell me about the baby when I kept bitching about Megan?" He makes a disgusted sound. "I don't care about Megan. I never cared about Megan, but I let my failed marriage get in the way of the best relationship of my life."

Asher gives me that serious, intent look of his, one that's become so familiar to me. "I love you, Wendy," he says. "I love your passion. I love the way you make me laugh, and even though it gets you into stupid bar fights, I love your willingness to stand up for what you believe in. I'm crazy about you. "

"Me too." Hudson's expression is uncertain. "I know I acted like a dick this morning, but I promise you, I'll cut it back."

I giggle. Happiness fills my chest, and I can't stop smiling. I'm nervous about the future, but I'm also really excited. "How much will you cut it back by?" I ask him with a grin.

"Just so I know what I have to look forward to." I can't believe that less than three months ago, I didn't know Asher and Hudson. Now, they're the most important people in my life. "I love you both," I say, throwing my arms around them. "So much more than I can put into words."

Asher chuckles in my embrace. "You're out of words?" he teases me. "That's a first."

I aim a mock punch at his strong bicep, which turns into a grope. "Your office door has a lock, doesn't it?" I ask him. "Let's use it."

They give me wolfish grins, and their fingers run down my body, and I stop thinking and kiss them back.

MUCH LATER, I lie awake in the middle of the night. It strikes me that we haven't discussed the baby.

Do I dare tell Hudson and Asher I want both of them to be the father of my child?

How will they react to my announcement?

I don't know.

34

The fear of death follows from the fear of life. A man who lives fully is prepared to die at any time.

— Mark Twain

Hudson:

The next morning, Asher finds me in the kitchen before Wendy wakes up. "I need to talk to you."

Something's bothering him. He's hiding it well, but I can read Asher like a book. "The night Thorne smashed the model," I guess. "You took a phone call."

He nods. "You remember Jean Nakashima?" he asks. "The head of Finance at Hancock Construction, the woman who drowned on a weekend sailing trip?" He pauses. "She's still alive. Miki found her. She's living in Hoboken under an assumed name."

"Why?"

He fills me in on Thorne's deal with Mikhail Vasiliev. I listen, feeling a chill spread through my body. *This isn't good.*

Vasiliev is dangerous. He's known to be unpredictable; it's rumored that he has a 'kill first and ask questions later' policy.

And Wendy might be in his crosshairs. Panic claws at my throat at the thought of something happening to her, to our baby.

"This is really bad, Asher."

He nods. There's a frown of concentration on his face. "I've been thinking," he says. "So far, all the attacks have originated with Thorne. The mafia isn't involved."

I realize he's right. Thorne tried to blackmail Asher; Thorne destroyed our model. Thorne orchestrated all of the petty inconveniences that we've been dealing with in the last two months. But none of the attacks have involved violence against Wendy. If Vasiliev were involved, we'd know. He always leaves a trail of blood in his wake.

"Okay, I can buy that."

"Well, why aren't they?" he probes. "There's sixty million dollars on the line. If Thorne doesn't become the CEO of Hancock, he can't pay them back. Why is the *mafiya* sitting on the sidelines, instead of taking a more active role in the situation?"

"I'm pretty happy they're sitting on the sidelines," I retort.

"As am I." Asher sips at his coffee, lost in thought. "But it doesn't make any sense. If Wendy were out of the way, Thorne would become the CEO of Hancock. So why doesn't Vasiliev act?"

"Let's go ask him."

Asher looks up sharply. "Ask him?"

I nod. I can't believe I'm suggesting braving the tiger in its lair, but we'll never get to the bottom of what's going on at the rate we're going. And with each passing day, the risk grows. Wendy's project is flourishing, and Thorne's highway build in South Carolina is failing. Any moment now, Thorne could snap. Stone Bradley has a couple of guards on Wendy, but I'd feel a lot better if Thorne was locked up in jail.

"Can you think of a better way?" I ask my friend. "We can sit here and debate this to death, or we can take a risk and talk to Vasiliev."

He reaches a decision. "Let's do it."

"When?"

He gives me a humorless grin. "No time like the present," he says. "Wendy's mother is flying in this afternoon to spend Christmas with her daughter. Wendy's going to pick her up at JFK. It'll take her three hours to get there and back. That'll give us enough time."

"You know where to find him?"

Asher nods. "Patrick Sullivan told me that he hangs out in a bar in Brighton Beach."

I nod. It's decided. We're going to confront Mikhail Vasiliev today. And before that? I'll be updating my will to leave my fortune to Wendy, just in case we don't make it out of our encounter alive.

FIVE HOURS LATER, Wendy leaves to pick her mother up at the airport in my Land Rover. "Are you sure you're okay with lending me your car?" she asks, her voice filled with hesitation.

I don't blame her for being tentative. After my bitch-fest about Megan's money-grabbing ways, her caution is understandable. "Of course," I tell her. "It's just a car, Wendy. It'll be rush hour by the time you pick up your mother, and the subway will be packed with people."

"Thank you." She takes the keys from me, then grins

wickedly. "My mother is dying to meet the two of you," she says. "Are you free for dinner?"

Oh God. It's proof of how much Asher and I love Wendy that we'll subject ourselves willingly to a parental inquisition.

"We'd love to," Asher replies to her question. "Shall I make reservations at *Tent* again, or would you prefer *Piper's*?"

"*Piper's*, please. My mom loves the mac and cheese there."

Once she leaves, I look at Asher. "Ready?"

He nods, his expression resolute.

We've both changed. After Lauren's death, Asher became wary about getting involved, unwilling to subject himself to the heartache. After Megan's deception, I closed myself off, believing that women were only interested in me for my money.

But this relationship has brought out the best in all of us. Wendy is more trusting, more willing to ask for help. I've realized that not all women are like Megan, and Asher is putting his heart on the line again.

We hit traffic on the Belt Parkway. As soon as we enter Brooklyn, we run across a three car pileup, blocking the two left lanes. It takes us forty minutes to get past the accident, and by the time we pull up in front of the nondescript bar in Brighton Beach, an hour and a half has elapsed.

Asher and I get a text from Wendy. She's just picked up her mom, and she's heading back.

"We're cutting this fine," Asher says tightly, getting out of his car and slamming his door shut.

I don't reply. We push open the front door and enter the bar, and as soon as we walk in, silence descends over the room. "Look at the suits," a thickly accented voice mocks.

We stand our ground. I look around the room slowly. The bar is shabby. A couple of men in torn jeans and black shirts play pool at the table in the middle of the room. A skinny blonde girl sits on the lap of a big burly guy in an Armani suit. He lifts his glass up for a drink as we enter, and I see the tattoos on his knuckles. *Bratva*. We're in the right place.

A man in a black leather jacket approaches us. He's a big guy—three hundred pounds of solid, tightly-packed muscle. "You must be lost," he says. "This is a private club."

Asher shakes his head. "I need to speak with Mikhail Vasiliev," he says clearly. "Tell him I'm an acquaintance of Thorne Hancock."

He gives us an incredulous look. "You want to speak to the *pakhan*?"

"Yes."

He stays exactly where he is, but the blonde girl slides off the lap she's sitting on and heads to the back. In a minute, she reappears and whispers something in the bouncer's ear, who nods curtly at us. "He will give you five minutes," he says, his teeth bared in a vicious smile as he pats us down for weapons, "for your bravery."

Nothing ventured, nothing gained. I take a deep breath and follow the goon through the back door.

The room we enter is much more luxurious. There's a soft teal carpet on the floor. A fireplace exudes warmth from a corner, and there's a massive tigerskin rug draped on the floor next to it. Plush brown leather armchairs are arranged around a card table.

Three men sit at the table, though I only have eyes for one of them. Mikhail Vasiliev is a short, powerfully built man. His bald head gleams in the warm light of the room.

His chin is covered with a goatee. An angry scar runs from under his left eye, almost to his ear.

"Mr. Doyle and Mr. Fleming." His voice is unaccented. "I was wondering if I'd see you here." He waves his hand to the chairs. "Please, sit down."

He knows who we are. My nerves stretched to breaking point, I take the indicated seat. Asher does the same. Vasiliev dismisses the bouncer who led us to the back room. "Would you like a drink?" he asks.

I shake my head. "I prefer to keep my wits about me," I murmur.

He nods. "A wise decision. I will have one, I think. Dmitri?"

One of the guards jumps to his feet and hurries to a side table holding an impressive number of bottles. He pours a shot of vodka into a crystal glass and adds a couple of cubes of ice from a silver bucket, then he hands it to his boss.

Mikhail Vasiliev sips his drink and regards us. "You're here," he says, "because I loaned Hancock some money."

"Yes." Asher takes a deep breath. "I'm going to lay my cards on the table," he says. "Wendy Williams is our woman. We're working with her on the Staten Island project. Is her life at risk if the project succeeds?"

"Normally, it would be." Vasiliev's voice is calm. "However, in this case, I've made an exception. I've made it very clear to Hancock that she's not to be harmed."

Relief floods through me. I lean forward. "Why?"

The men on either side of Vasiliev stiffen and tighten their grip on their weapons. I exhale slowly. *No sudden movements, Hudson.*

Vasiliev regards the little exchange without a change in expression. "Two years ago, your girlfriend represented a woman in a divorce case," he says. "She helped Sofia file a restraining order. She fought to keep her ex from getting custody." He steeples his fingers and surveys us. "Sofia is important to me, but I couldn't move directly against her scumbag husband without consequences. Ms. Williams helped me out of a tight spot. I owe her a debt of gratitude."

"Thorne Hancock is going to lose his father's contest." Asher's voice is flat.

Vasiliev nods. "The contest was *inconvenient*," he agrees. "Hancock didn't have a good read on his father. He thought he'd become the CEO when the old man died." He shrugs, indifferent to Thorne's fate. "It is unwise to borrow money from me and fail to pay it back, Mr. Doyle. There will be consequences if Hancock can't deliver on his promises."

Frustration fills me. Thorne knows that Vasiliev will kill him if he doesn't pay back the loan he took. Are we to sit back and watch Thorne's attacks escalate as he gets more and more desperate? We can't allow that to happen.

Then, in a moment of blinding clarity, a solution occurs to me. I can't believe I haven't thought about this before. "What if we buy out the debt?"

The Head of the Bratva gives me a searching look. "You would help Hancock?"

I'm afraid to look at Asher's face. For ten years, my friend has wanted justice for Lauren. Now, I've just offered to bail Thorne out of a death sentence, and I have no idea how Asher is going to react.

But I've misjudged him. Asher is nodding. "Yes," he mutters to me. "Of course. That's our way out." He meets Vasiliev's gaze unflinchingly. "We will do anything to keep Wendy safe."

Vasiliev sips at the vodka, lost in thought, then he shakes his head. "No," he says. "Hancock Construction will be a useful part of my network. I think I'll wait the year out."

My heart sinks. I turn to Asher, hoping my lawyer friend can think of some way out of this impasse. Then one of the bodyguards glances at his phone and leans toward Vasiliev, whispering something urgently in Russian into his ear.

Vasiliev listens, his expression unchanged. Then he turns toward us. "My associate tells me that Hancock just broke the terms of our deal," he says. "Under the circumstances, I will accept your offer." He pushes a piece of paper toward me. "Wire sixty million dollars to this account number by midnight tomorrow."

I tuck the scrap into my wallet. "And you'll leave Hancock Construction alone?"

His eyes harden. "Hancock Construction, yes. Thorne Hancock, on the other hand, broke my rules. There will be a price to pay."

"What do you mean?" Asher's voice is urgent. "He broke the rules? What rules?"

Vasiliev's expression softens. "A snowplow just slammed into your Land Rover, Mr. Fleming. Both passengers have been injured. They've been taken to Mount Sinai." His lips tighten into a grim line. "Hancock hired the guy who drove the truck."

The room sways around me. We're too late. Thorne has crossed the line, and Wendy has been hurt.

Please, I pray on that frantic drive to the hospital. *Please let Wendy be okay. Please let the baby be okay.*

35

To be happy we must not be too concerned with others.

— Albert Camus

Wendy:

When I see my mom standing in the baggage claim area of the airport, holding a large suitcase in each hand, my heart fills up with joy. I haven't seen her in almost six months, and I miss her. Running up to her, I hug her tight. "It's so good to see you," I mumble into her shoulder. "I'm so glad you decided to visit me."

She kisses me on the forehead. "I'm thrilled to be here, sweetie. Now, let me take a proper look at you." She holds me at arm's length and surveys me. "You're not showing yet."

"I will in a month, according to the Internet." I shake my head and take one suitcase from her grasp. "I'm going to be the biggest source of gossip at work."

"Ignore it," she advises as we set off toward the parking lot. "Most people won't give a damn after the initial shock."

My mother speaks from experience. Fredonia is a small town in which everyone seems to know everyone else. When Janet Williams came back from her short stint in the city, pregnant and unwilling to mention the father, it was the scandal of the year.

Janet Williams weathered it. I will too. I'm older than she was when she had me, and I have Asher and Hudson on my side. They'll help me with the baby.

I think.

"What's the matter?" My mother looks at my face and knows immediately that something is wrong.

I grimace. "I told Asher and Hudson about the baby," I tell her. "And after their initial shock, they were okay, but we never discussed the details. I don't know what they want." I hit the key fob, and the headlights flash as the car doors unlock. We get into our seats, and I start the engine and punch in Hudson's home address into the GPS.

"What do you want?" she asks me once we get underway.

"I want us to be one family," I confess, crossing my fingers as I reveal my heart's desire. "But am I being selfish, mom? Do I owe it to the baby to pick one of them and settle down like a normal person?"

"Sweetie," my mother says bracingly. "You've never been normal. Why start now?"

"What do you mean?" I ask indignantly.

She laughs. "Wendy, you got into fights in the playground on a weekly basis in grade school, remember? Who was that little girl that all the other kids used to make fun of?"

A long-forgotten memory surfaces. "Hannah. Don Jones and Randy Wright used to call her Hannah the Hippo, the horrid bullies."

"And you'd get into such scrapes, defending Hannah from those two." She sighs. "All you owe your baby is love and care, Wendy. Don't make yourself miserable because you think you're doing it for the child. You'll just end up resenting him or her."

"What if Hudson or Asher want something more conventional?" My voice is small. This is my biggest worry; that they'll ask me to choose between them. And I can't do that.

"Have they asked you to do a paternity test?" she probes. "Do they seem keen to know who the biological father is?"

I shake my head. Things have been so chaotic that I haven't noticed, but my mother's right. Neither Hudson nor Asher have insisted that I figure out which one of them is the father. "No, they haven't." I hit the brake pedal as we hit another red light. It looks like all of New York is out on the road tonight, shopping for Christmas presents. The traffic is demented and to add to the mess, a light snowfall has started. Thank heavens I'm driving Hudson's Land Rover. This car is built like a tank.

"Well then," she says. "That's your answer, isn't it? They aren't pushing the issue." She reaches out and ruffles my hair. "You're a silly goose," she says fondly. "Stop being so afraid of what might happen, and just ask for what you want."

My mom is right again; of course she is. "How'd you get so wise?" I ask her, glancing at her smiling face.

I'm looking at her; that's the only reason I see it. A snow plow is speeding up a side street, headed straight for our car.

Something's wrong, I think. *He's driving too fast. He's coming right at us.*

Then there's a crash.

And I can't think anymore.

Darkness envelops me.

36

I must not fear. Fear is the mind-killer. Fear is the little-death that brings total obliteration. I will face my fear. I will permit it to pass over me and through me. And when it has gone past I will turn the inner eye to see its path. Where the fear has gone there will be nothing. Only I will remain.

— FRANK HERBERT, DUNE

Asher:

My heart is in my mouth as I speed through the streets, taking the corners on two wheels, weaving in and out of traffic like a cab driver on steroids. It's started to snow. Large flakes fall from the sky, and it seems like everyone in New York has forgotten how to drive.

Mikhail Vasiliev's words echo in my ear. *A snowplow just slammed into the Land Rover. Wendy's been injured.*

Of course this is Thorne's handiwork; Vasiliev even

confirmed it. Normally, thoughts of revenge would be uppermost in my mind, but right now, the only thing that matters is Wendy. *Please let her be okay,* I pray as I maneuver past a stalled car in the left shoulder. *She has to be okay.*

Then I remember the baby, and my panic kicks up another notch.

To my right, Hudson's on his phone, trying to call Mount Sinai, trying to get any information on what's happened. No one is willing to talk to us. "We can't reveal any details on our patients," I hear a woman's tinny voice sound through the speaker. "I'm sorry."

"Try calling Wendy," I grit out.

"I did," Hudson replies. "It went to voicemail."

"Try her again," I insist. *Damn it, why is everyone driving so fucking slowly?*

Hudson doesn't reply. "Miki," I hear him say into the phone. "Have you heard from Wendy?"

Good thinking. Even if Miki's heard nothing, she might be able to hack into the hospital system to find out if Wendy's been admitted there. Normally, I'd frown on such flagrant violations of the law. Not today.

"No," she replies, her tone sharp. Hudson's put her on speakerphone. "Why?"

Hudson explains about the crash, and Miki swears. "I'll call Piper and Katie and let them know," she says. "We'll meet you at the hospital. Where are you right now?"

We've finally reached Mount Sinai. I screech into the hospital parking lot, pulling into the first spot I see. "I just got to the hospital," I tell her. "We'll call you as soon as we know something."

We sprint full-speed to the door, hurrying to the information desk. "Williams," I gasp at the receptionist. "A car accident. Two women in a Land Rover. I was told she'd been brought here."

A tired-looking nurse in wrinkled scrubs standing behind the receptionist overhears us. "Yes, they were," she confirms. "They had to pull her into surgery immediately." Her face is sympathetic. "It's a bad head injury," she says softly. "Her ribs are broken, and her lung is punctured. I'm sorry."

Oh God. Oh God, oh God, oh God.

The nurse's expression isn't encouraging. She doesn't tell us that the odds are low, but I can read it in her body language.

I can't breathe. I swore that I would protect Wendy and I've failed.

Hopelessness sweeps over me. I picture myself standing at Wendy's grave, lowering her body into the ground. I thought that Lauren's death wrecked me, but I don't remember this much pain. My chest is tight, and everything appears blurry.

Hudson's face is bleak. "Who can we talk to for more information?" he asks.

The nurse says something in reply, but I don't listen. Closing my eyes, I picture my fingers wrapping around Thorne Hancock's throat. I imagine squeezing, watching his face turn red, watching him kick out and struggle for breath, begging for mercy.

There will be no mercy.

The Surgery Department is on the fifth floor. In a daze, the two of us head to an elevator, riding up in silence. The hospital is brightly lit, and there are colorful pictures on the wall. *This isn't a place of death*, it seems to scream. *People don't suffer here.*

What a futile attempt to counter the pervasive gloom of the place.

The elevators open onto a small empty waiting room. I look around, trying to find someone who can help us. "Where the hell is everyone?" My voice comes out loud with frustration.

"Asher? Hudson? Is that you?"

I freeze. That sounds like Wendy, but she's in surgery, isn't she? Barely daring to hope, I look up, and it's indeed her. There's a large bandage on her forehead, and her wrist is in a sling. Her face is pale, and her voice is shaky, but she's standing in the doorway, *and she's alive.*

I take a step toward her, then another one, then I'm folding her in my embrace, holding her tight. Hudson hugs her from the other side, his face buried in her hair. "We were so worried," he chokes out. "The baby?"

"The baby's fine," she says. I release the breath I didn't realize I was holding. "But my mom..." Her eyes fill with tears. "They're not sure if she's going to be okay." She starts weeping, her body shaking with huge, shuddering, hiccupping sobs. "They have her in surgery," she says, "and the doctor," her voice falters, "told me she might not make it out alive."

Fuck. Wendy was raised by her mom, and the two of them are very close.

Hudson's face is etched with misery. This has to be bringing back painful memories for him. His father died in a hospital. I'm positive he'd rather be anywhere but here.

And yet, neither of us loosen our hold on Wendy. We stand there for what seems like hours, our arms around each other.

All we can do is hold her tight and offer comfort.

WE SPEND the next week at Wendy's mother's bedside. The first day is the worst. The doctors warn us that Janet Williams has lost a lot of blood and is dangerously weak. They've set her leg and removed the excess air from her punctured lung, but the injury has stressed her heart.

But the injury that the doctors are most concerned with is the contusion in her brain tissue. They've been forced to put Wendy's mother in a temporary coma. "The swelling needs to come down," the senior surgeon explains to Wendy. "Right now, her brain is being compressed against her skull." He sighs. "The next thirty-six hours are critical."

He clears his throat, sounding uncomfortable. "I don't want you to get your hopes up," he continues gently. "There's only a 25% chance that your mother will awaken from her coma without significant brain injury. At her age," he shakes his head, "the brain doesn't heal quickly."

"I understand." Wendy's voice is so quiet I can barely hear it. Her hands clench into fists, and her expression is bleak. "Thank you for your honesty, Doctor." She turns to us. "I can't leave her."

"Sit." I pull a chair up. "Whatever you want, we're here for you."

She grasps our hands in hers. "I don't want to be alone."

"You won't be." Hudson's voice is grim. "Asher and I have no intention of letting you out of our sight."

The staff at the hospital sets up a cot in Janet Williams' room so Wendy can get some rest. Hudson and I take turns staying with her. Miki's a constant presence at the hospital as well, and Piper visits every single day, bringing bags of food with her and coaxing her friend to eat.

Things get a little better on the third day. Wendy's mother is still unconscious, but the surgeon looks cautiously optimistic with the way her brain is healing. "We might be able to pull her out of the coma tomorrow," he tells us. "But you must be prepared for the worst. Your mother might have speech impediments because of her injury. She might have memory loss; she might not remember you or anyone else. It's going to be a long and expensive path to recovery."

"Money's not a problem," I reply at once.

Hudson nods agreement. "If I understand you correctly," he says slowly. "You're saying that Wendy's mother is well enough that her life isn't in danger anymore?"

We're searching for a desperate glimmer of light at the end of the tunnel. And we find it. "That's right," the doctor confirms, smiling for the first time in days. "If her vitals hold up, she's going to pull through."

Yes. Wendy's body slumps in relief. For days, we've been cautioned to expect the worst, but the doctor's words lift the cloud that's descended over us. Janet Williams has hung on the brink of death for three days, but she's going to make it. She's a fighter, just like her daughter.

FIVE DAYS AFTER THE ACCIDENT, Wendy's mother regains consciousness. "What happened?" she asks in a hoarse whisper. "Where am I?"

Hudson rushes out to find a doctor. I stay with Wendy, unwilling to leave her side. The doctor warned us that her mother might have lost her memory. We don't know the extent of Janet Williams' brain injuries, and I want to be around to comfort Wendy if she needs it.

"You're in the hospital," Wendy chokes out. "There was an accident. Do you remember anything?" Her body is tense as she asks her next question. "Do you remember me?"

A mixture of alarm and puzzlement flickers on the older

woman's face. "Wendy?" she asks. "What do you mean, do I remember you?"

I close my eyes as a wave of relief washes over me. Wendy's mom is okay. Her speech seems fine, and so does her memory.

Janet Williams struggles to sit up, but she's too frail. She falls back to the bed, exhausted by the attempt. "There was an accident?" she asks weakly. "Is your baby okay?"

Wendy clasps her mother's hands between hers. "The baby is fine." She sinks into a chair next to the hospital bed and puts her head on her mother's shoulder, sobbing in relief. "You remember the baby," she says, her voice tremulous. "Oh mom, you know I'm pregnant."

One of Janet Williams' doctors enters the room, Hudson on her heels. "You're awake," she says cheerfully to Wendy's mother, reading the chart at the foot of her bed. "How do you feel?"

"Like a truck ran over me."

Wendy laughs shakily. "That's literally true."

The doctor's eyebrow rises with surprise as she pores over the chart. "How is this possible?" she mutters. She conducts a detailed examination of her patient, and her findings confirm my hopes. Janet Williams appears to have no brain damage. The broken leg will need months of rehab, and her ribs will hurt for weeks when she breathes, *but she's going to be okay.*

It's five days to Christmas, but our miracle came early.

WENDY ACCOSTS us in the small reception area. "I need to talk to you," she says determinedly. "How did you find out I was in an accident? My cell phone was smashed to pieces, so I couldn't call you. How did you know?"

I fill her in on my meeting with Jean Nakashima, and on our interaction with Mikhail Vasiliev. As I explain, I brace myself for her anger. She has every right to be furious with us. We should have told her about our plan *before* we went to see the Head of the *Bratva*, not after the fact.

To my surprise, she takes the news calmly. "Don't do things behind my back again," she says mildly. "And Vasiliev told you that it was Thorne that did it?"

"Yes, he did."

Wendy nods grimly. "Good. Because I'm going to see to it that Thorne goes to jail for this. He nearly killed my mother. I won't let him get away with it."

"Hudson and I will figure something out," I reply. "I don't want you to put yourself in danger."

Her eyes flash in anger, and she gets to her feet. "Let me remind you," she says through clenched teeth, "that you had an opportunity to tell me about Jean Nakashima *and you didn't*. You should have told me about Mikhail Vasiliev, *but you kept quiet*. I'm giving you a pass on that because I can understand bad decisions motivated by fear. After all, I didn't tell you I was pregnant for similar reasons."

She's adorable when she's furious, but I'm smart enough to keep that thought to myself. "But it's time we stop hiding things from each other. We're most successful when we work together. All three of us."

"She's right, you know." Hudson's voice is amused. "Without us working together, we'd have never been able to get as far with Staten Island as we did."

I glare at my friend. "You're just sucking up to her," I accuse him. "What if she gets hurt? What if something happens to the baby? We can't let Wendy get involved." Fear rises in my throat. I can't go through this again.

"Asher." Wendy crouches next to me, her expression

gentle and understanding. "I know you're worried about me." She places her hand over mine. "I know you want to keep me safe. I know you can't stop thinking about what happened to Lauren and wonder if the same thing is going to happen to me." She takes a deep breath. "But I'm not a doll to be played with and protected. I'm always going to want to fight my own battles." She brushes her lips over my cheek. "Will you help me?"

I look into her pale blue eyes. The truth is, I love that she's a fighter. She's a beautiful woman, but it isn't her looks I fell in love with. It's her passion and her fire. "What's the plan?"

A smile breaks out on her face. "I don't know," she confesses. "Want to work on one together?"

Together. I can get on board with that.

37

Being deeply loved by someone gives you strength, while loving someone deeply gives you courage.

— LAO TZU

Wendy:

Two days later, we're ready to put our plan into action.

"Thorne is rattled," I tell Hudson and Asher, trying to convince them this is a good idea. "Jeff Choi emailed me this morning. The Attorney General is investigating Thorne's highway project for bribery and corruption." A mess I'll inherit if I win, but I can't worry about that right now. "I'm going to try and force the truth out of him."

Asher frowns at me. "I don't like it," he says for the millionth time. He opens a box and pulls out a decorative pin in the shape of a pair of boxing gloves. Though my pulse is racing with nerves, I have to smile when I catch sight of the brooch. "Very nice," I congratulate him.

He's obviously preoccupied because he barely cracks a smile. "It's a microphone," he says. "We'll be able to hear and record everything."

Hudson paces in front of the window, too tense to watch. Asher pins the microphone on my blouse. "Be careful," he advises. "Thorne is erratic. He's run out of options. His project is failing, and he thinks he owes the Russian mob sixty million dollars, money he doesn't have. He's cornered."

And cornered people are dangerous. "I won't take any risks," I promise Asher.

Hudson comes to a halt in front of me. "Please don't," he says. He brushes a kiss on my lips, then another one on my belly. Tears fill my eyes at the sweetness of his gesture, and I blink fiercely, pushing them back.

I've spent too much time crying during the last seven days, terrified that my mother might not make it, scared witless at how close my baby came to death.

It's all my half-brother's fault. Yes, I can see how he might think that the contest set up by our father was bitterly unfair. But he had every advantage in the world. He'd worked at Hancock Construction all his life; he knew how the industry worked, and he knew how to succeed.

All he had to do was play fair, and he would have probably ended up successful. Instead, he cheated. He blackmailed Asher. He smashed Hudson's model. And he almost killed my mother.

I'm done taking the high road. I'm going to deal with Thorne Hancock once and for all. I want justice for that poor girl Thorne raped back in college. I want to ease the shadows from Asher's expression. I want to complete the Staten Island project so that Hudson can finally fulfill his father's dream.

And I want us to live happily ever after.

MIKI PULLS me aside at the last minute, right outside my office. "We don't have a case against Thorne for the financial fraud," she says. "Yes, he tampered with the books, but as far as the law is concerned, Thorne hasn't stolen any money. In fact, he's injected sixty million dollars *into* Hancock Construction. Even if a court found him guilty, *which they won't,* Thorne will just get a slap on the wrist."

"What do I need to do?" I'm surprised at how calm my voice sounds.

"Get him rattled," she says. "Get him talking."

"Okay." I take a deep breath. "Wish me luck."

There's a ghost of a smile on her face. "You're the Barracuda, kiddo," she says to me. "You don't need luck. Go get the asshole." Her grin fades and her expression turns serious. "Before Hudson and Asher snap, and do something really stupid."

I MAKE my way to the top floor. There's no one in sight. It's two days to Christmas, and almost everyone is trying to do some last-minute shopping. All the offices on the executive floor are empty and dark, except for one. Thorne's office.

Stone Bradley, the detective that Asher and Hudson use, has been tailing my half-brother since the accident. He's reported that Thorne's spending twenty hours a day in his office, searching for a way out of the mess he's found himself in.

He's there now. His door is closed. *Courage,* I remind myself. *You have to do this. For the baby, for Hudson, for Asher.*

Without knocking, I push it open and march in. Thorne's behind his desk, reading something on his monitor. He's aged in the last week. His eyes are bloodshot, and his face is pale. When I enter, he almost jumps out of his chair in alarm. "You," he exclaims, outrage replacing fear when he realizes it's just me, "What are you doing in my office?"

"It won't be your office for very much longer, will it?" I smile mockingly before sitting down opposite him and leaning back in my chair. My heart hammers in my chest, but I keep my expression even. I can't let Thorne sense my fear. He cannot know I'm bluffing.

He snarls with rage. "You insolent bitch," he growls. "You think that because you sold a few units in your precious complex that you've won? We have a long way to go before the year is up."

I raise an eyebrow in his direction. "But you don't have a year, do you, Thorne?" I smile pleasantly at him. "You've made a string of bad decisions, and they're all catching up with you."

Thorne's scowl deepens. "I have no idea what you're talking about." He waves a dismissive hand toward his door. "If you don't mind?" he asks. "I don't have time for your crackpot theories. Some of us have work to do."

I'm getting to him. Sweat beads on his brow, and his hands clench into fists. I have him exactly where I want him. I just have to keep pushing at the cracks, and sooner or later, he'll blurt something incriminating.

"A string of bad decisions," I repeat. "It started with Barbados, didn't it? You shouldn't have bid on that bridge; everyone warned you that it was a disaster from the start. But no, you thought you knew better."

His face pales. His gaze narrows, but he doesn't say anything. *Damn it.* I need him to talk.

"So you involved the Russians." I shake my head. "You

made a deal with Mikhail Vasiliev. What were the terms, Thorne? He loaned you money, and in return, you turned a blind eye while they laundered their dirty drug money through Hancock Construction?"

Thorne grows still. "You're playing a dangerous game here, Wendy," he says. "I don't think you know what you're sticking your nose into."

"But I have proof," I lie calmly. "Jean Nakashima was onto you. When she drowned, you thought you got lucky, didn't you? All you had to do was delete her emails and appoint one of your cronies to her role. Of course, you had no way of knowing that she had backup copies of all her work." I twist the knife a little more. "Backup copies that I have access to."

Of course I'm lying. Jean Nakashima was careful to destroy all the evidence before faking her death. Even if she hadn't, Miki warned me we couldn't make this charge stick. I need Thorne to confess to hiring the guy who slammed into our car.

But I've done what I've intended; I've succeeded in unnerving Thorne. There's a trapped look on his face; he looks around the room as if he's searching for a way out.

"So what?" he says. "What are you going to do—talk to the Feds?" He sneers in my direction. "You're going to give them evidence that incriminates the Russian mob?" He laughs mockingly. "Please, be my guest. I didn't think you were stupid enough to make a move against Vasiliev, but I seem to be giving you too much credit."

Time to play my ace. "Mikhail Vasiliev won't hurt me." I lean back, holding Thorne's gaze. "He warned you not to harm me, and you didn't listen, did you?" I shake my head sorrowfully. "That was a bad move, Thorne. When the Head of the Bratva tells you to stay away from me, and you hire someone to drive a snow plow into my car..." I pause for effect. "You blew it."

"He'll never know," Thorne yells, his control snapping at last. He lunges out of his chair and comes for me, murder in his eyes. "I paid for the hit in cash. He'll never find out."

He grabs me by the throat and squeezes. I can't breathe. Spots of light flash bchind my eyes, and the room starts to go dark.

Then the door slams open and Hudson and Asher rush into the room, fury etched on their faces. They pull him off me and send him flying across the room. I draw in a shaky breath.

It's over.

~

Asher:

I keep hitting him, over and over. Blood spurts out of his nose, and his face is a pulp, but I don't draw back. I aim punches at him, my fury unquenched. Partly for what he did to Lauren ten years ago, but more so for what he did to Wendy and her mother, for putting her in danger, for the moments of mind-numbing fear I felt as we drove to the hospital, not knowing if she was alive or dead.

Through a fog of red, I feel Wendy tugging at my shirt, trying to pull me away from Thorne. "Asher," I hear her scream. "Please, stop. Enough."

I ignore her. I've made up my mind.

There will be no mercy this time. Thorne Hancock will never hurt us again.

He tries to put his hands up to block my punches, but he's no match for me. I aim another blow at his face, and then my hands lock around his neck. This fucker grabbed Wendy by the throat? He's going to learn what happens when someone threatens the woman I love.

My fingers tighten and squeeze, the way I'd fantasized about during those desperate hours at the hospital. His face is turning red; his breathing comes in gasps.

Then Hudson pulls me off Thorne and sends me flying across the room. I land with a sickening crash against the outer wall and blink up at my best friend, who looms over me. "She's pregnant," he says softly. "We're going to be parents. Don't you think you should stick around and be a father to our child?"

At his words, my haze lifts and my anger rushes away.

Hudson's right. I have a bright future ahead of me. I grew up without knowing my parents; I won't let it happen to my child.

THE POLICE ARREST Thorne and take our statements. "Did I do okay? Is there enough evidence to charge him?" Wendy asks me anxiously.

"You did better than good." I wrap my arm around her waist. "You did great. We have Thorne on tape confessing to ordering the hit on you. That's more than enough to send him away for a long time."

And if the justice system can't take care of Thorne, I'm sure Vasiliev will act. The head of the Russian Mafia rules by fear. He won't allow Hancock's infraction to go unpunished. Thorne doesn't know it yet, but jail's the safest place for him.

"What now?" she asks.

"Well," I mutter, nuzzling my lips against her neck, "I finally have my apartment to myself again. There's a soft bed waiting for you there. The doctors will probably discharge your mother tomorrow, so we'll move her to my place and hire a nurse to help out. Once she's ready for rehab, we'll arrange that too."

Hudson puts his arm around her waist too, linking the three of us together.

"About the baby," Wendy says, her voice nervous, "I don't want to find out which one of you is the father. As far as I'm concerned, you both are." She lifts her chin up and gives us a challenging look. "Is that okay?"

"Fine by me," I say promptly.

"Me too," Hudson says. "My realtor left a message for me earlier today. The apartment next to mine is coming up on the market. If we buy it, we can have the whole floor to ourselves." He kisses Wendy's cheek. "You are moving in with us, aren't you?"

She laughs breathlessly. "I guess I am," she agrees.

Happiness fills my heart. I give her a wicked grin as I move her hair out of the way and kiss her on the back of the neck. She shivers in pleasure. "Let's go tell Miki she's going to have the place all to herself," I whisper in her ear. "And then, let's go somewhere private, shall we?" My hand slides down her body and cups her ass. "Hudson and I have plans for you. Lots of plans. We're going to keep you busy for the rest of your life."

EPILOGUE

There are two great days in a person's life - the day we are born and the day we discover why.

— WILLIAM BARCLAY

Wendy:

Non-alcoholic champagne tastes like swamp water. Hudson's lips twitch as he catches my disgusted look when I see the bottle of fake champagne sitting next to the good stuff. "I know you prefer the Krug," he teases. "Are you sure you don't want a sip of the real thing?"

I shake my head. My obstetrician assures me that an occasional glass of wine will not harm the baby, but she's French, and I'm skeptical. "I'm good."

It's a hot, humid July afternoon in Staten Island, and we're finally ready to break ground on our project. We should have started building in May, but we ran into a delay getting a permit, and we're already behind eight weeks. Jeff

Choi assures me that delays are part of the construction process. "Should you be stressing?" he keeps asking me when I start panicking over our timelines. "Isn't the tension bad for the baby?"

He's right on all counts. Delays are part and parcel of the business, and I'm getting much better at figuring out which issues are important, and which ones are trivial.

Asher frowns. "What's the delay?" he grumbles. "Jeff, it's close to a hundred degrees today. I don't want Wendy standing in the sun for hours. Can we get this show on the road?"

"Oh for heaven's sake. I'm pregnant, not dying. The heat won't kill me."

He ignores me and stalks off to yell at someone. I gaze at him fondly. My two men are polar opposites about the pregnancy. Hudson is protective but laid-back. Asher, on the other hand, is a worrier. It's quite funny watching him fret.

Of course, I wouldn't have it any other way. The last six months have been magical. I'm the luckiest woman in the world.

Once she was discharged from the hospital, my mother moved in with us. She was in rehab for three months for her broken leg. I was afraid she'd never be able to walk again, but I didn't need to worry. Janet Williams has always been a fighter. She pushed through her physiotherapy sessions without complaint, and she made astonishing progress.

A couple of months ago, she announced her intention of moving to New York. "Don't worry," she'd said with a grin, "I'm getting my own apartment. But I'll be around to babysit my grandchild."

"Spoil the baby rotten, you mean," I'd retorted with a grin.

I'm thrilled for my mother. Her decision to move to

Manhattan shows me that she really did get the closure she needed from Paul Hancock. My mother's always wanted to live in the city. She's started to see someone too, a nice guy called Ben. It's still a new relationship, but Ben treats her like a queen, and I'm optimistic for her.

If there's anyone who deserves to be happy, it's Janet Williams.

"Ms. Williams?" Ricardo Baresi, the foreman of the project, comes up to me holding a silver shovel in his hand. "Are you sure you're up to digging in your condition?"

Kill me now; I'm surrounded by over-protective men. "Ricky," I say patiently, "I'm not actually doing any work here. There's a patch of dirt. I'm going to move a handful of it around. I think I can manage that just fine."

His expression is unconvinced, but he hands me the shovel anyway. "You're the boss," he says. "We're ready to get going."

My baby presses against my bladder at that moment. "In a minute," I reply. "First, I need to pee."

THE THING I didn't know about being pregnant? I'm horny all the time. Thank heavens Asher and Hudson like my baby bump, because I crave sex twenty-four hours of the day. I'm some kind of nympho-monster. Let's just say I'm very, very glad there's two of them.

Take this morning, for instance.

I wake up with Hudson's hard cock pressed against my butt. Asher is sleeping on his back, his face peaceful, and I decide to be a good girlfriend and let him sleep. As quietly as I could, I turn toward Hudson, but his eyes are shut as well.

Damn.

So I do the only thing I can. My hand slips between my legs, and I start to lose myself in a favorite fantasy, one that involves Asher and Hudson and the great outdoors.

Evidently, pregnancy makes me want to be an exhibitionist.

"What are you doing?"

I jump at the sound of Hudson's voice. "You startled me," I accuse him with a grin. "What does it look like?"

His hand closes over my wrist. "I don't think so, princess." There's a wicked gleam in his eyes. "It's *our* job to make you scream with pleasure."

Asher's awake as well. His finger slides between my tank-top and my shoulder, and he moves it out of the way before kissing my skin. Heat prickles in my body.

Hudson moves closer too. I'm trapped between their hard bodies. "I like the way you're doing your job," I whisper, shivering with desire as I respond to Hudson's predatory tone.

Hudson's finger dips into my core. "Wet already," he says, proud male arrogance in every syllable.

Well, yeah. Of course. "I have to be at work in an hour." Unfortunately. "We only have time for a quickie."

"You better follow instructions then," Asher replies with a nip against my neck.

I groan and grind my ass into him. "I will," I promise. Meeting or not, I need to satisfy this craving that pulses through my body.

"Take off your clothes," Asher orders.

I wriggle out of my tank-top and my thin cotton shorts, loving the look of desire in their eyes, knowing from their swift, sharp inhale of breath that my need isn't one-sided. They want this as much as I do.

Asher moves over me, his muscles flexing, and I watch greedily. I can't get enough of this sight. His abs ripple as he moves, then his hands and mouth are on my tender nipples, and I shut my eyes as pleasure overcomes me.

"Open your mouth." This time, the order comes from Hudson. He's hard, ready. "Suck my cock."

I turn on my side. My belly makes missionary uncomfortable, but that's made no difference in our sex lives. I've taken to studying the Kama Sutra—*hey, I said I was horny all the time, didn't I?*—and insisting that Asher and Hudson and I try out every sex position in the book. Of course, they're not complaining.

Asher slides into me as I suck on Hudson's hard cock. His clever fingers find my clitoris and strum on it steadily. I can't last. My limbs tighten and clench, and I moan as my climax hurtles toward me.

"Fuck," Hudson grinds out. "When you moan with my cock in your mouth..." His voice trails off, and his face contorts as his climax approaches. I pump him with my hand and suck harder, and he explodes in my mouth.

His orgasm sets mine off. Blood pounds in my head and desire sweeps in waves over me. Every muscle in my body twists and strains. Asher grabs my ass as he comes, and then the three of us collapse in an exhausted, sated heap.

BACK AT THE CONSTRUCTION SITE, Amanda, who is the newly appointed head of public relations, directs the company photographer. I see her look around for me, and I waddle as fast as I can. "Where's Wendy?" I hear her ask Jeff as I walk up.

"Here," I reply.

"Oh good. Let's start?"

The ceremony doesn't take long. I make a short speech, praising the team for the hard work they've put in. Then I stick the shovel into the ground, move a small patch of earth, and we're done. Jeff Choi pops open a bottle of champagne with a wide smile on his face, and he starts filling plastic cups with the beverage.

I watch, sipping my non-alcoholic swill, feeling a warm happiness in my chest. Less than a year ago, my life was completely different. As a divorce lawyer, I watched relationships collapse in the most bitter and acrimonious ways possible. Now, I preside over creating buildings, not tearing them down, and it feels remarkably fulfilling.

Thorne's in jail. His confession was enough to convict him, but Miki wanted to make sure there were no problems, so she used her ninja-hacking skills to find the guy who drove the snow plow into our car. Facing the prospect of life in prison for attempted murder, the guy cut a deal with the prosecution and identified Thorne as the man who hired him. My half-brother received a fifteen-year jail sentence. He won't be bothering us for a long time.

I was furious with Thorne for what he did to my mother, but once it was clear that she was going to be fine, I realized that I didn't want Thorne to die at the hands of the Russian Mafia. So I sent Mikhail Vasiliev a message, asking him to spare Thorne's life.

If I do this, he'd replied, *that will be the last favor. After this, you're on your own.*

I'd agreed without hesitation. I didn't want the Russian mob anywhere near Hancock Construction, and besides, I don't need Vasiliev's protection. I have Hudson and Asher watching over me.

Miki's divorce has been finalized. She's back in Manhattan, living in my former apartment. I still see her, and the rest of my friends, every Monday night. No matter what else changes, the Thursday Night Drinking Pack will remain a fixture in our lives.

At my old firm, Lara finally made partner in January and I couldn't be happier. We try to meet for lunch once a month. "It's not the same without you," she always tells me. "Can I talk you into coming back?"

Not a chance in hell. Despite my initial misgivings, I'm really happy about my new job.

"READY TO GET OUT OF HERE?" Asher frowns at me. "You've shaken the hand of every single person here and told them they're doing a great job."

"Sounds good." I'd never admit it, but he's right. The heat has sapped away my energy, and I'm exhausted. I really want a nap.

His intent gaze sweeps over my face, and I know he's on to me. I smile at him. "I know, I know, I should have let Jeff break ground."

His expression softens. "No you shouldn't have," he corrects me. "This is your baby. Without you, this project wouldn't have made it past the planning stage. You deserve all the recognition and praise in the world for your work here."

My fingers lace in his. "I'd have been lost without Hudson and you."

His lips curl into an amused smile. "So you say," he replies. "Yet Jeff tells me you're doing just fine without our help."

"Maybe," I pout, "but I miss working with the two of you on a daily basis."

Asher and Hudson are still around to help me if I need it, but now that the contest is over and I've been appointed the CEO of Hancock Construction, they've both cut back on their involvement. I do miss them, but I think it's for the best. It's not feasible for them to split their time between their companies and Hancock Construction. They're just too busy.

Of course, Asher still helps me with thorny legal issues, and Hudson's my first choice of architect. Even though he has a two-year wait list, he's promised he'll design an apartment complex in Chicago for us next year. Let's just say it helps to be in a relationship with the guy who heads up New York's best architecture firm.

I feel a pressure in my belly, and there's a weird popping sensation, followed by an immediate gush of warm fluid that soaks through my panties. *Oh my God,* I think in horror, *I just peed in public.*

Then it dawns on me that my water just broke.

Fuck me. The baby's not due for another two weeks, but it seems that my little monkey is done waiting.

I clutch at Asher's suit-clad bicep. "Don't freak out," I tell him, "but I think the baby's coming."

His face whitens. Hudson hurries up to us. "Is everything okay?"

Two men who love me. A little baby to expand our lovely family. Everything is more than okay. Everything is perfect.

EIGHTEEN LONG, exhausting hours later, I hold my baby in

my arms, marveling at my little miracle. She's beautiful. She has ten tiny fingers and ten tiny toes, and she can scream loud enough to wake the dead. "I wonder where she gets that from?" Hudson teases me.

I punch his bicep. "Cut it out."

"Have you figured out her name yet?" Asher brushes his lips across the baby's forehead gently, with so much love on his face that my eyes fill with tears.

Hudson looks up. We've been debating baby names for weeks. Somewhere at home, there's a piece of paper with a list of our top five baby names for boys and girls, but I've held off making the final decision until the birth.

"Yes," I tell them, holding the warm baby close. "Meet Natalie Janet Maria Williams."

They're lost for words. Natalie was Hudson's mother's name; Asher's mom was called Maria. And of course, Janet is my mother's name. Hudson and Asher's mothers are dead now, but I can't think of a better way to thank them for the gift of their sons than by naming our child after them.

I think Asher has tears in his eyes. He blinks rapidly and turns his face away from me, while Hudson clears his throat. "Wendy," he says, "there was something we were going to do after the groundbreaking ceremony. Asher, you ready?"

Asher gathers his composure and nods. He takes a small square box out of his pocket, and my heart starts to hammer. "I know what we have is unorthodox," he says, "but it works for us. The last six months have been the happiest of my life, and," he pauses, "I want forever."

Hudson laces his fingers in mine. "Wendy," he says, "I love you. I love everything about you. I love living with you. Well, except for the low-fat ice cream you stash in the freezer. That stuff is just disgusting."

"We'd go on our knees," Asher adds, "but you're in a

hospital bed, and you're holding Natalie. We should do this better, but I want to do this now." He opens the box and pulls the ring out. "Will you make us the luckiest men in the world?" he asks.

"Will you marry us, Wendy?" Hudson's expression is as serious as I've ever seen it. "Will you spend the rest of your life with us?"

The ring is beautiful. It has a large round diamond in the center, bracketed by two baguette-cut diamonds set on a platinum band. I barely have eyes for it; I can't take my gaze off Hudson and Asher. "Yes," I exclaim. Natalie twitches in her sleep, but doesn't wake up. "Yes," I repeat in a softer voice. "Of course I'll marry you." Tears trickle down my cheeks. "I want to spend the rest of my life with you too."

They slip the ring on my finger. "We love you, Wendy."

I look at my ring, then down at my peacefully sleeping baby, and finally up at the smiling faces of the men I'm going to marry. "I love you too."

∼

THANK YOU FOR READING WENDY, Asher, & Hudson's story! I hope you love them as much as I do.

∼

THE MENAGE IN MANHATTAN SERIES

WANT MORE? *Miki's story - The Hack - is next.* Read on for a free extended preview, or check out the other books in the MENAGE IN MANHATTAN SERIES.

The Bet - Bailey, Daniel, & Sebastian
The Heat - Piper, Owen, & Wyatt
The Wager - Wendy, Asher, & Hudson
The Hack - Miki, Oliver & Finn

DO YOU ENJOY FUN, light, contemporary romances with lots of heat and humor? Want to read *Boyfriend by the Hour (A Romantic Comedy)* for free? Want to stay up-to-date on new releases, freebies, sales, and more? (There will be an occasional cat picture.) **Sign up to my newsletter!** You'll get the book right away, and unless I have a very important announcement—like a new release—I only email once a week.

A PREVIEW OF THE HACK BY TARA CRESCENT

PROLOGUE

When it is all finished, you will discover it was never random.

— UNKNOWN

Miki:

Thanksgiving should be a time of gratitude and reflection.

Bite me.

The line inches forward. The terminals at Houston's George Bush Intercontinental Airport are always busy, but today, they're practically bursting at the seams. Swarms of tired and cranky passengers are everywhere. Several freak storms in the area have disrupted flight schedules, and the ticket agents are frantically rebooking the travelers, doing their very best to cope with the melee.

Miracle of miracles, my flight is still on schedule. Probably the only thing that's gone right in six weeks.

I queue up in the serpentine line, waiting to check in my luggage, two big suitcases, bursting at the seams with everything I own in Houston that I want to keep. My clothes, my computer equipment, my collection of silly and impractical shoes. My laptop I clutch to my chest—the the gate agents will pry that from me over my cold, dead body.

Twenty long minutes later, I finally reach the counter and hand the tired-looking agent my ID. She pulls up my details on her computer, and eyes my two suitcases dubiously. "There's a fee for checked luggage," she says, looking like she's bracing herself for an argument.

Poor woman. It must suck to work on Thanksgiving. "I know," I reply. "That's alright."

She punches in more keys, weighs my luggage, charges me for overweight baggage, and then prints out my boarding pass. I look at my seat assignment and wince. 31B. That's the back of the plane, in a middle seat. On a four-hour flight.

Pasting on my friendliest smile, I give her a hopeful look. "You don't have an aisle or a window seat open?"

She shakes her head. "I'm sorry, Mrs. Hickman. It's a full flight."

Ah well. A middle seat is a minor bump in the shit sandwich that has become my life in the last month and a half. "I'll deal with it," I reply. "Oh, and it's not Mrs. Hickman. It's Ms. Cooper. The divorce will be finalized in December."

In normal times, Thanksgiving is my favorite holiday. It's a day dedicated to eating. There are no crowded malls to wade through, no presents to buy. What's not to love?

These are not normal times.

Six weeks ago, I thought I'd surprise my soon-to-be-ex-husband Aaron at work on a Friday evening. We'd barely seen each other in the last three months, and I'd planned to surprise him with a spontaneous date night.

Except I walked in on his assistant Peggy giving him a blowjob in his office, bobbing her big blonde head on his junk.

Even worse? They'd been doing the dirty-dirty for eighteen months. Yup. When Aaron and I were standing up in front of a judge, promising to love and honor one another, he was having an affair with his assistant.

Let's just say I'm approaching the holiday with an emotion that does not resemble gratitude *in the slightest.*

Two hours later, we board the plane. I take my crappy middle seat. The other occupants in my row haven't shown up yet. *Maybe they missed their flight,* I think hopefully, then scold myself for that uncharitable thought. *Just because you're in a craptastic mood, Mackenzie Cooper, it doesn't mean you have to be a bitch.*

Coopers do not complain. Coopers square their shoulders, hold their heads high and carry on.

My family lives in Manhattan, but I haven't told them about the impending divorce. I'm sure my mother will try and talk me out of it, and I'm just not ready to deal with her yet.

I feel like such a fool. My friends tried to warn me that I was jumping into marriage with Aaron, but I wouldn't listen. Aaron was tall and handsome, and I was the nerdy computer chick. I'd been so thrilled that he noticed me that my common sense had fled.

I'd been wearing love-goggles, and I was blind. And stupid. And now I'm paying for it. When I get to Manhattan, Wendy, Piper, Katie, and Gabby will give me pitying looks and ask me questions about what Aaron did and what I'm going to do next.

I'm not ready to talk about it. *I'm not ready to face the future.*

Enough brooding. I pull out my dollar-store notebook with its neon pink cover from my backpack and start making a list.

Top Five Ways in which I'm Going to Reclaim My Life.

1. Move away from Houston. I'm done with this town. I'll always be the woman who walked in on her ex-husband's assistant giving him head under his desk at work, and I'm never going to be able to leave that memory behind.
2. Move back to Manhattan. Find an apartment.
3. Find a job. Manhattan is not a cheap place to live, and my savings won't last long.
4. Get a cat. I don't have to worry about Aaron's stupid *and imaginary* allergies anymore.
5. Sex is allowed, but love is off-limits.

I underline that last resolution several times until I stab a hole through the paper.

That's when someone clears his voice. "Excuse me," an amused male voice says. "If I could get to my seat—"

I look up, and my eyes widen. The two men standing in the aisle are absolutely gorgeous. The one laughing at me is big, blond, and broad-shouldered, like a modern-day Viking. He's wearing a carelessly un-tucked white shirt with dark blue jeans and worn sneakers, and he still looks like a million bucks. And his friend? His friend, with his custom-tailored gray plaid suit, dark hair, piercing blue eyes and lean, taut body, is just as drool-worthy.

I've won the plane lottery, ladies. *Pity I don't care.*

I get up, and the blond man slides into the window seat. It's a tight fit. His shoulders are broader than the seat, and his knees hit the back of the row in front of him. I'm five-feet-three-inches, and I don't have enough room. The Viking is easily six feet tall, and he must be acutely uncomfortable.

"Are you together?" I ask the dark-haired one. "Would you like to change seats?"

"No thank you," he replies. He has light blue eyes, the color of the sky on a cloudless day, and when his gaze locks on mine, my heart beats a little faster. The corner of his mouth quirks up. "I talk to Oliver all the time at work. Right now, you look much more interesting than he does."

Well, okay then.

Is he flirting with me?

What should I do?

I'm a hacker. Ask me about registry settings, and I'm your woman, but put me in front of a good-looking guy, and unless he's talking about brute force attacks or botnets, I'm a tongue-tied, stammering mess.

The noise that emerges from my throat is a mixture of a laugh, a snort, and a neigh. Lovely. *Thank you, universe.* You couldn't make me smooth and sophisticated, could you? No. You had to make me sound like a donkey with a head cold.

My cheeks flushing with embarrassment, I slide into my chair, my shoulder bumping into Viking-guy. "Sorry," I murmur and try to hunch so I'm not making contact with his body.

His smile widens. "Hi," he says. "I'm Oliver. Tell me why you want a cat, who Aaron was and why he pretended to be allergic, and most of all," he bends his head toward me, lowering his voice to a conspiratorial whisper, "why sex is allowed, but love isn't."

"You read my list." Shock makes my voice indignant. *Aren't people supposed to pretend they aren't reading over your shoulder?* "You're rude."

He laughs easily. "I've been accused of that and more," he says. "But you're right. That *was* rude of me. Allow me to make it up to you." He raises his hand, and like magic, a flight attendant is at our side, beaming radiantly at Oliver the Viking.

Good-looking-guy-magic. Aaron had it too.

"I know it's against the rules," Oliver says to the attendant, his smile charming and ever-so-slightly-apologetic. "But you couldn't grab some orange juice from your cart for us, could you? As well as three of your mini-bottles of vodka?"

She simpers at him. "Of course," she says. "It's a four-hour flight, and these seats don't recline. It seems the least I can do."

In about thirty seconds, she returns with a handful of bottles. Oliver takes them from her with a smile, and the dark-haired guy slips her a folded bill. "Thank you," he says. "I really appreciate it."

Whoa. Smooth. I'm pretty sure that was a hundred dollar bill, unless they've started putting Benjamin Franklin's face on smaller denominations.

Oliver hands me my share of the spoils. "Will you accept my peace offering?" he asks, his eyes twinkling.

It seems silly to pout for four straight hours, and this might be exactly what I need. Though I've cried and I've fumed in the last six weeks, I haven't gotten shit-faced. Maybe I do need to get good and drunk.

Closing my notebook, I tuck it into the seat pocket in

front of me. "Okay," I say. Opening my OJ, I take a long drink from it before adding the vodka. "Truce."

Two hours later, I'm chatty, and I'm well and truly on the way to being drunk. Which sadly only takes three of the little mini-bottles, because I'm a lightweight.

I'm sitting between Finn and Oliver, their thighs brushing against mine. Drunk-Miki is much better at flirting than Sober-Miki, or so I think. "Now that we're friends," Oliver says, a smile dancing on his lips, "Who's Aaron?"

"My husband."

Finn's eyes fall to my left hand. I lift it up. "No ring," I announce. "I'm getting divorced." Unbidden, my eyes fill with tears. I was such a fool. I wanted so much to be loved that I ignored all the warning signs.

"Hey, hey." Oliver's voice is soothing. "Don't cry." His big, strong hand covers mine. "It's okay."

Finn hands me a tissue and a bottle of water. I dab at my eyes and take a long sip of the cool liquid. "Sorry."

"It's okay," Finn replies, exchanging a glance with Oliver. "You're not the first person to cry over a failed relationship, and you won't be the last. Let's talk about something else. What do you do?"

I'm a hacker. In today's world of shell corporations and offshore bank accounts, people hire me to track down some-one's assets. I'm not a lone wolf; I used to work for a company that gave me some protection from getting sued or worse. But the work I did was quasi-legal, and I'm too cautious to talk about it. *Even when tipsy.*

"Computer stuff," I reply vaguely. "It's very boring. I stare at spreadsheets all day."

Oliver's hand is still on mine, and I don't know if I

should leave it there, or if I should pull it away. I don't want to be rude.

Finn's face is turned toward me, and he's close enough that if I fall forward, my lips will land on his. It's a tribute to Aaron's asshattery that I resist. His lips look soft. His face is covered with dark stubble, and there's a tiny part of me that wants to rub against it and purr, just like a cat.

I should stay away from vodka.

For the rest of the flight, I sip my water and make conversation. They're easy to talk to. We like the same kinds of what-if TV shows: Person of Interest, Fringe and Sense 8, and the journey passes as we squabble good-naturedly about whether the second and third Matrix movies were any good. There's still an undercurrent of sexual tension in the air, but for the moment, it lingers in the background.

I don't want to leave when the flight lands; I'm having such a good time. I might be fooling myself, but I don't think I'm the only one. Finn and Oliver linger in their seats, ignoring the rapidly emptying plane. It's only when the aisle is almost clear that Finn gets to his feet. "We should go," he says, his voice reluctant. "Miki, it was great meeting you." He smiles warmly. "And my initial assessment was right. You are much better company than Oliver."

I get up as well, grabbing my backpack from underneath the seat in front of me. Call me paranoid, but I don't like leaving my laptop in the overhead bins. I didn't even like leaving it behind when I went to the bathroom, but I also didn't want Oliver and Finn to think I was crazy.

The three of us make our way out. Once we're in the airport terminal, Oliver puts his hand on my arm. "I'd like to keep in touch," he says. His expression is intense, and suddenly, he's not the guy I've been talking to for the last four hours. He's in good-looking-guy mode, and sure enough, I'm back to tongue-tied-and-awkward.

He pulls a business card from his wallet and holds it out. "Call me?"

My heart lurches. What the hell am I doing, flirting with these guys? My marriage has just ended. I don't have a job or a home. My life is one big, tangled, complicated mess, and Oliver and Finn will make it worse.

I swallow hard. "I don't think that's a good idea," I say, unable to meet their eyes. Then, before they can try to talk me into it, I run away.

～

Finn:

I watch her leave, my gaze lingering on her back until she disappears into the crowds at JFK. *So that's Mackenzie Cooper.* "She's not what I thought she'd be," I say out loud.

Three months ago, a prototype security system at Imperium got breached by a hacker. One of our clients, Howard Lippman, had hidden his assets in shell corporations during a contentious divorce. The mystery hacker uncovered the scheme and unmasked Lippman's fraudulent behavior.

I don't give a shit about Lippman's troubles—he violated our terms of service by breaking the law, and we terminated his account as soon as we found out. But I do care, passionately, that my code was cracked.

It was a few minutes' work to close the vulnerability that led to the data breach. It's taken us considerably longer to find the hacker that pulled off the feat.

Then yesterday, we were able to get a hold of a name.

Miki Cooper.

At my side, Oliver's lips curl up into a sly grin. "You mean, she's a girl. You got hacked by a girl."

I roll my eyes. "Grow up, Prescott. I'm not being sexist. My grandmother is the strongest person I know, man or woman." My lips tighten. "Until Miki, we've never been breached. She's a problem."

He nods. "Let's look at the bright side," he says. "She's not a rogue operator. She cracked Imperium as part of her job."

"A job she quit last week." We know as much about Mackenzie Cooper as it is possible to know legally in twenty-four hours, which isn't much. "She's a free agent now. That makes her dangerous."

She's not on social media; she doesn't post her pictures on Facebook, and she doesn't tweet about whatever is on her mind. She's someone who knows that everything she does online is a link back to her, and she's careful.

"Let's keep an eye on her," Oliver says. "She's on DefCon's forums. We'll find her there and make contact."

Imperium, the company Oliver and I founded five years ago, is going public in six months. "We can't risk another data breach."

"I know," he replies, his expression grim. "It won't come to that."

We walk out of the airport and hail a cab. It's Thanksgiving. Nana will have made a feast, as she does every single year. There will be three kinds of pie, maybe four. For the moment, work can wait.

But only for a moment. Tomorrow morning, it's back to the grind.

"We need to stop working with high profile clients," Oliver remarks in the cab. "We're spending far too much time vetting these guys, and assholes like Lippman slip through. I don't want to be in the business of protecting drug lords and mafia dons."

Our private security division is one of our oldest groups, but it's increasingly become a liability for Imperium. This breach is the last straw. "Agreed," I reply. "You want to close it right away?"

He shakes his head. "There'll be too much chatter ahead of the IPO," he says. "Let's take it slow. No more new clients, and we won't renew any packages that expire."

"The board isn't going to like this."

Oliver shrugs. "I'm not going to run our business by Ambrose's ethics, Finn. I'm going to run it by mine."

We both fall into silence. The taxi navigates the snowy roads and the back-to-back traffic, inching its way into the city. I should be reading and replying to the hundreds of emails I've received in the last six hours, but my thoughts are elsewhere.

I was attracted to Miki Cooper. And I haven't been attracted to someone in a really long time.

∼

CHAPTER ONE

Yield to temptation. It may not pass your way again.

— ROBERT A. HEINLEIN

Miki:

Three months later...

I'm not awake before noon very often, but today's a special day.

'Special' is code for 'craptastic.'

It's my thirtieth birthday. It's also Valentine's Day. For someone still shaken by the end of her marriage, it's quite a double whammy.

"Surprise!" A chorus of voices cries out. My bedroom door is thrown open, and the gang crowds in, Piper in the lead, holding a birthday cake covered with candles.

I cover my head with my blanket and pretend I'm not here.

"Happy birthday, Miki," Bailey says cheerfully. "I'm going to tug the cover free. If you sleep naked, now's the time to let us know."

"You guys, I'm pregnant," Wendy quips. "If I catch a glimpse of Miki's pasty ass, I can't even drown my sorrows in drink."

I stick my head out of my blanket fort. "Pasty ass?" I ask indignantly. "Do you mind? Isn't it traumatic enough that I'm turning thirty?"

"Yes, yes," Gabby says. "And you're divorced, and Aaron's dick was in Peggy's mouth. We've heard it before." She perches at the foot of the bed and gives me a hopeful look. "If you blow the candles out, we can eat cake. It's Katie's carrot cake."

Ooh. Fine. I guess I can get out of bed. I sit up, and the five of them launch into a rousing rendition of 'Happy Birthday.' Once they're done singing, I blow the candles out. Piper gets a knife from the kitchen, along with some plates and forks, and efficiently slices each of us a piece.

Wendy waddles over to the armchair in the corner of the room and sits down. "Okay, Miki," she says. "Eat some cake, because you're going to need it."

I take the plate that Piper hands me. "Why?" I ask warily. When Wendy gets a look of battle in her eyes, anything can happen.

"Because this is an intervention," she replies. "Right, ladies?"

The other five nod. "Let's wait for her to finish eating," Piper says kindly.

I sit up straighter. "Why am I getting an intervention?" I ask, though I already know the answer.

Top Five Reasons I'm Getting an Intervention

1. I haven't left Wendy's apartment in four days.
2. I stay up all night and spend all day in bed. I'm like a vampire, and Wendy's comment about my pasty skin is dead on.
3. No new job. I'm living off my savings and the cash I earn by doing one-off jobs for people.
4. I've worn the same pair of sweatpants for a month. Every single day.
5. In preparation for the horrid awfulness of my thirtieth birthday, I drank a bottle of wine last night. My mouth feels like sandpaper.

Well, hell. If I'm going to get an intervention, I need another slice of cake. My mother's not here to tell me that I need to watch what I eat. I can already hear her voice in my head. *Oh dear, Mackenzie,* she'll sigh. *You're going to get fat, dear. You just turned thirty. How will you meet someone? Failed marriage, wrong side of thirty, and carrying an extra ten pounds?*

I hold out my empty plate and Piper, bless her Southern heart, gives me another slice. Armed with cake, I'm ready. "Okay," I tell my friends. "The intervention. Bring it on."

Once they leave, I get out of bed and into the shower. Instead of wearing my navy blue sweats, I slide on a pair of jeans and a red sweater. "You're going to conquer the world this year, Miki," I tell the too-pale woman in the mirror. "Forget Aaron. Look at the future, not the past."

I don't know if it's the intervention or the pep talk or even just the shower and clean clothes, but I'm feeling positively hopeful by the time I crack open my laptop and navigate to DefCon, where there are three private messages waiting for me.

I open Lancelot's message first. *Happy birthday, mouse.*

Grinning widely at the fact that he remembered, I click on Merlin's message. *Lancelot and I have a present for you, mouse, but since you won't tell us where you live, you'll have to pick it up yourself.*

Merlin's attached an address to his message. I instantly type it into Google Maps. It's a furniture store. Huh.

Lancelot doesn't appear to be online, but Merlin is. Ignoring my third message, which is from someone called User0989, I click on his icon. *You're buying me furniture? I don't have an apartment yet.*

He replies almost immediately. *Is your friend kicking you out? Do you have another place to live?*

His concern warms my heart. I hastily type out a reply before he worries too much. *Of course not. I can stay here as long as I want. They threw me an intervention today.*

Is that a New York birthday tradition?

I giggle. *No. They're worried about me. They don't think that it's good for me to sit in my sweatpants all night, glued to my computer. They think I should go out, be more social.*

Are they right?

A little, I admit. *I promised them I'd work on it.*

I've never been the most social person in the world, but before Aaron cheated on me, I enjoyed going to movies and listening to jazz bands play in small, intimate venues. I've meant to do all those things again, but I can't seem to find the energy. Maybe my friends are right. Maybe I do need a metaphorical kick in the pants.

Then there's money. My bank account took a serious beating from the divorce—Aaron decided to be a pig and contest it, and I had to hire a lawyer, Wendy's friend Lara, to help me deal with my uncooperative ex-husband. Lara didn't come cheap. I'm living rent-free at Wendy's, and that helps my finances somewhat, but I need to find a steady job.

I don't bore Lancelot and Merlin with all this. I haven't given my online friends my real phone number, and they don't know my real name, just my handle—*Mouse*—but I still tell them almost everything. I've told them about my divorce, my difficult relationship with my parents, my feelings of failure when I compare my life with my sister's, and they're always there to listen, to offer comfort and bracing advice.

It's weird. I don't know anything about them, but they're my best friends.

Merlin doesn't reply right away. I stare at the screen, waiting for his answer, but after three minutes of nothing, I click on my third message, the one from the person I don't recognize.

It's a job offer. *I'm looking for someone with your set of skills,* User0989 writes. *The job pays a hundred grand. Interested?*

Whoa. I'm barely making minimum payments on my credit card bills. A hundred grand sounds amazing. Unfortunately, I doubt it's real. I don't believe in unicorns, I don't believe in fairies, and I don't believe anonymous users who promise mysterious jobs with huge payouts.

I'm about to delete the email when a chat window pops up. It's User0989. Persistent dude.

Are you interested?

I roll my eyes and type out a sarcastic reply. *In a hundred grand? Yes. In your job? How the hell would I know? You haven't told me anything about it.*

What does this guy think? He says a hundred grand, and I'll pant all over him? I might be bummed about Aaron, but it hasn't interfered with my ability to be snarky.

I need you to get me Imperium's client list.

This guy's a lunatic. Imperium is a data security company, one of the best in the business, if not the best. They can't be hacked. Dozens have tried; all have failed. The person in charge of their operations is a genius.

It can't be done, buddy, I type. *Don't waste your money.*

You're wrong, he writes back, oddly confident. *It can't be done from the outside. But if you're inside their firewall, you might have a shot.*

Imperium isn't hiring. About the first thing I did when I moved back to Manhattan was ask around to see if they had any openings, but they were in the middle of a hiring freeze.

If I get you in, are you interested?

Okay, I've had enough of this guy's fantasy. It's my birthday, and I have better things to do with my time. Talk is cheap, and this guy hasn't given me anything tangible. I switch to Merlin's chat window.

Where were you? he asks.

Since I like Merlin, I refrain from pointing out that he's the one that disappeared first. *Some guy's trying to offer me a job.*

Who?

Merlin and Lancelot are entirely too nosy. They don't think I can look after myself. Then again, given that I've been moaning on and on about Aaron for the last three months, I don't blame them.

I'm about to answer, but User0989's icon is flashing at me. I switch to that conversation to tell him to knock it off, but then I read his message.

I've put you on the guest list for the Imperium party tonight. If you want more details about the job, show up and tell them you're M. Mouse.

There's an attachment. I open it to see a flyer for the party, and I immediately realize this event is way out of my league. I'm a hacker, most comfortable with chatting anonymously with people I don't know. The Imperium event is a themed, formal party. I'll have to talk to actual flesh-and-blood people.

Well? User0989 prompts. *What do you think?*

One hundred thousand dollars to hack into a company and steal their client list.

You'll get arrested if you get caught, Miki.

I hesitate, frozen in indecision. I don't want to go to jail, but my financial situation is getting desperate. Call me stubborn, but I don't want to ask my parents or my friends for help. My husband cheated on me. I'm staying rent-free in Wendy's apartment. All my friends have successful careers and happy, healthy relationships. I already feel like a failure; I don't want to make it worse.

A minute later, another message appears on my screen. *What do you have to lose?*

He's right. I have no job. No money. No husband. It's my thirtieth birthday and my plan for the evening is to sit at home and watch TV.

I don't want to be pathetic and miserable any longer. Aaron cheated on me, and I'm the one who's suffering as a result. It doesn't seem fair, and I'm tired of it. I want to take matters into my own hands. I want to control my own destiny.

Before I can second-guess the decision, I type out my reply. *Fine. I'll be there.*

I switch back to Merlin, who's still waiting for me to tell him who wants to hire me. I'm starting to type my answer when a thought strikes me.

Merlin and Lancelot are protective. They're going to talk me out of hacking into Imperium. They're going to point out I'll get into trouble if I get caught. They're going to warn me that I don't know who User0989 is and what his motivations are. They're going to tell me it's not safe.

Just some random guy, I reply, my cheeks heating as I lie. *Dunno who he is.*

I've never lied to them before. *It feels wrong.*

Click to keep reading The Hack.

ABOUT TARA CRESCENT

Get a free story from Tara when you sign up to Tara's mailing list.

Tara Crescent writes steamy contemporary romances for readers who like hot, dominant heroes and strong, sassy heroines.

When she's not writing, she can be found curled up on a couch with a good book, often with a cat on her lap.

She lives in Toronto.

Tara also writes sci-fi romance as Lili Zander. Check her books out at http://www.lilizander.com

Find Tara on:
www.taracrescent.com
taracrescent@gmail.com

ALSO BY TARA CRESCENT

MÉNAGE ROMANCE

Club Ménage

Claiming Fifi

Taming Avery

Keeping Kiera - *coming soon*

Ménage in Manhattan

The Bet

The Heat

The Wager

The Hack

The Dirty Series

Dirty Therapy

Dirty Talk

Dirty Games

Dirty Words

The Cocky Series

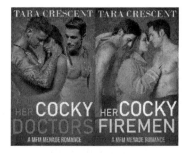

Her Cocky Doctors

Her Cocky Firemen

Standalone Books

Dirty X6

CONTEMPORARY ROMANCE

The Drake Family Series

Temporary Wife (A Billionaire Fake Marriage Romance)

Fake Fiance (A Billionaire Second Chance Romance)

Standalone Books

Hard Wood

MAX: A Friends to Lovers Romance

A Touch of Blackmail

A Very Paisley Christmas

Boyfriend by the Hour

BDSM ROMANCE

Assassin's Revenge

Nights in Venice

Mr. Banks (A British Billionaire Romance)

Teaching Maya

The House of Pain

The Professor's Pet

The Audition

The Watcher

Doctor Dom

Dominant - *A Boxed Set containing The House of Pain, The Professor's Pet, The Audition and The Watcher*